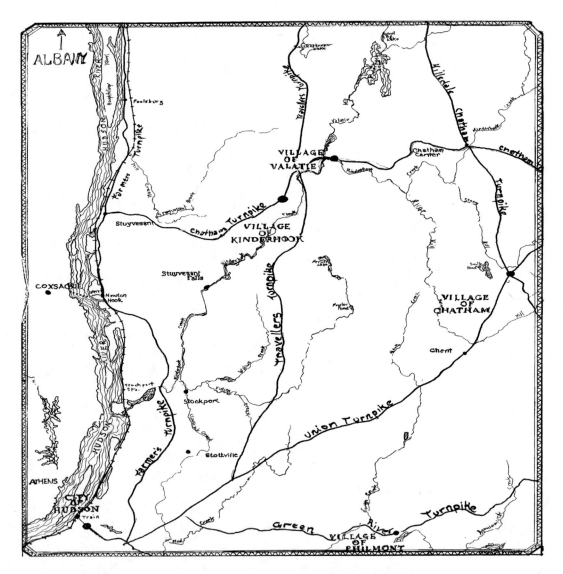

Map of nineteenth century Columbia County by Melanie Burrows

One More River

a history

by N.E. Sartin

ISBN 0-7414-4941-2

Published by: Infinity Publishing.com, 1094 New DeHaven Street, Suite 100, West Conshohocken, PA 19428-2713
Info@buybooksontheweb.com
www.buybooksontheweb.com
Toll-free (877) BUY BOOK
Local Phone (610) 941-9999
Fax (610) 941-9959

Printed in the United States of America

Printed on Recycled Paper

Published November 2008

Cover design by Katrina Ellis.

Illustrations

This book is dedicated to all the wise and goodhearted people of Kinderhook Village and Columbia County, New York, whose care and tolerance have eased our stumbling social progress in the twelve decades since the events portrayed here. We cannot change the past, but we can learn from it, and act as if what we do matters, as if we can make some small difference. As for the past, we were not there to know all the circumstances that led to failures and triumphs in those bad old, good old days. We are in this fragile present, captive to our own ways of thinking and being. Our forebears dealt with another time, another reality. We should, perhaps, weigh their shortcomings gently. A time will come when the way we are perceived will depend on the leniency of our descendants.

Acknowledgments

Ann Cooper of Columbia County Tourism suggested the idea. Dr. Charles Swain, Official New York State Black Historian, inspired the presentation of this bit of history. Thank you, Ann. Thank you, Charles.

Blessings on all keepers of records. I cannot name each of you, but here are some of you: Holly C. Tanner, Columbia County Clerk, and Deputy County Clerk Patrizia Gallo; Helen McClellan at the Columbia County Historical Society; Fern Apfel Pelletieri at the Chatham Public Library; Babette Ryder, editor of the Chatham *Courier*; staff and resources of the New York State Library and Museum in Albany; Julie Johnson, Lois Sealock and other friends at Kinderhook Memorial Library; Kinderhook Village historian Ruth Piwonka.

Blackwood and Brouwer is not a library, but a bookstore. Nevertheless Jean and Rondi Brouwer stock their shelves with hard-to-find resources, and their lively curiosity often provides impetus for the next phase.

Special thanks to Gail and Elysia Astle for information on Thomas Oliver, to Kenneth Esrick (Esq.) and Charles Oliver Wolff (Esq.) for legal guidance, to Leif Solem for editorial advice and criticism, to Vik Solem for technical expertise and determined prodding, to Rachael Solem for timely encouragement, and to Robert Bisson, best listener and spiritual guide. Thanks also to numerous friends and acquaintances in Kinderhook, Stuyvesant Falls, and Hudson, New York who supplied varieties of local lore, dates, reminiscences, and support.

Carl G. Whitbeck, Esq. of Hudson New York, great-grandson of John V. Whitbeck, kindly made available his trove of John V. Whitbeck's papers and shared family memories of the attorney who is at the center of this history.

Note to the Reader

      The following recollection was gleaned from untitled and unpublished papers of Royce Tilden, which were entered in the archives of the State University of New York at his death in 1939. They are presented here essentially as found, except for the addition of newspaper reports from the time of the Jackson trial. Tilden's version of events, coupled with the old news reports, recreates an event of singular significance and factual authenticity. Anyone who reads this history and finds in it echoes of family traditions or references passed down from earlier generations is invited to contact the author. Anyone who believes this history describes situations or injustices that belong only to the past is urged to consider the present state of our social contract.

      Anachronistic terms of reference to African-Americans, and any other obsolete expressions, have been left as set down by Royce Tilden.

N.E.Sartin

at Kinderhook, June 30, 2006

One More River

Chapter One

Complaint is made concerning a death from natural causes (heart failure) of a colored woman in the presence of witnesses, after which by reason of undue delays and laggard attention, an inquest had to be summoned, to which only whites from Chatham were called as jurors, though Chatham Center residents, knowledgeable and eligible to serve, were not notified or called. Unnecessary misery and expenses were thereby caused to the people of Chatham Center by highhandedness of Chatham officials.

J.W. (John Whitbeck) in a letter to the Chatham *Courier,* August 10, 1887

April 4, 1933, at Loudonville, New York

My name is Royce Tilden.

I have been a teacher for forty odd years now, and before that, back in the 1880s, I spent a year clerking in the law office of John V. Whitbeck in the bustling little town of Hudson, New York. I was just out of Columbia University Law School then, perhaps somewhat bumptious about it, and certainly green and unpractised in my understanding of human nature. I was, then and now, susceptible to the emotional emanations of those around me. It is a failing of shy, sensitive people of drab exterior, accustomed to rebuffs and practised in overcomng indifference, even turning to account the telltale looks and gestures of others. I like to think I am a hopeless romantic. In those days I was one, hiding my flamboyant attitudes and dreams behind my generous girth and owlish spectacles.

John Whitbeck, my employer, was at that time approaching his fiftieth year, a seasoned and successful, even distinguished lawyer with settled views about the sanctity of law and the primacy of reason in effecting progress. He was married with a young family His son, John Jr, who later succeeded him in the practice of law, was then but ten years old. In appearance Whitbeck was in every way unlike me. He was very tall and slender and usually grave of countenance. He had been a captain in the County Regiment during the Civil War. His GAR pin was always in his lapel. His voice, high and penetrating like Lincoln's, could be very overbearing when he chose. Prospective clients who climbed the stairs to his two-room office on Warren Street might find us oddly matched, my eager obsequiousness an odd match to Whitbeck's stern interrogatories.

When we'd walk down Warren Street for our daily lunch at Vanderhagen's, Whitbeck striding along with his overcoat unbuttoned and flapping in the breeze, swinging his gold-headed walking stick that he used to poke the air to emphasize his points of legal lore and opinion, and me trotting along to keep up, in my foppish bar-exam suit and thick-lensed spectacles, peering up at him vacantly like the veriest sycophant, people would step smartly out of our path. Many would nod, but few attempted to speak, giving both honored veteran and unmemorable clerk a wide berth. John Whitbeck was then a Surrogate Court Judge as well as a friendly pleader in opposition to District Attorney Aaron Gardenier. He was, in short, a well known local figure. In his company, my presence hardly registered.

In those days I had large dreams, a doctorate in legal history, a professorship, perhaps, a meteoric political career like my relative, Samuel Tilden, whose rise to national eminence was sparked by his crusade against Tammany Hall. Then, perhaps I would join a reputable Albany law firm and finally retire in mellow country seclusion while I penned my colorful memoirs, surrounded by adoring progeny. So much for dreams. My life has too little incident to rate a biography. Here I shall merely set down the facts of the Jackson case as completely as I can recall them. The extant record lacks substance.

People versus Jackson is a trial I recall very well, a formative experience for me, one that remains clear in my mind while events of later times have faded. It is a sign of encroaching age, perhaps, when early experiences, turning points in our lives, stand out more and more vividly, while their aftereffects blur and overlap like echoes in a canyon. I made discoveries then, glimpsed wellsprings of human behavior until then unknown to me. The Jackson case also revealed unsuspected aspects of myself, painful and saddening truths. Since then, remaining hopeful, if not entirely convinced, of the potential of law to regulate human conduct has been my finest achievement. That precept was my chief legacy from John V. Whitbeck, whose adherence to the ideal of law never yielded to the contradictions and buffets of time or the shafts provided by the company of rogues, bluffers and manipulators he represented.

The Jackson case was not the first case in my year with John Whitbeck. We pled before Judge Samuel Edwards, who then presided in the Third Circuit Court of Columbia County. Edwards was in his eighties, a massive, imposing figure with wisps of white hair in a halo around his ears and a nervous tic in his left eye that made him appear constantly impatient, seeming to wink at the jury, urging disregard of all pleading and every sworn statement. His big gnarled hands caressed the gavel as he listened to testimony, as if he might knock a faltering witness on the head to speed things up.

As a matter of fact, we lost the first case I worked as Whitbeck's second. Our client was judged guilty of doing away with his wife's aged mother and sealing her up in an abandoned cistern on her property, which he then inherited. Judge Edwards, his cadaverous face jerking and grimacing all through the day of testimony, leaned from his polished oak perch to instruct the jury after final arguments.

"Be sure, be wise, be diligent. And do not keep this Court waiting overlong."

They took less than half an hour to return a guilty verdict, to my great dismay (and the defendant's horror). Whitbeck handled most of our defense, but at the end he let me question the defendant and do the summation. I believe he felt I could not hurt the case and could use the practice. I sat with the scowling, defiant murderer while we awaited the verdict. Whitbeck pretty much ignored us as he tidied his papers and consulted his pocket watch. Ten minutes after it was over, I found him at the Iron Horse chatting with two cronies. He signaled me to bring him another tankard.

"This is my young colleague, Royce Tilden," he told his jovial friends. "He did a fine closing for me today. Sometime soon I shall give him first chair."

Not fine enough. We lost the case. The fellow declares his innocence, but he'll be hanged.

"Better hope you don't get Edwards then." Ike Pomerance, the stouter of the two men, told me. "He'll not let you meander so another time

Until that moment I had thought my handling of the witness was exemplary and my summation a model of reasoned argument. Whitbeck, whose longwindedness was legendary, chuckled along with the others and avoided my eyes. I could tell he was not promising me a chance to shine. He was going to throw me to the wolves. But I smiled and asked a dumb question. "Do I get to choose which client I defend?"

"As surely as you choose which suit to be buried in."

All three laughed at my expense. But in the following months, as John kept me busy with writs and filings and searches through dusty records, I did not once appear in court.

I was planning to leave him, leave Hudson, in the autumn of 1887 when the Jackson case began on a bright, brisk, golden afternoon. You could not but be glad of life on such a day. I had a letter in my pocket from Lillian Roeder, my first and nearly-promised love. The whole broad Hudson Valley was ablaze with the tawny flames of sugar maples. When I rode down into Hudson that afternoon, after a visit to old Vossie Van Louwen, our wealthiest client, I could see the russet peaks of the Catskills to the west and the hazy line of Berkshires far to the east. My horse frisked in the sharp October breeze, and I clutched my broad hat and whistled tunelessly as we trotted between stubbled fields of corn stooks and past white farmhouses sheltering under russet oaks and golden willows. I felt ready to save the world.

I was still smiling when I stabled my horse, and whistling as I climbed the stairs to our office. When I opened the door, which let directly onto the anteroom I usually occupied, a woman was waiting there on the bench, a colored woman. She appeared hardly more than a girl, very slim, in dark suiting, white shirtwaist and a pretty rust-colored bonnet. She clutched a reticule in both hands and had a handkerchief tucked in one sleeve. I think she had been weeping, for when she looked up at my entrance, tears glistened in her dark lashes. She had extraordinary eyes. Even at that moment, with her face distorted by desperate anxiety, I couldn't but note that she was a handsome negress. I don't claim my sympathy was instant, or my emotions engaged, but I do confess that her winsome appearance made it easy to listen to her appeal when I had ushered her into Whitbeck's office.

Whitbeck was not there. He likely would not have allowed her past my desk. He was a bit stiff with black clients. Whitbecks had once owned slaves, and though he fought in the Great War on patriotic principle, his attitude toward emancipation and suffrage and the rest was more complex than among the Tildens, who had been unqualified abolitioniists. It was legal principle Whitbeck upheld, rather than moral values or individual rights. I never heard him argue against the thirteenth amendment, and he did condemn both major parties for their hypocrisy on race. But he himself scorned, or seemed to scorn, any obviously liberal outlook.

Which was odd, for I do believe he hired me for my name, my connection to Samuel J. Tilden, who was an unapologetically liberal abolitionist, of the Free-Soil, Barn Burner variety. When I met Whitbeck, he surveyed me sharply while we exchanged names and shook hands, as if seeking a resemblance in me to my famously elected non-presidential relative. Beyond similar stature and fair hair, there was none.

After an awkward pause he said, "Ah," It was a sound like an unoiled hinge. "Well then. Never mind. Tell me about your background, since you are without experience in the law."

So we got off on the wrong foot for that reason; and my rosy-cheeked naivety and cheerful sanguinity, along with my lack of anything like his stature or presence, put me quite out of consideration for promotion into his law firm.

Apart from that disappointment, I quite admired John Whitbeck. He was an honorable and respected attorney. As could be expected in a town no larger than Hudson, New York, he accepted all sorts of cases and defended some miserable examples of humanity, as well as handling a variety of family and business matters. He was neither known for defending nor refusing colored clients. My guess is that when he took such cases he charged a smaller fee, but I don't believe he served colored clients with less dedication. He had not, until then, challenged the inequalities of post-Reconstruction society as manifest in the courts. As I remember, much of our practice was the most basic sort of legal defense. We dealt in simple crimes like robbery and battery, and defended obviously guilty suspects. We did not concern ourselves with civil rights or racial distinctions under lingering pre-emancipation statutes and attitudes. Whitbeck's approach to legal discrimination was in keeping with his deep respect for legal principles.. He saw the imperfections of the system as part of the larger imperfection of oue society, as circumstances that would yield to the progressive nature of legal science.

In his defense it should be pointed out that it was then only two decades after emancipation. Reconstruction had abruptly ended with the election of 1876, when Samuel Tilden ceded his hard won victory at the polls to the political victory of Hayes. That standoff left behind it a slow hardening of racial barriers. Black enfranchisement and other entitlements were still subject to various sorts of footdragging in New York State, as everywhere else.

So, to return to my story, there I was, on that gorgeous afternoon, with my spirits soaring, and my gallant instincts fully engaged, without the restraining influence of my employer. Faced with this pitiable example of the fair sex ~ well, in her case, the fair if dusky sex ~ I ignored the dictates of customary prudence. I sat the young lady down in one of Whitbeck's client chairs and listened to her sad story.

It's always a sad story. There is always special pleading and extenuation and the iteration of innocence. But every time, even now in my seasoned prime, I find myself drawn into a circumstantial telling of woeful error. I accept, for the nonce, the claim of injustice, the petition for defense, for exoneration from mistaken blame, for rescue. It is my calling.

Her name was Cynthia Ann Van Houck Jackson. She was barely nineteen, married and a mother. Her husband was accused of murder, a murder committed in 1885, two years before, soon after Cynthia Ann Van Houck's marriage to Jay Jackson. The victim, a white woman of advanced years, had been beaten or stabbed to death in her home, apparently in the course of a robbery, since an amount of money she was believed to have kept in her house was missing when her body was found several days later. This woman, Gertrude Margaret Hover, was neighbor to the Jacksons and Cynthia Van Houck, having her residence in the midst of the negro settlement at the edge of Kinderhook, a charming old village one stage stop up the post road from Hudson.

I could have made her plea for her, so predictably did she begin: "I know my Jay, sir. He couldn't have done such a thing! He's a good man, maybe something wild when he was younger, but he's a steady worker now down at Powell's farm, and in the dairy right opposite us. He's a church-going man. He sings in our choir. That's where we met, Jay and I, in the choir at Bethel AME right on our road there in the village."

I was listening carefully, not so much to her tale, as to her manner. This was not an ignorant housemaid or field worker. She was the sort of negress I knew from New York City, an educated blackamoor. There had been such a one in law school with me, well spoken, intelligent, not merely literate, but bookish, generations away from slavery. This girl was more ladylike than my own young sister, and disturbingly self-possessed, though she was shy of me, mostly gazing down at her gloved hands clutching her reticule. Or she would pull the lace handkerchief from her sleeve to dab at her nose or wipe away a stray tear. When from time to time she raised those remarkable eyes to meet mine in earnest pleading, I could feel my heart catch, and restrained an impulse to reach out a hand to comfort her.

"They accused Jay's brother William first. Now William ... William's tetched, you see. He can't always talk sense so you can understand him, poor dear. And sometimes he gets upset at that and shouts, and that scares people. But he's harmless. He won't squash a bug. He works down along the railway. He walks the line and finds broken ties and washouts. Some days he just walks the roads. He can't always tell you where he's been. But everybody knows him. Specially those nasty boys that tease him all the time." She stopped suddenly, her gloved hand over her mouth. Nasty white boys was what she meant; and she'd nearly said it to my white face.

"I understand," I told her soothingly. "Children can be pretty mean sometimes."

"That's as may be," she said tartly, steadfastly regarding her hands, now folded again in her lap. "After they found Miss Hover, her body I mean ~ it was days, days before they found her, poor soul ~ it wasn't long till they started in accusing. A lady was over on the Albany road and said William was at her house, Miss Hover's. Well, he could have been. She lived right there, in the next house over from Jay's father's place, our place. William doesn't live at home. He has a cabin in the woods over near Ghent town, but he comes home to visit sometimes. He'll stay with us a day or two, so I can cut his hair and do his laundry and get some hot food into him. Far as we can remember he was with us that weekend, or part of it, anyway. That was all I could remember after they arrested him over Chatham way."

Now she did look up at me, those fine eyes wide with pain. "They put him in the lockup for shouting. Some old busybody women claimed he was yelling at them. He just yells, you see. He doesn't really yell *at* anybody. Then they said he was the one killed Miss Hover. And William, he can't tell you whether it rained yesterday. How can he say where he was when an old neighbor lady died? So you see, it's only because Jay wanted to get William out of jail that he let them take him in. Jay wasn't ~ Jay didn't ~" Now the lace handkerchief was snatched to cover her sobs. I felt like a gross lout, sitting stiffly in the client chair beside her, not offering a touch or word of comfort. After a while I took out my own folded pocket handkerchief and offered it. But she shook her head, regaining control with an effort.

"Jay's very protective of William," she explained, quite unnecessarily. I had figured that out for myself. "He won't let anything happen to William, so ~"

"Wait, now. Back up, ma'am. Are you saying that your husband turned himself in not out of guilt, but just so that his brother could get out of jail?"

"Well, not exactly. It wasn't only that. It was Emma. Emma Briggs sent them after my Jay. Emma ~ well, I don't like to speak ill of my neighbors, but Emma Briggs told tales about my Jay to the police. That Emma, she can be spiteful. I know it to my sorrow. She set her cap for Jay the minute he joined the choir at the Beth-El. And her an old married woman! It was a scandal how she prinked and paraded to make him notice her."

I could sense old animosity here, Cynthia the smart young canary vying for top diva in that tiny country church choir, and Emma the old crow, bigger and louder, pulling rank, blocking her way. I wondered if the woman across from me had a voice to match the sweetness of her face, and had an irrational wish to hear her sing. I smothered a grin. She was continuing.

"... found out Jay was courting me, she was fit to split a gusset. I think her husband finally settled her down about that, or it could have been Pastor Oliver. Then Jay and I got married, and after that Christmas Pastor Oliver left. He was so nice, Pastor Oliver. He was up from New Jersey. He was a graduate from the divinity school at Princeton. How he could preach! And he brought us all those new songs. He truly saved my Jay, and some others too, from the drink and from ..." She paused searching for a tactful phrase. "... youthful indiscretions. He was bound for greater things, Pastor Oliver. We all knew." Her expression softened, remembering a happier time, and then became intently serious as she looked up at me again.

"So then, for that year, until we had the baby, there was no trouble at all. That is, Miss Hover had died right there on our road, which was a great trouble, but other than that ~ My little Jemmy, Jeremiah, was born in September last year. And Emma, well, Emma never had children. She grows berries for the market, and does her good works for the church. And she's a fine singer, of course. She leads the choir. But I think never having a child is a great grief to her. So when Jay and I had Jemmy she just couldn't bear it, to see us so happy, I mean. So she went and told the police a tale to get him in trouble about Miss Hover. That's what I think, Mr. Whitbeck, Sir."

"Oh, dear," I suddenly realized I had failed to introduce myself to her. Was it her color or her beauty that blew away my basic social skills? "Miss Cynthia, that is, Mrs. Jackson, I'm not John Whitbeck. You must have told me this expecting him to take your case, but I'm only his junior in the firm, Royce Tilden. However, I am at your service, if you'll accept me."

At that inopportune moment John Whitbeck came creaking up the stairs and advanced into his office, filling it with his dignified and proprietorial presence.

"Ah, Royce," he began, before he took in the woman seated in front of his desk. The reproof he was about to fire off at me for invading his private chamber (My usual spot was the desk in the anteroom.) died on his lips, as he pointed his stick at Cynthia Jackson. "An appointment I was not apprised of, missy. How did you find your way up here?" Then he turned to me with a look of stern severity. "You must warn me, Mr. Tilden, when you plan to conduct your affairs in my office."

"Allow me," I rose and faced him as starchily as I could manage, "to introduce our new client. Mrs. Cynthia Van Houck Jackson. This is Mr. John Whitbeck, for whom you have mistakenly taken me."

Whitbeck tapped his cane impatiently and nodded once at the girl, who had risen and was regarding him gravely from those enormous eyes. Then he stepped around me and seated himself behind his desk. "So, Mr. Tilden, we have been engaged by Mrs. Van Houck Jackson. Is that it?"

"How do you do, Mr. Whitbeck." Cynthia answered as smoothly as if he had addressed her rather than frowning at me. "I have been relating to Mr. Tilden the circumstances of my husband's detainment for a crime he did not commit. My hope is that your firm ~ Whitbeck and Tilden is it? ~ will defend him against the false accusation of murder that has been brought against him."

I had never seen John Whitbeck flummoxed until that moment. He had not expected the girl to speak at all, and certainly not to speak with such almost legal clarity. Nor had he ever heard our very unequal relationship described as a firm with my name attached to it. He regarded me as his legal aide, a mere factotum who incidentally had passed the New York State Bar exam. But he did recover pretty sharply.

"Has Mr. Tilden discussed terms or retainer with you, Mrs. Van Houck Jackson?"

"You may call me Mrs. Jackson, Mr. Whitbeck. It's less ungainly. I am prepared to offer a retainer of one hundred dollars. I have it with me. It represents the support of Bethel AME Church and their firm faith in my husband's innocence."

She and I had not discussed anything so practical. I realized how lax I had been, how dazzled. I had not introduced myself, nor explained my menial position. I had not taken down her address nor asked for bonafides of any kind. I had simply walked her into Whitbeck's office and listened to her tale, hoping to distract her from the ready tears that coursed down those soft brown cheeks, hoping to coax a smile onto that woebegone countenance. I had a sudden flash of joy at the thought of how a jury would react to this lovely young woman.

"Well, well." Whitbeck turned a chilly stare on me. "You must be prepared to give this account of yours many times and to less sympathetic ears than Mr. Tilden's. I shall be obliged if you begin again now. Tell me how your husband came to be accused of this crime you say he did not commit. You need to apprise me of every circumstance, no matter how trivial. Mr. Tilden will be assisting me in every way, but I shall handling the case."

He sat back in his overlarge chair, his walking stick, as usual, propped against his desk, and his expression placid as a feeding lion. He had astonished me twice in one sentence, by accepting her entirely inadequate retainer, and by taking as his own a client I would have eagerly volunteered to serve. Ignoring my open-mouthed surprise, he encouraged Cynthia Jackson to retell the events, from two years before up to her husband's recent indictment for Gertrude Hover's murder. This time I took notes.

After he assured Cynthia Jackson of our intent to do everything possible in Jay Jackson's defense, my employer brought the interview to a close. When I offered to accompany her immediately to the jail to visit her husband, he reminded me of a deposition I was to take down that afternoon. So I saw the charming Cynthia down to the street and returned to face my mentor and his searing disdain.

"Such a puppy!" he began, before I had even closed his office door. "I can't leave you for five minutes but you soil the floor. Did you manage to get Van Louwen to sign that codicil?"

I nodded.

"And did you have his signature properly witnessed by nonlegatees?"

I nodded.

"And how did you manage that? He has every cow and gatepost listed in that will of his."

"I persuaded two of Van Wie's fieldhands to ride over with me. They were glad of the break." They were also glad of the strong drink I treated them to afterward in the tavern at Chittenden Crossing.

"Ah. Forethought. So what caused your forethought to desert you when this high yaller in ruffles came flouncing into my office? Can you not recognize a lost cause when it stumbles into your path on the way to perdition? A murder unsolved for two years! Of a propertied old woman in Kinderhook Village! A negro defendant? A hundred dollar retainer! How many dismal markers do you need, Roy?" He did not wait for my reply, which was in any case not forthcoming. "And there you were, ready to mount and ride to her rescue, rush over to the jail to hear another tall tale from her scoundrel husband."

"Scoundrel? She says he's a model husband and father. Churchgoing. Signed the teetotal pledge probably. Sings in the choir, for God's sake. Steady worker, protector of his demented kid brother. And dresses his wife in good gray worsted, did you notice?"

"I certainly noticed the wife. Who could avoid those eyes? Roy, Roy. You can't defend a murderer merely because he has bedded an extremely attractive mulatto girl. Gertrude Hover's murder was the most grisly crime in the history of Kinderhook. And it has remained unsolved for two years. Twenty-five months! That's more or less the number of times she was stabbed with a butcher knife. Her heirs have battled before me in surrogate court over the prime bits of property she owned, and her orchard with frontage on the main street of the village. Her house has been scoured of her blood and repainted and sold. Now that they have finally arrested a credible suspect, a negro suspect, can you, in your wildest knight-errant imaginings expect to plead him down or get him off on reasonable doubt?"

"I expect us to defend him with due diligence," I retorted huffily, standing in front of his desk as rigid and flushed as only a hopelessly compromised young lout could be, "and hope that the victim's blood will cry out against false accusations and miscarriages of justice."

Whitbeck leaned back in his big chair and looked up at me with disgust written all over his narrow face. "And when that poor little girl can't wheedle any more money out of her friends, family and any dogooders she sets those tearful eyes on ~ what then? Do you plan for me to defend Bat Jackson *pro bono publico*?"

I let my shoulders relax a degree and put a quizzical expression on my face. "And who, pray, is Bat Jackson?"

"Your client, Roy. The beautiful Cynthia calls him Jay. Some say he's John Jackson, or maybe sometimes John Thompson. Or he's none of those, but the local rags refer to him as Bat, or Battice Jackson, a fellow with a certain notoriety hereabouts and up in Albany, where he apparently got his sobriquet, and whence he scuttled off just ahead of the law. His return to Kinderhook was more a matter of avoiding arrest across the river than coming home to mend his ways."

"But what...?"

"What felonies did he commit up in Albany? Receiving stolen goods, promotion of gambling, things like that as I recall. Yes indeed." He shook his head at my ignorance, but surely all this had happened before I came to Hudson. "That may be the least of it. The sheriff's men up in Albany County have been cleaning up our fair capital. Scrappers like Bat Jackson have in recent years been relocating down here in Columbia County, where there are wild areas, like Guinea Hill over east of Kinderhook, in which the lawless live quite unmolested and prey on the stages and God knows what else. The allout boxing crowd has been over here all along. Bettors aplenty and coin to be made from bruising your knuckles and bloodying your nose in front of sweating ranks of well dressed men who wouldn't know how to make a fist, let alone lash out with it. Like highway robbery, prizefighting is illegal here, my boy. However, our local sheriff is a fan of the sport. Sheriff Halz patrols the site while the mob inside lay their bets and scream for blood and yell for the fight to continue until the combatants are so battered and exhausted they stumble and slip in their own gore and lean on one another for support, for the first one to fall is the loser."

"Obviously you have attended this sort of entertainment," I chided, getting in my first counterblow of the afternoon.

"Obviously you have not," he retorted, "or you might have figured out how little sympathy you will elicit from a jury on behalf of a felon who probably makes a living carrying stolen goods across the river, and surely got his nickname in brawls. His peers on the jury will find it only too easy to imagine him using his lethal strength against a frail old woman to wrest from her some paltry sum of money."

"But you accepted her retainer," I pointed out. "You agreed to defend Jay Jackson."

Whitbeck smiled the smile of a predator about to pounce. "Indeed. I have agreed to take the case. You will assist me in defendng Bat, the delicious Cynthia's Jay." He stood up and ran his forefinger lazily along the leather bound row of New York State statute books. "There is a weighty legal principle involved here, Royce, which I am sure coincides with your liberal leanings. It should be a tonic for both of us, and a challenge too."

Chapter Two

I would liken you to a night without stars
Were it not for your eyes
I would liken you to a sleep without dreams
Were it not for your songs.

Langston Hughes, "Quiet Girl"

I remember being torn by contrary emotions as I descended to Warren Street and made my way to Mrs. Bullock's where I was a boarder. John's prompt seizure of command with our new client(s) had nettled me somewhat. His presumption that a dry legal wrangle was to be the center of the case eclipsed my rather more idealistic (I assured myself) motive for undertaking the defense of an accused murderer. Meanwhile, my heart leapt in anticipation of a delightful turn of events. According to word just received, I was about to have a visitor. Fortunately my rather formidably starchy landlady was agreeable to letting the parlor accommodation for the weekend on this very short notice. It was a pair of rooms she seldom let, since her charge for the two days was as much as my own room let by the week. But I needed to make a show of style, if not affluence. The letter in my breast pocket, which had me smiling to myself whenever I thought of it, was from my dear Lillian and announced her imminent visit to me. Indeed, the tardy mail had put it in my hands only on the very day she would be debarking from the steamer at Hudson landing.

Such a pleasant surprise gave me reason to hope that her view of our relationship coincided with my own, that she was confident of my serious intentions toward her. Perhaps she had even suggested to her father that I might soon ask... Well, that was my sanguine mood as I put on a fresh shirt and brushed my coat and shined my shoes. Almost giddy with the prospect, I stopped at Pulcher's Livery where my horse was stabled, hired a trap at exorbitant cost, and so arrived at the landing in a manner more befitting a junior partner than a mere legal clerk.

I caught sight of Lillian, well wrapped against the river breezes, when she fluttered her handkerchief from the rail as the steamer docked. We soon managed to gather her luggage from the purser, a formidable weight of bags to have loaded in the trap, for which I gave the porter a formidable tip. I would like to say that I noticed the man's blackness and the shabbiness of his thin jacket, that the guileless pleading of Cynthia Jackson had worked a change in my consciousness. But I cannot so deceive myself. The stableboy who cared for my horse, who readily hitched up the trap at my order, the maids and kitchen help at Mrs. Bullock's ~ all of them were pretty much invisible to me. I knew Tom, the black bartender at Vanderhagen's, and Willa, who owned the stationery shop on Warren Street, but only because they were persons of some standing and authority, removed by their occupation from the anonymity of negritude. I suppose that makes me an elitist of race, or something. With race, as with female suffrage in those days, I endorsed the idea of equality but quailed at the consequences, except for certain individuals. I would solicit Tom's or Willa's vote if I ran for office. In fact, years later when I did run for the state senate, I shamelessly used my negro clients to gain support among the black community. But populism ~ liberalism if you will ~ did not prove to be my path into politics.

Lillian greeted me, offering her rosy face for a brief kiss, and took my hand in both of hers. I could feel her stiff, icy fingers inside her gloves, the slender bones pressing hard. She had been in dread the whole trip up the Hudson that I would not have received her warning, would not be there to take her in charge, that she would be left to make her own arrangements without my guidance and protection. I gave her all the reassurances proper to a public place, then tucked her hand securely under my arm as we made our way up the landing. I handed her up into the trap with considerable relief that I had thought to hire it. She allowed me to tuck the travel blanket around her knees (not strictly necessary on that sunny afternoon) and smiled when I chirped the horse into motion as if I did it every day.

"So, Lillian my dear, what shall we do first? Have you eaten lunch, or would you like a cup of tea? Or shall we settle you into your lodging before we see the town?"

"Oh, Royce! Let's get inside somewhere! I am so grateful to be off that grumbling boat and safe with you at last. No wonder people take the train! I had no idea it was so far up here from the city."

"And still only halfway to Albany our fair capital," I reminded her placidly, remembering my own dismay when I first found myself so far from familiar sights and faces, a full day's ride from New Lebanon and home. A year had made Hudson's single muddy commercial street familiar, if not lovely to my eyes. Indeed, I nodded to several acquaintances as we trotted up Warren to Mrs. Bullock's big square house with its ample porches and neatly kept front garden.

Lillian was soon made welcome and settled into her rooms, with a fire in the grate and tea served to us by Mrs. Bullock herself, who would cheerfully have joined us if invited. She did have sense enough to leave us after fussing about with the cups and biscuits and poking earnestly at the little fire for more time than one would think possible.

"Well, then. I'll leave you for now," she said, finally rising and turning to the door. "You do understand, Mr. Tilden, that the rooms are let to Miss Roeder for her visit. You'll not be overstaying your welcome in her parlor." It was her warning. Lillian and I were to behave at all times with propriety. Mrs. Bullock had appointed herself chaperone for the weekend. Lillian giggled as the door closed behind the stiff matronly figure, armored in rectitude and brown bombazine.

"I am so glad that high moral standards obtain up here in the provinces." She bit into a biscuit, smothering a most delicious grin. The promise in that grin had kept me in Lillian Roeder's orbit for nearly two years now, since before I had passed the bar, since a law school reception for alumni which she attended with her distinguished and rather distant father, a partner in the law firm of Gould, Martin, Roeder, in whose august assemblage I might someday be included. She had been barely nineteen, newly returned from a tour of the continent, and dauntingly aloof and sophisticated. When we met she offered a slender hand and that self-mocking grin. Her father, as I remember, had momentarily left her side to confer with the dean of the law school.

Now she topped up my tea and then looked at me slyly. "Are we to spend this whole weekend with both feet on the floor and our hands folded?" she asked, quoting her finishing school rule for gentlemen callers.

I certainly hoped not. "Only if you keep to my landlady's parlor," I assured her. "We are not without entertainment up here in the piney woods. There is a concert tonight at the opera house, if you would like to attend. And Mr. Whitbeck and I are to defend an accused murderer in the New Year. What do you think of that?"

"I think it's a bit sordid, Royce, the murder, not the concert. You surely can't enjoy the prospect of consorting with the sort of people who do each other to death." She sipped her tea, looking at me wide-eyed over the rim of her cup. Lillian's intense gray-green gaze brought back to me Cynthia Jackson's timid dark-eyed glance, her gentle pleading, her calm determination. They could not be more different, the two women who relied on me that day: Lillian in confident expectation that I ~ that the world ~ would do her bidding; and Cynthia resigned to constant rebuffs yet brave enough to mount those stairs, to beg a white lawyer to save her husband. Lillian, I know, thought herself meek, obedient to her father, to the demands of her social position, but she controlled her life, would control mine if I managed to win her. Cynthia Jackson had the meekness of a subjugated lifetime, but under her manner I sensed an unyielding and resilient core, cloaked by her beauty as Lillian's meekness veiled her will.

"People who do someone to death, my dear, are not always the ones accused of murder," I said rather stiffly. "It is in the public interest to investigate carefully and sift the facts of terrible crimes, so that justice does not miscarry, that the innocent not be punished." I was sounding destressingly like Whitbeck. Before she could give me a poke for such pomposity, I downed the last of my tea and proposed that we go for a ride in the trap, so she could enjoy the beauty of the day and the countryside.

We spent a very enjoyable afternoon rattling over the winding, hilly roads of Columbia County. We stopped to view the Van Buren mansion, and then rolled into Kinderhook Village, our wheels sending up flurries of bright leaves behind us in the road. Past the impressive row of stately homes that lined the way, we pulled into a layby, and found the post office so Lillian could send a card to let her father know she had arrived safely. We glanced into shop windows, paused at the millinery store, peered into the dim interior of the Kinderhook *Rough Notes* office and printshop. In front of the staging inn with its barns and stables a crowd of hostlers and errand boys and idlers occupied much of the walkway. Apparently the coach from Albany was due. We kept to the opposite side and crossed the post road to continue along the main street, walking on a soft carpet of fallen leaves, which Lillian culled for a few bright maple stars to press in her album. At the crossing before the hat factory, I guided us into a winding lane called Sunset.

Lillian, who had earlier expressed delight at the charm and prosperous look of the old settlement, surveyed the curving road dubiously. "This seems quite the end of the village, Roy. There's no more walkway. And look ~ it's all fields on that side of the road."

"Let's just go a little way. We can turn back at the crossing. Van Buren is supposed to be buried somewhere near here." I urged, not wanting to reveal that we would be passing the scene of the very crime described to me by Cynthia Jackson earlier that day. And pass it we did, but not before we observed a number of placid dairy cows and a flock of pickaninnies filling sacks with chestnuts, and chasing one another about, as carefree as any antebellum plantation. There was a neat white church, Bethel AME, quite modest compared to the fine Dutch Reformed edifice back on the post road. There were several farmhouses, and a row of cottages, presumably a colony of freedmen. Interspersed with this shabby collection were a few older dwellings in the style locally called eyebrow colonial. One of these, the one adjoining an apple orchard, was the house where Gertrude Margaret Hover had lived till she was murdered. The orchard lay between us and the gravestones and monuments of Kinderhook's cemetery over past the main street.

"We should turn back now, Royce. I don't want to poke around some old headstones to find Van Buren's tomb. To have seen it from this distance is quite enough. Please, let's go back now."

"But you said how much you liked the place," I chided, content with what I had seen of the physical aspect of the crime. "You said how nice it must be to live in such a pretty, peaceful village."

"I also said it could do with better pedestrian walks and a tea shop or two."

"Ah! Your appetite has returned. Shall we stop at the inn then for early supper? Or is it late dinner? I have heard their wine list recommended."

We were treated to a quite sumptuous supper, during which I did not raise the unseemly topic of the murder. She would think it too sordid for mealtime conversation, though my mind kept returning to that neat white house, a short walk from where we dined, where fatal violence had shattered a life. Nor did I venture on the matter of our relationship, which seemed with Lillian's sudden visit to be entering a deeper phase. Once or twice Lillian seemed about to embark on whatever topic sparkled in her eyes, but each time the waiter came eeling around filling our water glasses or pouring more wine. For my part, just to have her there with me was pleasure enough for the moment. I confess to pondering words of proposal as we spoke of mutual friends, our glances meeting and sliding away from the candle gleam.

We barely arrived back in Hudson in time for the concert, a pastiche of scenes from what I took to be Shakespeare plays, though they seemed to have strayed dismayingly toward *commedia del'arte* in the presentation. Mrs. Bullock let us in before locking the door, and remained in her parlor, plinking idly on her spinet, until I bid Lillian goodnight. Under those circumstances, we did not attempt any serious or extended conversation.

I was sure Lillian was on the verge ~ as I was ~ of some revelation, each of us on tiptoe but unready to leap. We lingered over our goodnights as we had lingered over supper. I watched her face in the lamplight, half shadowed, half rosy, and the way a chance spark in the grate fire glinted golden-red in her hair. I remember her slender, graceful hands, occasionally touching my own. What we did say, I can't recall. I was a very happy man that night, teetering on the edge of commitment, frankly enjoying the anticipation. Where I found the confidence to believe she might accept me, I cannot imagine. Her lips were soft against mine at our whispered parting. I carried her scent with me up to my chilly bed.

It was a remarkable day, one of my happiest memories.

The one that followed was more decisive. After a grand breakfast, with Mrs. Bullock presiding over a full table of three other boarders and me, with Lillian the honored guest, Lillian proposed to visit the shops on Warren Street in company with Mrs. Bullock. I had an appointment at the jail.

The room where Cynthia Jackson and I met with her husband to affirm that John and I would represent him in the matter of Gertrude Hover's murder was hardly more than a closet with a window. It had a battered table and three chairs and was gaslit, as were all of Hudson's municipal buildings, including the courthouse. I was turning up the flame as Jay Jackson was led in. He was shackled, but still wore the checquered suit and bright boots he was arrested in.

What newspaper accounts of the trial later described as his 'well set up manner' was immediately apparent. He was a bit darker complected than Cynthia, with a broad brow and high cheekbones and crinkly hair cropped close to his head. There was an intensity to his expression, as if fierce fires were damped within him. He was not much above middle height, half a head taller than I, and wiry, even muscular to judge from his movements, which were springy and lithe in spite of the trammeling irons on his wrists and ankles. His eyes were deepset and very bright as he leaned to kiss his wife with great tenderness, ignoring the presence of the guard and me. He was older than Cynthia, in his late twenties I judged, and when he turned to me he was smiling broadly, as if we shared some delightful secret. I had never before been so impressed by a colored man. I regarded him intently as I tried to discover the character behind the skin, judge how this defendant would be perceived by a jury. Already I was calculating John Whitbeck's chances of success in pleading him innocent or painting him mad or seeking mercy on his behalf. *A dandy and a rake*, I thought, as I told him my name and that Cynthia had engaged John Whitbeck and me to defend him. *The jury will hate him. I dislike him already.*

His cocked eyebrow dismissed me. "Well, Cyn, that was quick. You said you'd go the rounds of local firms to find one who'd serve me. You didn't look far." He measured my face, as if I were a horse for sale. "He looks far too young and soft. Did you hire the first counsel on offer? Or the only one? Perhaps you ought to look further." He turned from scolding her and looked me up and down, as insolent as an anarchist. "Tilden, is it? Any relation to the fella almost got to be president?"

"Not close enough to matter," I told him, to his apparent amusement.

"Did you take my girl's money with the thought of getting me hanged, Lawyer Tilden? 'Cause if you did, you can give the money back to her now. I did not kill dear old Miss Gertrude. Nor did my brother William, who was jailed for the same crime, and beaten too, while they held him down over there in Chatham jail. I couldn't let William stay in that hole, so I gave myself up to free him. But it's all a cockup, a story invented to calm the white folks of Kinderhook, so they don't have to hide under their beds any longer in case the fiend who killed her comes after them all."

His speech, while there was a bit of drawl in it, was as literate as his wife's. Their voices were northern bred, centuries away from Africa, with more education behind them than my landlady, for instance, if I were to guess. According to the public accounts, William Jackson had not been beaten while in custody, only restrained because he was violent and raving and might harm himself or others. Also, one report of Jackson's first arrest had him giving a false name and attempting to fast-talk his way out of custody before he was identified and later accused of the Hover murder.

I could see why this Jackson was a choice candidate for indictment. He was too brash, too glib, too good looking, far too self-assured to be allowed free rein. I took him for a confidence man, though even growing up in New York City I had not encountered a negro bunco artist until that moment. I did not relish the prospect of defending him in court before a jury of white farmers, nor did I like that he had captured such an exquisite example of dusky womanhood as the girl Cynthia, who sat silently drinking in every bold word he uttered.

"I hear you declare your innocence, Mr. Jackson. Do you desire Mr. Whitbeck's counsel and representation, and mine, in this matter of which you are accused?" That was my formal interrogatory. If he refused me, I could with honor return the fee Cynthia Jackson had left with my employer the day before, and be out from under what I now saw would be an unpleasant and unsuccessful defense.

Jackson looked over at his wife, who softly told him, "I tried four others, Jay. None of them even gave me the time of day." A hint of outrage crept into her voice. "He's the only one who granted me an interview, him and that kind Mr. Whitbeck."

I smothered my gasp of surprise at this description of John Whitbeck, whom no client in my experience had ever referred to as kind, and who would be much displeased to know of it now.

"You got both for the one price? That's not bad, Cyn. I guess I'll have to go along with it." He turned to me again and reached his manacled hand across the table. I was too startled to do anything but grasp it in my own. His pale palm, dry and smooth, the scarred knuckles enclosing my grip with effortless strength, momentarily overwhelmed my senses. I had a sudden flash of dreadful awareness that I had been hired, that we had not taken on a case, but instead had been taken on, that Jackson was in charge here. Fortunately the impression was fleeting.

Cynthia said, "I am sure you have a busy day ahead, Mr. Tilden. Jay and I need a few minutes more. I will call on you next week to hear how you progress."

So was I smoothly sent away, after promising that Mr. Whitbeck would soon pay the prisoner a visit. Such matters as the accused's whereabouts when the crime was committed, his possible motive, his relationship to the deceased if any, his credibility in the community or as a witness were yet to be determined. He had offered no proof of innocence except an almost certainly spurious claim of presenting himself as a suspect in his brother's stead. He had disparaged my ability, questioned our motive in taking his case, cast doubt on my experience, set me against him without even trying. Defend him? I'd sooner have run him out of town on a rail.

It was still shy of ten in the morning. Plenty of time to stop at the Hudson *Register* office before reporting to my employer. Lillian would still be somewhere there on Warren Street inspecting the shops with Mrs. Bullock as guide. She would meet me for lunch, I hoped, at Vanderhagen's, which would be quiet on a Saturday, and perhaps conducive to the revelation of whatever it was Lillian was saving to tell me. I assured myself that she would have delivered calamitous news (that she was betrothed to another, that she was about to sail for the continent, that her father had died and left her penniless) with merciful speed. I savored the memory of her warmth at our parting the night before, her acceptance of my embrace, the caressing way she whispered my name before she closed her parlor door and sent me stumbling up the stairs, fuddled with desire.

Thinking of befuddlement, Cynthia Jackson came swiftly to mind. My first impression of her was a besotted girl, overwhelmed by the charm of a city black, a criminal or even a killer. Not surprising for a naive country girl to be attracted to a hint of danger or violence, to enjoy his wildness, his mastery. I had half expected Jay Jackson to be a thug, and so he had seemed. But Cynthia continued to surprise me. She was well spoken, but then so were many northern colored folk. I suspected some schooling, perhaps even a high school diploma, had contributed to her manner. Now that I had seen how she stood up to her husband, I realized just how remarkably sure of herself she was, Jackson's child bride. If she could persuade her husband to tone down his flashy style and glib tongue ... If Jackson could be proved unconnected to the crime... If I could work out a possible reason for someone else to have taken a butcher knife to Gertrude Hover, to stab and stab her as she fought frenziedly for her life...

I remember standing in the chilly back room of the Hudson *Daily Evening Register* poring over back issues for their account of the gruesome murder of Gertrude Margaret Hover, who had been stabbed seven times in the face and neck and beaten so that her nose was broken and her lip split. The struggle which led to her death apparently occurred in the course of a robbery. Relatives of the dead woman testified that a sizeable sum of money she was reputed to have kept in her home was missing when her body was found on September eighth of 1885. She was believed to have been slain during the afternoon of September fifth, a Saturday.

The Hudson *Daily Evening Register* first reported the crime on Wednesday, September ninth, under the heading 'THE KINDERHOOK MURDER'.

The discovery of the body was described, the search for a weapon, the discovery of a broken butcher knife , probably from Gertrude Hover's own kitchen, in her trash heap, and the assembling of a coroner's jury. The column began: "The people of this beautiful village are wonderfully excited over the tragedy, and nothing else is talked of. The suspicion that rested upon the colored people living in this locality and their friends is hardly warranted, except from the general impression that the murder was committed by someone familiar with the premises and the mode of living of the deceased."

Among the colored men questioned or detained was William Jackson, arrested in Chatham for vagrancy and creating a public nuisance by shouting at women who passed him as he was raking the bed of the railroad track. William Jackson was held and questioned about Gertrude Hover's murder, but released when his whereabouts at the time of the murder could be established. Other colored men had been questioned or detained and later released.

The Hudson *Register* for September tenth that year mentioned a telegraph dispatch from Albany (publicizing its use of modern technology) describing the involvement of Albany police under Chief Willard in the search. That day, Coroner Waldron was quoted as saying,"Thus far there is not a shadow of a clew to the perpetrator of this crime."

In the *Register* for September eleventh, John Jackson was reported to have eluded capture. On the twelfth, a reporter's reconstruction of the crime traced the course of Gertrude Hover's last moments: "The murderer entered the house by the back door, opening into the kitchen. The victim was then in the kitchen. He demanded money and clutched her throat to enforce his demand. She resisted and he then struck her with his fist square in the face. She got away from him and ran through the south room and into the hall and tried to open the front door. The murderer grabbed her again and struck her with the knife, one of the fatal blows, and she fell to the floor. He dragged her then into the parlor and stabbed her again. From a thief he had changed into a murderer. The crime having been committed about two o'clock Saturday afternoon, he remained in the house until evening.... Marks made by a bloody foot are found in the south room. He left by the same door he entered. The door is secured by a bolt and thumblatch....The intruder was known to the unfortunate woman; and when she fled to the front door he resolved to murder her." It was a plausible reconstruction of the crime, but rather fanciful. If the prosecution used it, I would challenge every word.

After that account, developments in the Hover murder went unreported.

I knew about William Jackson's arrest, and that he was held and questioned about Gertrude Hover's murder. Beside the early mention of tracing Jackson to Albany, in the two years since, several other colored men had been arrested and accused of the murder and later released. Jay Jackson had not been charged with the Hover murder until a few weeks ago.

There were no eye-witnesses to the crime. Bat Jackson's principal accuser was his neighbor Emma Briggs, who lived on a patch of land west of Kinderhook where she grew and marketed berries, raspberries, huckleberries, blueberries. She claimed to have seen Jackson mounting the fence that separated Miss Hover's back yard from the adjoining apple orchard. All those wounds, the bashing of her face, the damage to both parlor and kitchen, the broken furniture and crockery sounded to me like a crime of passion rather than a robbery turned violent. I could certainly imagine Jay Jackson's powerful fists battering an old woman. What I couldn't envision was a woman in her sixties putting up a prolonged struggle against him. Fighting for your life is understandable, but fighting against a physically superior assailant for a few dollars tucked away under the mattress or in the cookie jar? Even if she kept a 'sizeable sum' in the house. I personally would not wager my chances against that quick, sinewy body. Nor would I challenge the intensity that occasionally flashed in that handsome face. I could not imagine an old woman doing so.

I could see Bat Jackson robbing an old woman, but he'd do it with a grin and a bow. He'd have a plausible tale of woe, a believable reason to come begging. He'd have charmed her. Jackson was known to Gertrude Hover. His father lived just the other side of her orchard. His loopy brother probably gathered her windfalls and shoveled her walk in winter. I could fit my client into the role of thief, but this was a murder committed in rage, a very personal and sustained assault. What animosity could there be between a young negro just settling into married life and an old woman who chose ~ on my walk through the village with Lillian I had scrutinized that little cluster of houses out on Sunset very intently ~ *chose* to live among the village colored population, parceling out apples to the children and employing the adults to clean her house and yard and tend her garden.

I was thoughtful as I continued up Warren Street to Vanderhagen's to reserve a table for lunch and almost certainly to find John Whitbeck holding court over his third or fourth cup of coffee. He and three others were indeed settled around one of the round tables in back. Whitbeck waved me over and signaled for a new pot of coffee.

"And where is the lovely Miss Roeder this morning?" he demanded as soon as I had hung up my coat and hat and found a chair.

"Shopping with my good landlady. I have been to see our new client," I told him.

"Have you? Well?" He looked at the three men with him, the local druggist, a doctor, and the owner of Stuyvesant Landing's icehouse, deciding their discretion could be relied upon. "And your impression, young Royce?"

"A likely suspect if it were merely a robbery. But apparently he knew the old lady. They were neighbors. He could have chosen a time when she was out of the house. He could even have coaxed her into giving him her jam jar of coins. He seems far too slick to go at her like a madman. I have also read the accounts in the newspaper, and Dr. Pruyn's findings from the scene. There must have been an almighty racket when she was attacked. She fought back all the way from her kitchen to the parlor. The killer got hold of a knife and went from bashing her with his fists to stabbing her. All the cuts were to her face and neck. She bled to death from a severed jugular."

"Oh, thank you for that vivid description, Roy. We were going to order another round of toast and sausage, but I have quite lost my appetite."

"Sorry. Sorry, sir. This is a most unpleasant case, in every aspect. It's been two years and more since she died. This Jackson fellow seems more a convenient solution than a viable suspect."

"Pleading him already, are you, Royce? Or stepping up brave for his charming woman? He sent a handsome mulatto girl to seek our counsel, complete with bonnet, bells and tears, and an inadequate retainer," Whitbeck told his friends. "I'll be surprised if she's actually his wife, as she claims, though the baby may be real. They always produce a pickaninny or two to soften up our uncharitable hearts."

"Uncharitable, certainly," I said icily, as I poured myself a mug of coffee. "We'll need more cream here. And I'll have sausage and toast," I told the waiter. The others nodded their seconds, already recovered from my description of violence and gore. "After all this time it will be difficult to establish either culpability or alibi. Except for gossip and assumptions, there's no proof the victim kept any amount of money in the house. For a few dollars or a silver spoon or two, why do bloody murder, if you'll excuse my ghoulish curiosity."

"Why indeed. That's the rationale for putting the crime on a colored fella. You don't need to explain his motive or his bestiality. His race does it for him. Except for a bunch of Bible thumpers and bleeding heart social reformers, there wouldn't have to be a trial. Any violent crime that erupted up here in our fair Eden, we could just seize the nearest young black boy and hang him from a handy oak tree."

"Now, John," the druggist chided, "you surely, as a lawyer, uphold the constitution, including the thirteenth, fourteenth and fifteenth amendments. And most of your clients, the ones you got off and the ones Gardenier sent to prison, are white men like Beckwith." (Beckwith, the notorious ax murderer of Canaan, was at that time still awaiting execution, having failed to achieve clemency in a series of appeals too numerous for even a lawyer to track.)

"Now that's what will make this case truly interesting." Whitbeck left off badgering and assumed his genial sage persona, elbows on the table, long hands raised with a forefinger ready to make his points. "Under federal law and the thirteenth, fourteenth and fifteenth amendments the accused is equal before the law and entitled to the rights and privileges of citizenship. Twenty years before the crime was committed of which he is accused, he was in some states chattel, mute before the law, unable to testify for himself or witness for another, unable to inherit, purchase or own property, without claim of ownership even to a wife or children, barred from any authority or office that could afford social acceptance..."

"But, sir," I cut in before he could embark on his whole broadside against the two major political parties and their hypocrisy over race. "It was slaves who had no rights or claims. Slavery was ended in New York State nearly fifty years ago. Neither our client nor his wife was born into slavery. They may have family pedigrees of freedmen going back generations. And you know black families with property and business ownership. As surrogate judge, you yourself have handled a few disputes over inheritance among colored heirs."

"That's as may be," he sailed on, gesturing me silent. "There are some rabid and outspoken abolitionists up here still, the ones who haven't turned their attention to abolishing demon drink or enfranchising women." John Whitbeck's position on both these was so well known that a groan cascaded around the table. "Yes, well. A certain liberality infects the idyllic reaches of the Hudson and Mohawk Valleys. Colored freedmen have taken on the airs of Dutchmen and the speech of Bostonians. They hold positions of authority in more trades and businesses than I care to number. They attend school with our children and mingle freely on the streets and in stores. If we are not vigilant we will find ourselves in another generation in a position of mere equality with people we once bought and sold and despised as inherently inferior."

"Surely that was the intent of abolition, the aim for which we fought the most terrible war ever known." That was the doctor. He'd been a surgeon in the war, and had a more personal and harrowing experience of its cost than most. John Whitbeck's distinguished service in the Great War had risen out of principled conviction, rather than deep sympathy for the abolitionist cause, or so I believe.

"If actual equality was the aim, why have the national parties and their elected members in Congress left to the disposal of the various states how they shall achieve and insure it? There are local laws and regulations all over this land which prohibit or limit the exercise of equality by negro citizens. The old Blackbird laws are still in force in many places. Did you know that? All the trick clauses designed to make a profit out of capturing and returning fugitive slaves to Dixieland, all the delays built into the ending of slavery here in New York ~ Why ~"

"Yes, John. We know. You've told us before," the icehouse owner broke in. Most of his crew were black. I wondered how he felt about them voting or attending school, or forming a union. This was not an entirely new thought to me. in Albany and New York City these were very hot issues indeed, though they seemed distant to what concerned us in Hudson, mainly the railroads and gas companies and how the spread of the new electrical energy would affect them.

"Well, it will be fun to see how old Sam Edwards handles our murder case," Whitbeck raised his mug, sharing a sort of toast with me. "He'll either adhere to the old rules that blacks cannot testify (except as in Roman times, under torture) or make a clean break with old law, and allow coloreds to speak in open court. If he denies negro witnesses, it will weaken the prosecution's case, perhaps fatally. If he allows them, I can call every darkie in Kinderhook Village to testify for Jackson, but no one will believe a single one of them. This I can assure you, denial will cost the prosecution dearly, for I shall battle it all the way to the supreme court of this nation over that one issue; and you'll be an old man, Royce, before our case comes to trial."

THE SUNDAY JOURNAL PRINT.

Grand
Masquerade

AT THE

OPERA HOUSE,

HUDSON,

THURSDAY EVENING, FEBRUARY 7,

1889.

MUSIC BY PROF. E. LEE.

≪ PROGRAM. ≫

1 Grand March.
2 Quadrille.
3 Lanciers.
4 Waltz.
5 Saratoga Lanciers.
6 Quadrille.
7 Schottische.
8 Quadrille Basket.
9 Lanciers.
10 Polka.
11 Quadrille Cheat.
12 Saratoga Lanciers.
13 Waltz.
14 Quadrille Irish.
15 Schottische.

INTERMISSION.

≪ PROGRAM. ≫

1 Grand March.
2 Quadrille.
3 Lanciers.
4 Waltz.
5 Saratoga Lanciers.
6 Quadrille.
7 Schottische.
8 Quadrille Basket.
9 Lanciers.
10 Polka.
11 Quadrille Cheat.
12 Saratoga Lanciers.
13 Waltz.
14 Quadrille Irish.
15 Schottische.

INTERMISSION.

Dance Program from an entertainment at Hudson Opera House, 1890,
used by permission of the Hudson Opera House Archive, Hudson, New York

Chapter Three

Do you mean to propose?

You'll be looking into the victim.

I found Lillian chatting amicably with Mrs. Bullock before the parlor grate. She rose at once to greet me, a sign that she was royally impatient with the landlady's company, though good breeding enabled her to conceal it. I suggested a walk around the town before going to lunch; and she gratefully agreed to it, snatching up her shawl without a moment's delay.

"You live in a lively place, Roy," she confided as we turned up the street in the direction of the common. "I have not seen gaudier dresses in any shop on Broadway. And there were men lurching about or sitting on the curbstone in front of the taverns. I could not believe they were taken in drink so early in the day, but Mrs. Bullock assured me it is a common sight."

"Perhaps not every day," I qualified. "This is the weekend, after all. The dockers and roustabouts from the lumber yard and the goods station get their pay on Friday night; and some of them drink it up as soon as it jingles in their pockets. It's no different from those streets along the westside piers in the City. I hope you were not accosted or incommoded, my dear." She took a firmer grip on my arm, but only shook her head in reply. I seized the moment to ask, "Now, Miss Lillian, what's this weight of news you have carried all this way and not yet offered to let me bear?"

"Oh, Roy!" She suddenly skipped away and danced in a dizzy circle before coming to a stop facing me with her hands clasped and her eyes alight. "I have such a secret to tell you; and nobody knows that I know it; and you must never tell how you found it out!"

I regarded her solemnly and said in my gravest tone, "Miss Roeder, I shall never reveal your confidence, on pain of death."

"Oh, don't be a stick, Royce! It's not a state secret, only my father's. And it isn't that he's concealing anything, just that no one is supposed to know." She took a breath and anchored herself, holding my hands, as if without her gloved fingers clasping mine she might lose touch with the moment. "Old Mr. Gould has taken ill. The doctors think it's his heart this time, but he's been failing all this past year, so it's not a great surprise that he will have to leave the firm. That leaves only Kenny Martin and Daddy ~ with the juniors, of course, but they don't really count. Their names are all wrong."

She must have seen my bewilderment, for she suddenly smiled and turned to take up our stroll again. "Gould, Martin, Roeder was originally Anderson, Baker, Gould. That was long before Daddy's time. They have always been in the City. All three were out of Columbia Law School. The firm has only ever taken partners from Columbia: Kendall, Martin, and then Daddy. There are clerks and juniors from elsewhere. It wouldn't do to snub everyone else, or give the appearance of an exclusive club. Since they do corporate accounts and estates and things, the Columbia connection has worked well; and they are discreet about how strong the ties are to Alma Mater." She wrinkled her nose at the reference to Columbia's proud emblem. Lillian, of course, as a female, could not have attended Columbia College or the law school.

"My father is always so very busy. When he joined the firm, Anderson was still alive, though not very active, but Bryce Baker was there. After Anderson died, the partnership became Baker, Gould, Kendall. Then Kendall died, so it was Martin. When Daddy became the fourth partner he was let in on the firm's other tradition, that of listing partners alphabetically. Kenny Martin brought clients with him who about doubled the practice, but even he couldn't persuade them to charter as Martin, Baker, Gould. They're very prickly about precedents and tradition. So Daddy fit right in, you see. Roeder after Martin. There was some distress when Walter Baker had to leave, something about funds missing from trust accounts. I was away at school, so I don't remember much about it."

We had climbed the hill toward the post road, and were making slow progress toward the bustle of the coaching inn, so I steered us onto Union Street where it was quieter. The wind off the river fluttered the fringes of Lillian's shawl. A curled leaf had fallen onto the brim of her bonnet. I plucked it away gingerly and showed it to her. "This cannot be an intentional adornment, Milady, but if you like it, I can put it back."

She chuckled and took it from me, crushing it and scattering the bits. "When you rearrange my millinery, Mr. Tilden, you must not do it with dead leaves." She glanced at me sidelong, from under her lashes, with that gamine smile. And, for a moment my heart was so deep in her spell I could not speak or even move.

"So, you see, Roy Dear, what I have divined?"

"That I would make a poor milliner? That I must always provide you with fresh posies for your hat brim? That Gould, Martin, Roeder made up for the thievery of Walter Baker?"

"Yes, yes, yes. And no. That's not what I have divined. You haven't been listening."

"Oh, I have. I have. You are a delight and a wonder, my dear Lillian. Gould, Martin, Roeder is swamped. Its extremely lucrative legal defense of corporate America has become too heavy a burden for all those doomed Harvard and Princeton Law graduates with names far down the alphabet, and even for the few from Columbia Law who qualified on merit but now toil in vain at Gould, Martin, Roeder, since their names are too far up in the alphabet to allow them into partnership. You have overheard your father divulge this dismal state of affairs; and you believe you can turn it to your advantage."

"Clever. I knew you were clever, Royce, the cleverest man I have ever met. But the advantage is not mine. I haven't a Columbia Law degree and experience with a distinguished attorney who can give me an exceedingly flattering letter of recommendation when I offer to join Daddy's firm and take over their knottiest litigations. My name doesn't begin with one of the last seven letters of the alphabet."

Ah.

We walked in silence nearly all the way to Fifth Street. Then we turned again toward Warren where a table awaited us at Vanderhagen's Restaurant. Lillian had revealed so much to me in the space of those few blocks, those ten minutes of time. She had clearly anticipated my own intention to ask for her hand in marriage. That she might be agreeable to such a proposal was astounding. She was apparently willing to use what was a private tradition of her father's law firm to land me in a position where our union could be a possible result. A partnership, even a toehold at Gould, Martin, Roeder, might make me acceptable to her formidable father, would insure Lillian the income and social standing she required to live in the city she loved, in the style to which she was accustomed. To say that I was overwhelmed and astonished would be like describing the War Between the States as a pillow fight. Lillian, my distant dream, was willing to connive to make me her husband! I was dizzy and weak at the idea, too overcome to be delighted.

However, quickly on the heels of this tidal realization, the reasons swept in that had prevented me from proposing to her months earlier. Gould, Martin, Roeder had not been among the law firms I applied to when I passed the bar. My interest was not in corporate law, in civil litigation, malpractice, liability ~ all that sort of endless plodding and bickering. Criminal law was what interested me. I aspired to command a courtroom, convict or exonerate, to argue motive and circumstance, eventually to pass judgment, cite obscure precedent, make actual the law's ideal of equal justice, and so on and so forth. Criminal pleading was my reason for enduring that weary year as John Whitbeck's clerk.

Much as I was drawn to Lillian from the moment we met, her devotion to her widowed father was an obstacle for me. All her brilliance was aimed at pleasing the hard-to-please Robert Roeder, at being his proper, shining star of a daughter. In Hudson she was like a princess among savages. It never entered her mind that I might want to make a career outside of New York City, or give up years of income to earn a doctorate so I could teach the law I loved. Such ambitions would not suit her plans for me. Her plans for me were so far out of tune with my dreams as to be unimaginable. So she had blindsided me with this idea of hers, this wonderful chance she offered, the shining promise of herself as prize.

I was still stunned as I took her shawl and gloves and settled her at our table in Vanderhagen's, where the manager had produced a snowy tablecloth and polished cutlery for the occasion. The waiter was smiling and deferential, as if he had not aimed me at Whitbeck's booth hundreds of times with no more than a jerk of his thumb. Lillian ignored the menu he put before her, regarding me with bright-eyed expectancy. I looked at her, at the way she sat so primly erect with her head tilted just so and her rosy mouth ready to tease and one soft tawny curl dancing down her cheek, and was struck suddenly by the contrast of her elegance and cool composure to the sharp electric tang of that little room where I had met Jay Jackson, whom the newspapers called Bat. A hint of menace leapt from him, a kind of feral energy. I wondered again if that wildness, that unpredictability, was what had attracted his wife to him. What did Lillian find in me? I am not physically prepossessing. Even at that time I was a bit pudgy, my round face rather florid. I still had hair then, and wit, of course. I suppose she thought me brilliant. Curious what constitutes acceptability in a mate. It was more Lillian's beauty than her cleverness I found desirable. Easy to see what Jackson had found in Cynthia Van Houck, exquisite beauty and unawakened virginal yearning ~ the eternal substance of male fantasy. A jury would hate and envy him in equal measure. The case would be lost before the judge even entered. How foolish to have become entangled in the hopeless defense of a black man so obviously meant to be hanged. Meanwhile, here, across the table from me, was my sure escape from all that, and the promise of pleasure and ease to boot.

"Beautiful Lillian," I murmured, "You have trumped my ace before I even played it. What would you like for lunch? I recommend the sea bass. They fetch it fresh from the river."

"I shall have some soup first, while I think about it, and while you consider how to deal with my idea."

I looked up from the menu (which I knew by heart) and regarded her with what I hoped was affectionate sternness. "The mulligatawny is good. We'll have that then." I signaled the waiter and gave him our order, quizzing him at length about the freshness of the day's catch and choosing a light wine for it. Lillian waited, tapping an impatient finger on her knife handle, kneading the folds of her napkin, watching me as a cat eyes a mousehole.

I smiled a complicit, cheshire smile at her. "My plan is to take you riding in the trap again. We can see a bit more of the countryside. And you can tell me what you've been doing, beside plotting my future." Her expression at this was smugly serene, though a faint blush warmed her cheeks. "Also," and here I paused to take a deep breath as if about to plunge from a great height, "I need to tell you... to ask you... to propose..." (For a legal pleader not given to waffling, I was making a poor job of this.) "... a serious matter that has filled my mind... In particular, I want you to give me your opinion of one or two houses in the area which are on offer for purchase, should I, should we..."

Lillian's eyes opened wide, her hand flew to cover her mouth. I had managed to astonish her.

"Yes, my dear. Our thoughts have taken similar paths. Until you told me ~ what you just told me ~ my intention was to ask your advice, or even urge you to choose one of several fine houses I have noticed in nearby villages, houses you might find worthy of interest, that you might want to decorate and furnish to your taste and comfort, that you might want to live in with ~

"Stop! Stop, Royce. You are babbling. Do you mean to propose that we live up here when we are married? I can't believe it! You are being whimsical, as usual. I know you have family over there in New Lebanon, but really! Here you are, rusticating among these old Dutch farmers, letting your keen legal mind waste away. Ridiculous! And when I suggest a means for you to change that, to come to the City where you belong and take up a civilized practice with Daddy, you tease me with jaunts through the cornfields and sightseeing among the stately homes of ~ what county is this again?"

"Columbia County, my dear Lillian. So, does this mean you expect that we shall marry? Do I hear a yes in that scolding?"

"You hear me insisting on a proper course for us, Roy. Don't let your soup grow cold."

And with that she turned her full attention to the fragrant, steaming bowl the waiter was bringing to the table. A delightful lady, Lillian Roeder. She married a lawyer named Staunton, who did, of course, join her father's firm. When I returned to Columbia to earn my law doctorate they had me to dinner a few times, the odd bachelor to balance out an aunt or cousin at the dinner table. She did have the grace to visit two stately homes with me that afternoon, not that I retained much hope of persuading her that she could be happy living so far upcountry, so far from her father. We parted on Hudson Landing early Monday morning under a misty rain that slicked the cobbles and turned the river a soft pewter. We were at that moment unofficially engaged, but I never did ask her father for her hand, the chilly, gloved hand that clasped mine in farewell. I remember how sweetly she smiled at me, so assured that I would come round, that I would become the copy of her father she wanted me to be.

After she was safely aboard I returned the trap and horse to Pulcher's Livery and found John Whitbeck at Vanderhagen's reading his paper. His coffee had not yet been brought; he was uncharacteristically grumpy. He had invited Lillian and me to dinner with his family on Sunday, after our inconclusive tour of local mansions. (No farmhouse would have been acceptable for Lillian Roeder.) His cordiality apparently exhausted by entertaining my fiancee, no opening of mine could rouse him on this rainy morning. As we left for the office he gave me my agenda for the day.

"You'll be looking into the victim, I expect." (That was his way of giving an order.) "I have some reading to do in the statutes." That would be the New York State Statutes, of course; and I could bet which ones, New York state emancipation law preceded the Thirteenth Amendment to the national constitution by a generation. Runaway slave laws and freedmen's statutes and county and town regulations were even older. Local traditions were older still, going back to the treatment of Indians and indentured laborers under the Patroons in the seventeenth century. John would be reviewing his knowledge of the statute books, culling instances of abuse, inconsistency, and legal discrimination against negroes in and out of bondage during all of New York's hypocritical and unwholesome past. My task was much simpler: to find out who Gertrude Hover was, her family, her character, her social and economic standing, her attitude toward her colored neighbors and their regard for her. With a supreme bit of luck I might learn why she was beaten and stabbed to death on a quiet September day two years past. Perhaps I could form an idea about her killer, Unfortunately, Jay Jackson, that cocky, glib hustler, seemed on first acquaintance capable of almost anything overheated local minds could fantasize into nightmarish brutality. He would be a supremely unsympathetic defendant.

So why did I not do as Lillian desired? I could have resigned from the case, left Whitbeck's employ, asked him for a letter of recommendation to Gould, Martin, Roeder. I could have returned to New York City, and begun to gather handsome retainers instead of scrabbling along on meager fees of petty felons. You will think, perhaps, that my motives were idealistic, that I was an early crusader against the sordid outcome of Reconstruction, that I was an advocate for justice, equality and the American dream. Please continue to think so. I admit to a less noble impetus. I was young then, and my *amour propre* had been deeply wounded by Lillian's refusal even to entertain the idea of making a life with me in my home county, though she was willing to marry me on her terms. I could not help but compare her intransigence, her assurance that she could dominate me, with the soft, trusting loyalty of Cynthia Jackson, whose grace, intelligence, charm, and beauty offered everything in Bat Jackson's defense that his own demeanor lacked. That was the other aspect of my own intransigence. I wanted to be part of this case.

Was I drawn to Cynthia Jackson? Of course. Was I, suddenly at odds with the woman I planned to wed, in danger of disloyalty to her? At these forty years remove, I cannot with honesty answer that question. I do know, however, that as we conferred and struggled and supported one another through the months that led up to her husband's trial, I came to understand on every level how constant interchange and conversation can erode conventional barriers between people who think themselves fundamentally different, can expose our artificial racial distinctions for the flimsy sham they are.

Chapter Four

There's a school. Do you know it?

In Columbia County (New York) for example, the Second School District maintained a separate school to serve the other towns in the district. Its location in Kinderhook (with a population of 143 Blacks in 1865) posed hardships to Blacks who lived in other towns. The thirty pupils were taught in winter by a Black man and in summer by a Black woman in an inadequate "room formerly occupied as a store".

Ena L. Farley in *The Underside of Reconstruction New York*

As I trotted beside Whitbeck on the post road up to Kinderhook that Monday, my mood was one of sober determination. The rain had given way to a brisk wind, though it was still a damp, chilly morning, gray as my outlook. I thought of Lillian and wondered if she felt aggrieved at my resistance to corporate law, or rather my reluctance to submit to her father's domination. For that, I realized, was the crux of it. As dazzling and attractive as I found Lillian to be, I had never warmed to her father, a large, hearty, redfaced man who talked expansively and at length on any topic that arose, and seemed incapable of listening to any voice but his own. Was I refusing my chance at a lucrative career in the City for such a trivial reason as dislike of a prospective colleague? He would also, of course, be my future father-in-law, the grandfather of my children. Ah, Lillian, did you see in my deferential manner toward you a malleability that would make me compliant to your father's will? It was you, Lillian, your peculiarly graceful reserve, your exquisitely tasteful manner to which I was deferential. I had never until then met a woman of such charming elegance. She could, and did, draw me across a room full of people and keep me at her side, trading sallies that promised so much. Unwise of me to presume from the promise of that soft manner that I could turn her loyalty to me, guide her into my life, away from her father. Perhaps ~

All the years gone by, my whole life, and still I sometimes wonder, as I did that morning, what I could have done to change the outcome of that weekend. If had been more eloquent, more forceful, perhaps, if I had made myself a person of more consequence in her eyes ~

That dangerous perhaps was pushed from my mind as the sky began to lighten. Whitbeck drew my attention to the Catskills rising out of the river mist and Kinderhook's outlying farmhouses shimmering palely among their dark windbreaks. A day inquiring into the life and character of Miss Gertrude Hover would provide me with some entertainment, and might even be useful in Jackson's defense. Indeed, I was surprised that my employer had given me this aspect of the case to investigate. It would have been more his style to put me among the old lawbooks and court records, and visit those involved in the case himself to establish what he might use as a defense. It was usual, of course, for Whitbeck to order me about. I was his only employee except for the cleaner who brought up coals for the Franklin stove and took away the crumpled discards of Whitbeck's voluminous writings. My senior was careful and serious in his personal life, protective of his family. The dinner for Lillian was the first time I had been entertained at his home. One trait we shared was a dislike of flamboyance. He was coming to tolerate me, but it was an uneasy regard; and I did not presume on it. So I did not ask him why he had assigned me to what might prove a pleasant day querying Gertrude Hover's neighbors. Nor did I question his decision to join me for this one interview, since it was with a prominent and influential citizen.

We were to call at the home of John Powell and his wife, whose large holding lay across the soft hills south of Kinderhook Village. Powell was a person of standing in the county, a major contributor to conservative causes. His fields stretched nearly to the river, with his house perched on high ground back from the road. To the north, his dairy herd grazed the field opposite Gertrude Hover's house.

Powell's wife, a large, comfortable, garrulous woman, welcomed us effusively, offering hot coffee and sweet buns. She knew Whitbeck well, apparently, but I think she similarly welcomed anyone willing to sit in her parlor and endure her rambling monologue. I settled gingerly on the stiff horsehair of her settee, sipped my coffee, and listened.

"Gertrude? Of course I knew her. My John hires them darkies live over by Gertrude's place. Well it's not hers any more. That nevvie of hers took it over right off, but the brothers wouldn't let him keep it. Sold it all at auction last year, house and barn. That nice orchard of hers: Now my John offered good money for that orchard. It's on the road past our far meadow, you see. I could have done with that crop of apples. But the church there, or was it the village? came in with double. Double! John was that upset. I hear they want to extend the graveyard. That's why they want it. Want to keep plenty of space around the Van Buren plot. Big on monuments the village. But the brother, one of the brothers ~ lives down Stockport way ~ well, he kept two acres for himself, nice stretch that fronts on the Albany Road. Very high-handed the village is, when they want something.

"Here now, let me just warm that coffee. And you take another bun, Lawyer Whitbeck. You could use some meat on you. Some of you fellas don't eat proper." She glanced, then, at my well-fed self. "Come winter you'll wish you had. Strengthen the blood, I always say, and it'll strengthen you. My John, he never goes out of this house without a good meal inside him. Day in, day out, he has his steak and fry-potatoes and eggs for breakfast. Never sick a day, my John. Never. Now where was I? Oh, yes, them Hovers ~ well the nevvie, he's not a Hover. His mother was Gertrude's sister Nettie, Jeanette that is. She married a Van Epps from over Canaan way. She died, must be ten years ago now. She was consumptive. Her husband and the son, George, they don't get along too good.. Not a nickel between them, and George, Gertrude's nevvie, he doesn't amount to much. Worked in the icehouse at Stuyvesant Landing for a while, till they, him most likely, lost the house Nettie left, gambled it away, my John says." Suddenly her hand flew to cover her mouth, as if she had said something forbidden. Whitbeck cleared his throat. Two sips of coffee and a keen glance at my mystified expression elapsed before she continued.

"George he used to hang around Gertrude's place, helping her with chores and that. I saw him once up on her roof. I was passing in the buggy, and there he was up over them little eyebrow windows at the front of her house, nailing down shingles, and Gertrude yelling up at him the whole time how he was doing it wrong, nailin' in leaks stead of fixin' 'em, how he better come down and let Amos do it. I laughed! Old Amos, he must be eighty if he's a day. Used to work for my John sometimes. Come up here before the War, a runaway slave most likely. He talks that soft drawl from down there. Used to work in the print shop till he got too old to see the type. And Gertrude wanted him up a ladder to her roof. Can you imagine?

"She was a great one for hiring her neighbors for whatever she needed done, you see." She smirked at us to indicate that by neighbors she meant negroes. "She was a bit odd, Gertrude, used to go clear over to Seneca Falls, for them abolitionist meetings. Very big on helping the niggras. A great one for causes was Gertrude. I remember once she came back from one of her abolitionist gatherings and she was tricked out in them Bloomers. For a while she'd work in her garden wearing them, parading herself around like she was the cat's meow. You couldn't pass the time of day with her but she had to preach about Votes for Women. Silly old bat. No wonder she never married. Who would have her, with that tongue of hers and her opinions."

She paused to nibble at her bun. I held my rapt expression so as not to interrupt such a font of lore. Whitbeck nodded encouragement.

"She was a great one for meddling with her neighbors too. She'd see one of the pickaninnies from those little houses over next to her ~ She owned that land, see, and the houses where the coloreds live. Used to be slave cabins back before ... you know, back when." She gave a conspiratorial smirk and cast her eyes heavenward, as if slavery were a fondly remembered Eden. When neither of us responded, she nodded to herself as if she'd found us out in a lapse. "Anyway," she went on relentlessly, "Gertrude was that nosy, always peeking out her parlor window. She'd spy a child playing outside on a school day and she'd march out and lay into them like hellfire. What were they doing wasting their time in games when they could be over at the school learning and bettering themselves, and like that. There's a school, do you know it? a school for the coloreds. Right there in the village, in one of the old tannery sheds. It's the only one in the county, has maybe twenty, thirty children, got a darkie teacher and all. So anyway, about Gertrude, my John told me. He'd hear her when he was over seeing to the milking. My John said she was the best show around when she got going on one of her rants. The kids would say to her, 'Miz Hover, we got no shoes. Can't go to school barefoot.' And she'd take a willow switch and whip them over to Trimper's and buy them stockings and boots so they'd have no excuse to stay away from school."

She got up to fetch the coffee pot from the well-stoked kitchen wood stove, and filled our cups with her strong, steaming brew without asking. "You know we have the Academy too, a very fine school that is, right in the village. The Quakers were the ones started it. They take scholars from all over and beyond, live right there at the Academy some of them. That Cynthia Van Houck ~ ~ well, she's Jackson now, Bat Jackson's wife ~ she graduated from the Academy. I don't know, maybe she was the first one ~ not the first girl I guess, but one of the first colored to go there. Her Aunt was so proud, I tell you! Her Aunt Margaret that owns the hat shop on Hudson Street in the village ~ she was so puffed when Cynthia got the history prize there was no talking to her. I said to her, 'Margaret, That's so fine your niece won that prize and all, but what will she do now? She gonna wear that medal on a ribbon while she sews feathers on your hats? She gonna give history lessons while she helps us try on your spring bonnets?' She wasn't half upset I can tell you. I didn't go near that shop again till I heard the niece was marrying Bat Jackson. In the AME Church, too. Never thought to see one of them Jacksons in a church! Now that was a wedding I wouldn't have missed for all the tea in China. Margaret made the hat I wore to it; and you never saw such a spread of good food as that day at the Beth-El." She smacked her lips, remembering.

"Cynthia never went back to helping in the hat shop after that. She does some seamstressing and that. But Bat Jackson wouldn't have his wife working, not in a shop anyway. He's a uppity niggra that one, but smooth talkin' when he wants sum'pn' from ya. He was happy enough for her to turn out that old house of his father's and make it respectable. She's forever washing the windows, beating the carpets, whitewashing the walls, scrubbing. Clothesline full every time you go by there. She nursed Bat's father when his back went bad last year; and Bat's brother William ~ he's tetched that William, talks like a loon ~ he just worships Cynthia. He didn't used to visit his father much till Cynthia married Bat. Now he's there all the time. He comes over from Chatham ~ he works for the railroad ya see, walks the tracks and reports damage. So he comes over to his father's for a hot meal and stays a day or two. I think Cynthia does his laundry, cuts his hair, and like that. Now she's got that baby too. I wonder how she manages it all, with Bat in jail and no money coming in. He's a hard worker, that Bat Jackson, a good provider. He works for my John sometimes."

Her hand covered her mouth again. Her spate halted as if she'd been dumbstruck. In a way she had. My-John Powell had arrived. I could hear his boots thumping in the mudroom off the kitchen. He'd be wanting his hot meal before returning to his afternoon chores. Mrs. Powell got up without another word and swept into the kitchen. I heard her setting the table. When she took the lid off a pot on the stove the rich, savory aroma of soup wafted through the open parlor door. Then John Powell himself filled the door and we stood to greet him. He was a burly, massive man, with a wind-blasted face and big rough hands sticking out of shirtsleeves not quite long enough for him.

"Whitbeck," he nodded to my employer. He had probably washed under the pump, for the hand he extended to me was damp and bright red with cold.

"John Powell." he said, and then told me, "You're the other lawyer gonna keep Bat Jackson from hanging. The missus says you're both welcome to lunch if you like. You want help getting that nigger off, don't look at me. Jackson helped out here sometimes." He paused, studying our faces for a reaction. "If they ask me, I'll testify he was here that Saturday, before he killed the Hover woman. He's wild, Bat Jackson." He seemed about to turn away, but then added, "I never had trouble with him. I just heard tell he was a bad'un. He's quick as an eel, and glib, and sly. You don't ever want to turn your back on Bat. That's what they say. But he never bothered me." Then he did clump his way back to the kitchen.

We offered our excuses to his wife and made our exit. When we reached the post road, Whitbeck set off back down to Hudson, urging me to complete our planned interviews. I rode north toward Kinderhook wondering about what John Powell had not told us. What sort of work had Bat Jackson done on the farm that made him 'a good provider'. Farmhands, then and now, earn hardly enough to feed themselves. Yet Bat Jackson dressed like a dandy and clothed his wife in good worsted. And what was Powell looking to have known or acknowledged in those wordless exchanges with my employer? The wife, too, had hinted at something in among her ramblings. What did she start to say that she didn't want her husband to hear? What savory plums could be plucked from her overabundant pudding of local lore and gossip? What use could we make of her revelations about Gertrude Hover?

In the village I hitched my horse outside the coaching inn and found a table with a good light. I jotted down some of what we had just heard before the waiter came to take my order. Half the day was spent, and Gertrude Hover seemed to hover, so to speak, in the river mist. A stern, prickly old woman, stubbornly independent in her views, benevolent in the abstract but not the personal. She seemed to occupy a moral pinnacle too rarefied for just about anyone else to reach. I could imagine how she might inspire resentment, even be avoided, but battered senseless and stabbed repeatedly? The account in the Hudson *Daily Evening Register* of how she had been found, the state of her house, indicated a viciousness of attack that was out of all proportion for a robbery. Somebody had harbored a deep hatred for old Gertrude; and it had boiled over into uncontrollable rage that September day two years ago. The struggle, the terrible act, was playing itself in my mind to the exclusion of the placid village reality in front of my eyes.

After my meal I strolled through Kinderhook's tiny, bustling center, passing the shops, including a shoe store and Layton's millinery, which I took to be the one owned by Cynthia Jackson's Aunt Margaret. The livery stable and ticket office for the New York-Albany stage took up one whole corner, with the coaching inn and an adjoining sadlery. Willcoxson's Drygoods and General Store occupied another. There was a bank, a grocer, an apothecary, a sweet shop, and lawyers' and doctors' offices. On Hudson Street I could see a feedstore and the printshop, or rather the glass-fronted premises of the local weekly, the Kinderhook *Rough Notes*. Gold lettering announced the paper, with Fine Printing, Notices, Calling Cards, Invitations strung out in an urgent line that advertised the shop's true trade. Behind the window loomed a bearded, melancholy face with a starched collar beneath it. That would be C.W. Davis, editor of the newspaper and presumptive master printer.

He soon dismissed that idea. "Not at all, sir. I leave the printing side to Daly. He learned from old Amos; and I never interfere. I am a historian by calling, and a vigilant observer of village life, as you noted before entering. Everyone in Kinderhook comes within my view sooner or later. I can see the village center from here, the stages passing through, the inn where our businessmen congregate and confer, the shops where the ladies meet. I hear the clatter of wheels and hooves, the grumble and buzz of voices, the shrill cries of the children. I am the village scribe, occasionally the town crier."

"You are managing editor of the *Rough Notes*," I insisted. I'd like a look at your issues of two years ago, and perhaps even the benefit of your knowledge of a case I am currently examining."

"Ah. You must be John Whitbeck's clerk." I gave him my name. "You've taken young Jay Jackson as a client. Surely you don't expect to get that rascal off. As for my old news, I can provide the account of Gertrude Hover's death. Dr. Pruyn, who examined the body, lives here in the village. I also published a report of Jackson's arrest, but little else. We avoid printing what reflects poorly on the life of our village," he said primly. "A President was born here. His memorial graces our cemetery, his stately home brings tourists to visit. We have a certain reputation to maintain."

"You censor the news, then. What about your recollections? Can I have access to what you have seen and heard from behind your plate glass window?"

"Censor is too strong a charge, sir. I consider the sensibilities of my readers. My wife, for instance, who is the paper's owner, approves every issue." His lips formed a painful smile. "My personal observations, however, are considerably more complete. I am a historian, after all. Come into my office, where we can talk privately."

Indeed, Charles Davis's personal observations were readily to hand, and of an unexpected acuity, once he was ensconced behind his cluttered desk with his door closed, though I had not seen another soul in his establishment who might overhear us. From a back room the clank of a letterpress sounded intermittently. Davis, as he told me, was a comparative newcomer to the county, having arrived some twelve years earlier from Buffalo, where he taught history at DeWitt

Clinton College, to deliver a lecture on the Erie Confederacy to the ladies of the Kinderhook Historical Society.

"The invitation came to my department head, but nobody senior to me had any wish to make the jolting journey downstate to the Hudson Valley. My dear wife Fanny, Frances Van Alen Winters that is, was then president of the Society. She met me when I alit from the stage. A remarkable woman my Fanny. She founded the local Browning Society. She chairs the women's group at the Dutch Reformed Church. She is the daughter of Randolph Winters, who then owned this printshop and edited the *Rough Notes*. So, as you will have surmised, I married into the newspaper business. Randolph died seven years ago. He was apoplectic and loved his wine."

"So you left teaching for this ~" I indicated the dim and dusty interior outside the office.

"Not entirely. I still teach, at the local academy. The scholars are young, of course, but many show considerable aptitude and promise. I confess to putting far more energy into that avocation, and take more pride in my students' progress, than I invest in this weekly gazette. Very little of news value or abiding interest occurs in the village. It was a placid place before the first Dutchman persuaded the Mohawk to cede hunting rights over a tract of Hudson Valley forest. It has changed little in the centuries since. Martin Van Buren was born here, not a distinguished president, but a national figure all the same. That does make for a certain smugness, an exalted notion of Kinderhook's importance. I find it ~ impolitic ~ to challenge established ideas and prejudices."

I wondered about that formidable wife of his, who seemed to have him nicely haltered. Surely my Lillian would not... For all his apparent compliance to local strictures, however, Davis expressed views of recent history that fell aslant of local traditions. His face grew more animated as he spoke of events in the recent past. I leaned toward him and nodded slowly, urging him to continue confiding such small nuggets of local history as came to his mind.

"My son Randolph is now seven," he explained. "I insist that he be exposed to a good deal more of the world, and of regional history, than is expected at the academy, or than I can comfortably teach there. I do include European history, as well as colonial and American history in my courses. Sometimes, when the school year ends in June and the graduates have been honored and the prizes given, I feel as flat as a punctured hot-air balloon. I miss my students in the summer, and return to them eagerly in the fall. They keep me sane, those earnest, not to say adoring, upturned faces, the timid questions, the bright-eyed speculations." He looked at me keenly before proceeding.

"Cynthia Jackson was my student until two years ago." He leaned forward and spoke more softly. "Cynthia Van Houck that was. She received her prize in history from my own hands. No college for her, of course. She'd have needed more than her beauty, those luminous eyes, that talent she has for analysis and speculation, to land a place in any college. If she'd had a sponsor with influence and funds maybe... Have you met her yet, Jay Jackson's wife?" I nodded. We smiled at each other, sharing that pleasure.

"Jackson met her the summer after she graduated, blew into town and saw that one flawless gem, that lovely brown child, and just dazzled her into marrying him. She sang in the choir at Bethel AME. Just a slip of a girl, but she has a voice clear as fresh water, sweet and high..." His eyes closed, Davis listened briefly to harmonies in his mind, before he shook them away and continued. "I don't attend the Bethel Church, of course, my wife being very active in the Dutch Reformed, and the AME being a colored denomination. But if you walk along the road there sometimes you can hear them singing... At any rate, that summer Bat Jackson was suddenly an avid churchgoer. And he was up in the choir loft before you could say Nelly Bly. They say he sings a fine tenor, that his singing won my Cynthia's heart. But I do believe it was his soft tongue. Young Jackson's a talker, sharp and witty, full of fine sweet words. They say, those who know him, you have to keep your hand on your wallet with Bat Jackson. He's so slick he'll charm the shoes off your feet and sell them back to you. I don't know this for a fact. I also hear Bat's got quick hands in an altercation, and a quick and clever mind. And Cynthia is an excellent listener, attentive, perceptive..." He paused, remembering, "I can see those eyes of hers glowing with fascination when I lectured on the Century of Progress, my view of American history since 1776." He nodded at my unexpressed admiration for his up-to-date approach to the past.

"It wasn't that she was my most brilliant student," he raised a cautioning hand. "That was probably the Potts boy. But Cynthia was so bold, her ideas so original." His face turned inward again, remembering, "those soft eyes of hers, that light voice, and her questions! She'd ask things like *Why did the New York State manumission law of 1799 free slave women at twenty-five but men only at twenty-eight? How come they made the New York freedom law in 1817, but it only freed people ten years later? Three emancipation amendments to the constitution? Three? And still Mr. Daly who prints the ballots, he can't vote. Why is that?* She just sheared away appearances and laid bare the underlying political substance."

"You were a bit in love with her, I think."

Davis smiled again, that tight, unhappy smile. "Every man who meets Cynthia Van Houck falls a bit in love with her," he shrugged. Then a kind of painful judder spasmed across his face.

"At her graduation," he said dreamily, "she wore white broderie and ribbons in her pigtails. She swayed up between the rows of parents as if she were made of willow fronds, head bowed, hands clasped at a broad green sash. I slipped the history medal over her head on its silk ribbon, and presented her with my own leather-bound translation of Tacitus. And then she looked up and thanked me. And the soft look in her eyes just made me tremble, she was so lovely. Right then, the idea of her venturing unprotected into a hostile world full of rough and predatory males filled me with rage, and yes, I suppose, with envy. But you must understand that my feelings for Cynthia Van Houck, now Jackson, are paternal, purely paternal. I want what's best for her. And," he glared at me. "if being rid of that scoundrel Bat Jackson who seduced and married her is what's best for Cynthia, then I will do what I can to bring that about. So you cannot look for my help in defending him, Mr. Tilden. I'll not bend the truth to convict him, but there's no innocence in Bat Jackson, whether or not he killed the Hover woman."

His expression went from sharp distaste to brooding sadness, dark eyes challenging mine to persuade him out of a stance he knew to be unworthy of his character and calling. Then he stood and led me down a ladderlike flight of steps into the shop's basement where old issues of the paper were filed. "You'll find them in order, I believe. Please return them where you find them." He turned abruptly to leave me to it.

"Please, before you go, Mr. Davis, are there others in the village who knew Miss Hover, who know Bat Jackson, and might be willing to talk to me?"

Now a faint smile was discernible on that melancholy countenance. "Anyone you meet will talk to you, sir. The trick is to glean anything useful from what you are told."

I started with September of 1885, when the murder of Gertrude Hover was reported in a black bordered announcement on page one, and plowed through two years of C.W. Davis's four page notices. Most of the paper consisted of postings before and after local meetings, local concerts, social events, including holiday parties at the big, comfortable houses on the main street, Albany Avenue, and such national and international news as Davis could squeeze in among the advertisements for women's fashions, patent medicines, and the fluctuations in grain and meat prices.

From the death of Ulysses Grant, to Gladstone's proposal for Irish home rule, to the craze for all things French at the dedication of the Statue of Liberty, national news merited hardly more than a paragraph or two. I supposed that those wanting to know more of the world subscribed to other newspapers. The most daring insertion I found was a notice that Karl Marx's *Das Kapital* had appeared in English translation.

The report of Gertrude Hover's death in the Hudson *Register* was far mare informative, so I decided to rely on it, rather than the dour "Terrible Death on Sunset Road" provided in the *Rough Notes*. I did glean a few names, Emma Briggs, whose accusation had led to Jackson's arrest, the Sitcer family, who lived close to Gertrude and claimed knowledge of what went on there that fatal Saturday in September 1885. Drs. Woodworth and Pruyn, who had examined the body, needed a visit. I must also spend some time with Jackson's family, his father, maybe the brother, and with his wife, of course, the enchanting Cynthia who inspired the keenest protective feelings not only in my vulnerable self, but in the staid and mature Charles Davis as well. No doubt there were others caught in that dark Helen's spell. Could I make use of that in Jackson's defense, imply that his indictment could be part of a plan to put him out of the way so another could rescue his child bride (and his child) from his unworthy grasp?

The cold dankness of Davis's storage cellar was causing me to shiver and sneeze. I became aware that the printing press had ceased its thump and clatter some time previously. In fact, there was no detectable sound from above me. Had Davis and his employee left for the day, forgetting that I was there? I scrambled up the steep steps and burst out into the narrow hallway, nearly crashing into Davis, on his way to fetch me.

"Ah. Good. You have finished?"

"Yes, thanks. You keep tidier files than some."

"Actually Daly keeps the files. He stays late sometimes putting them in order. Amos set up the racks long before my time. He was ~ is ~ a remarkable old fellow, Amos. Born before the War of 1812, and remembers pretty much everything that's happened here in this century. He was a printer for the Chatham paper before he came to the village. They use a lot of boiler plate there. You know, those 'Darkie Jim an de tree button boot' stories that fill up the inner pages between the painless dentist and whalebone corset ads. I think Amos liked working for the *Rough Notes* because I try to avoid using such material, if I can. People who read them, who are amused by how they demean black folks, don't seem to realize how that sort of thing demeans everyone. When I lay out an issue I always have in mind that Daly, or Amos before he retired, will be reading it as he sets the type. Anything printed that portrays negroes as stupid or incapable will be known to every darkie Daly meets before he has walked from here to Valatie. And, of course, anything that sullies the shiny image of this charming village will bring calumny on my head. Between my sensitivities and my convictions, and the expectations of this community, I tread a very narrow path, Mr.Tilden. I envy the pioneers and crusaders of print who have no ties of kin or coin to restrain them. John Whitbeck's advocacy for Battice Jackson I find truly admirable, sir. I'd wish him and you success in this case, but you would rightly doubt my sincerity. Bat didn't do it, of course. You are required to assume that. And it may be true. All the same I hope he hangs."

"Thank you, Mr. Davis. You've been a great help, with or without intending it."

We had made our way to the front door. Davis stood with his hand on the knob, unwilling to let me go. "We are an impatient people, Americans." he told me. (Indeed, I was at that moment impatient to be on my way.) "We want the problem solved and put away. We are hot to tackle the next mess the old world has left us. But do you see the danger of that boasted Can Do American attitude?"

I was certain he would explain it to me.

"It goes with a very short attention span. Like our politicians, who can't think past the next election, we set encompassing goals like Equality and so forth, but then expect to reach them with a sudden great effort. Abolition took up the moral imagination of reformers for a generation. But abolition did not achieve equality among our citizens. Equality could not be reached in a single bound from slavery. However, disregarding the ills Abolition and Reconstruction left behind, we have rushed on to the next social ill we perceive: Liquor, which threatens family welfare and economic stability.. So now all our moral energy is focused on prohibiting strong drink. In that arena we will battle until some grand law is passed that we will expect to solve that problem. Then on to the next, whatever that will be. My great-grandchildren will see laws passed to enforce universal education or prohibit poverty or give the vote to women or whatever. There is always another river ahead of us. We don't look back to see the flood still rising where we've been."

"That puts us firmly on the great wheel of history, Mr. Davis. You have expressed admirably the historian's view. Like the weight of the law, it can utterly squash you if you let it." On that note I bid him a hasty goodbye before he could start off on another rant.

The afternoon was fading toward dusk, golden leaved maple trees pouring long patterns of dancing shadow across my way as I crossed the village center again, making for the meandering cart track of Sunset road that left the village proper and followed the edge of a pasture till it became a seam between harvested fields. A colored farmhand with a big, rough voiced dog was rounding up cows for milking. Opposite the field, a little white church, Bethel AME, began to glow from within as the lowering sun filled its tall clearglass windows.

Farther along the road stood the cluster of houses that Mrs. Powell had called slave cabins. They looked too new and far too sturdy for that. Several had additions and picket fences. They occupied a nicely shaded acreage adjoining the Hover house and its orchard.

I found it difficult to wrap my pleasant anticipation in Davis's cloak of fatherliness as I asked the three small children dancing giddily among the fallen leaves which house was the Jacksons'. Mutely shy, they pointed me to a two-story dwelling, painted gray with dark green shutters, fronted by an enclosed garden. There was no answer to my knock for a long minute. Then a faint response and slow footsteps brought the elder Jackson to the door. He was stocky, with a thread of gray in close-cropped hair and deep lines scouring a dark, craggy face that might once have been as handsome as his son's. He was grumbling, scowling, until he saw me, whereupon a rictus of smile formed to wall me out.

"Yessuh. What can you be wanting?"

"Mr. Jackson?" He nodded. "My name is Tilden. I am assistant to John Whitbeck. Your son Jay has engaged us to represent him when he comes to trial." The forced smile remained, but the dark eyes looked out at me bleakly. He stood without speaking, meeting my gaze with an almost malevolent distrust. After an excruciatingly long interval he motioned me ahead of him into a small, neat parlor. As he crossed to what must be his accustomed chair and sank into it, the painful twisting of his back was clear, the crippling injury that Cynthia had nursed him through.

"Sit," he told me. "My daughter's not here. What you want with me?"

"I am hoping you will tell me a bit about your son, what sort of a person he is. Whatever you remember about what Jay was doing, where he was, around the time of Miss Hover's death would be helpful. You may know something that would serve to clear him of this charge ~ something you don't think is important."

For a long period there was no response. Jackson sat very still, gnarled hands on the chair arms, head bowed, almost as if he were dozing there, while twin shafts of sunlight spilled through the paired windows and crept across the patterned wall toward him. The silence was long enough that when he spoke, in a soft, mellow baritone, I was startled.

"You got my boy in jail, where he shouldn't be. You got the girl running about, as she shouldn't be, for money to save him. You got half this town ready to lynch him and some others would do anything to get him loose and keep him quiet. You got people lying, paid to lie, and people scurrying to hide the truth. What you don't have is one white man ready to stand up and witness to it. What I know, what I remember, won't be listened to. I'm his kin and I'm a black man." He raised his head at last to glare at me. "You have to find an honest white man. That's what my son needs. If you find one, will you want to hear what he says?"

"Perhaps if you tell me what to listen for it will guide me," I suggested mildly.

"And have you build a tale to suit you? And send my boy to the gallows?" His voice had risen, and then cut off suddenly as he turned his head to listen. "My grandson is awake," he told me. "I'll see to him now. You can go. Talk to some others, like Tom Warren or that snake Van Epps, or Asa Gillet. Asa might be willing to talk to you. Not many will."

As he rose slowly from the deep chair, I noticed again that he favored his left side, carried one shoulder higher than the other. His expression, grim and impassive, masked whatever pain he felt as he shuffled ahead of me to the door before calling out in answer to the fretful sounds that began to drift from a room beyond.

Asa Gillet: a name that had not appeared in any public account of the crime or the investigation. Outside, the children were no longer playing in the leaves. I made the rounds of the snug negro settlement, knocking on doors that did not open to me, accosting two women who hurriedly told me they knew nothing, not even their names, it appeared. My very presence there was a threat to their fragile security. I had never, in my two years defending Hudson's lawbreakers, felt so distrusted, so much the oppressors' emissary, as on that bright autumn day in Kinderhook Village. After an hour of it the white woman who came to the door of what had been Gertrude Hover's house was a welcome sight, though she was as unforthcoming as her neighbors. With some reluctance she did point me toward the property of Asa Gillet before firmly shutting her door on any further queries.

Kinderhook Village Common, ca. 1880 (detail)
used by permission, Columbia County Historical Society, Kinderhook, New York

Chapter Five

Let us compare the prejudice of today (1887) with that of the emancipation (1863). Is prejudice as evident now as then? Why no ... Whereas the Negro was set free penniless and ignorant, (which was his condition) with the keen blade of prejudice ready to cut him down (which was the result of slavery) he is now a citizen, and in accordance with the progress made in intellectual development and acquisition of property he is a farmer, a mechanic, a merchant, a preacher, a teacher, a lawyer, and a physician.

Junius C. Ayler, in a lecture at Princeton, New Jersey, 1887

Back on the road I turned to the right, continuing away from the village. I could see Asa Gillet's cottage nestled at the edge of a harvested cornfield. Gillet, a burly, bearded fellow of middle years, whom I found by following the sound of his curses to the chicken coop he was mending, offered me a grudging five minutes and a tot from his bottle of execrable whiskey in the kitchen of the cottage he rented along with the portion of Gertrude Hover's land he had farmed. He had lived and worked there, a virtual sharecropper, as he complained to me, for twelve years past on the promise of a lifetime tenancy when she died. Gertrude, however, had died intestate, a circumstance Asa Gillet found incredible.

"I know that old witch didn't like me much. She didn't much like anyone. Could be she was just toying with us all. Whatever she told anyone else, I had her promise of this godforsaken little plot ~ land that used to be Gillet land. She promised me a life tenancy if she died before me. She gave me her solemn word she had it wrote down. 'I'll do right by you, Asa,' he mimicked in a rusty falsetto. "That's what she'd say when she wanted me to haul her apples to the market boat, or paint her damned shed. Then she dies sudden and I'm out in the cold, whistling for my right to what I should have clear till I die."

"If she left no will, Mr. Gillet, who inherited Miss Hover's property?"

He laughed, a single short bark, and spat, before pouring himself another tot of whiskey. He offered me the same, but I shook my head. One dose of his paint thinner had cured me. "Ask your partner. He was the judge handled it. That nephew of hers, George, he thought he'd get it. He was in there after they found her body, pulling up the floorboards, tearing out the walls, looking for Gertrude's will that he said favored him. He took over the house and put the land up for sale before she was buried ~ for all the good it did him. Gertrude's brothers stepped in and put a stop to that. When the dust finally settled a year ago, the property was parceled out between the brothers. The one from over Albany way got the best of it. He had the best lawyer, as I hear it." He glanced slyly at me before continuing. "Her orchard's been sold to the village. So if you're fixing to lay a claim, it's too late. Now I have work to see to, and your five minutes is up."

I was thoughtful as I started back along the dusty track toward the village. The little I had learned in a long day of tramping about and listening to the silences and rebuffs and half-truths of Gertrude Hover's neighbors seemed hardly worth the cost in time and boot leather. So it was a decided treat to my spirits when I caught sight of the shawled figure coming toward me. How I knew it was Cynthia Ann Jackson I cannot explain at these many years' remove. A slight tilt of her head, perhaps, or that swaying walk that set her skirt floating above her boot tops. She clutched the shawl close to her waist, a reticule hanging from one slim wrist. I hurried to stop her as she turned into the path that led to her father-in-law's house.

"Mrs. Jackson! Mrs. Jackson, a moment, please."

She froze, startled, but then recognized me with a brief smile that mended my tattered day. "Mr. Tilden? What are you doing up here? Has something happened? Is Jay all right?"

"No, nothing. No, he's fine so far as I know. I'm here trying to learn who Miss Hover was, and maybe find someone who can testify that your husband didn't ~" how avoid the word murder? ~ "commit the crime he's charged with."

"And did you have any success, Mr. Tilden?"

"Very little, I fear. Most of Miss Hover's neighbors are reluctant to speak to me. Understandable, perhaps."

She nodded, catching my reference to the mutual distrust that was widening between the races since emancipation. Then she looked up, a vertical crease slicing her smooth brow. "No one wants to talk about Miss Gertrude now she's dead. Speak her fine and you must be lyin'. Speak her ill and her ghost could hear. The way she died, she can't rest easy in her grave. She didn't have friends, Miss Hover. She had ... causes. It was a trial, sometimes, to live close by such ... righteousness. I do believe one reason Jay left home so early was to be away from her. He was just a boy when he quit school and went over across the river. I never knew him, really, till he came back that summer two years ago."

She smiled, remembering. "I was new graduated from high school that year, and proud of myself. Then Jay came along. He's so much smarter than I am; and he's very wise, too, in ways that I am not. You can't imagine what Jay is really like, Mr. Tilden. You only see him in that wretched place, that jail, wild with anger to cover his dread. You can't guess at how tender his spirit is, wounded and hidden away. No one here will tell you about him, no more than they'll talk about that old white woman. Everybody is afraid. Can't you feel it?"

I thought of my afternoon spent knocking at doors that never opened, and recalled the distrust that met me up and down Sunset. I thought of Charles Davis's evasions and asides, the village politics and gossip he must know that never reached his little news sheet. Then I regarded the woman who faced me in the path.

"You are not fearful, Mrs. Jackson."

"No, Mr. Tilden. I have not learnt yet to be afraid. I hope I never do. Now, I must get home to my child. Mr. Jackson will be wanting his supper." She turned abruptly and started off toward the neat gray house where her family waited.

I watched her go before calling out, "Goodbye then! I'll see you soon again."

She raised a hand, but did not answer as she sped swiftly and silently away from me, the late sun shimmering green on her black shawl, boots flashing under the hem of her skirt. Amazing, I thought. Even now, after all the years between, when I think of Cynthia Jackson it is with a brief thrill of amazed delight.

John Whitbeck, however, did not share my reliance on either Bat Jackson's wife or Charles Davis as possible future sources of understanding, and certainly not as possible witnesses in our client's case. "You can't believe," he scoffed in that sharp voice of his, "that little quadroon knows something that will get her lout of a husband off ~ if she's even allowed to testify. All she knows is what he's got her charmed into believing. That's a very sharp fellow we have for a client, Royce. He'll have us dancing a jig for him and never tell me anything worth setting before a jury. Didn't you learn anything from the Matthews case, or the Vandergroot mess? We are not the trusted agents of negroes who come to us in desperation. We are the wrong color, the wrong side of the law, the wrong class. They walk. We ride. They carry the ineradicable stigma of an enslaved race. We bear the ineffaceable guilt of a slave-owning race. You can't just cross that chasm with a smile and a promise."

I gathered from this that his interview that day with Bat Jackson had not gone well. "But surely, sir~"

He cut my protest off with a gesture and a grimace, and stood to pace the room impatiently before turning back to me. "Don't start with your windy idealism. You will not alter a blade of grass in this wretched country by hoping. Blessed Columbia had more chance of building a truly egalitarian society under the Puritans than it will ever have under the rule of political expediency." He scowled fiercely. "It would have been a grim sort of society with them in charge, but equally grim for all. What we have now is the nasty inheritance of slavery without its few advantages." He stopped, pointing at me to emphasize his ridiculous argument, "and only the Law itself to stand against barbarism.

"You are too young to remember when Abolition was a religious cause, Royce. Massachusetts Bay Colony imbedded emancipation in its charter, and scorned the federalists for including a runaway slave clause in the constitution. Prissy George, he of the wooden teeth, couldn't retrieve his own slave when he escaped to New England. And he was president at the time. But now! Now we have one party, my own party, pretending to be the black man's friend but denying him the vote, and the other party, yours, not even pretending, just pitting Irish and German immigrants against black laborers who threaten their toehold in the promised land."

When he stopped for breath I draped my coat over one client chair and settled into the other. John Whitbeck in lecture mode could neither be stopped or deflected. He drenched me with some form of it each time a political event displeased him. So I had heard it all before: the sectarian state, the intentionally godless state, the fallen state of man, the fallacy of free will in a state of grace, the supremacy of reason over passion, of law over savagery. Whatever rationale surfaced from the cluttered attic of his mind would be used to float his argument.

"You haven't brought up Beriah Green and More's Utopia yet," I reminded him. "There has hardly been time to dismantle the Underground Railroad; but already you speak as if it never existed, as if no white folks ever wished the negro well or tried to help him or passionately desired the withering away of slavery or demanded its abolishment by whatever means it could be achieved. There was a war, Mr. Whitbeck, a very savage war. You fought in it. Are you implying that only principled reason, or worse some sort of mass hypocrisy, fueled the mounting of that terrible conflict?"

"You were a babe in arms when that war ended, Roy," he reminded me with sudden gentleness. "You have no idea what egregious moral judgments, what obdurate principles, what sectional and territorial, and economic loyalties motivated our actions. We were two national identities allied by a passion for independence. Now we are a single federal body with feuding factions strewn throughout. There is no single will now that can override the selfish purposes of those in power. That's why our elections are so fiercely contested. Politicians are marauders after spoils. The battle becomes as corrupt as the greed that fuels it. There is no moral or ethical guidance to contain our purposes. Capitalism is not a system of government. Royce. It is the licensing of greed, the legalization of self interest."

"You speak as if the country is irrevocably lost, as if simple justice or even due legal process cannot prevail, as if the foundation of equality on which this nation was framed no longer has a part in its nature."

"I am merely warning you, Tilden, that our defendant has already been adjudged a miscreant and a murderer. There is little I can do to exonerate him, since any facts that do not support the case against him have been suppressed, and if rediscovered will not be allowed to surface during his trial. What I can, I shall do, but do not expect to prevail."

"You have been consulting with your courthouse experts, I see. The district attorney has witnesses lined up and well coached, I'm sure. Our local politicians have had two years to work out a way to close this case without riling their generous supporters here or up in Kinderhook, before they stand for re-election."

"Yes. Well, that too. You allude to the narrow span of attention that rides on special influence and political expediency. Judge Edwards' decisions reflect views that will extend his term past next November. He will not urge or sustain a verdict that alters the status quo by a single comma. He wants to keep his place on the bench, not point the way toward a more just and honorable society. My argument, however, was more general. I was referring to the current state of justice in our fair democracy."

"Let's ignore the grander issues for now, please sir. My day up in Kinderhook has yielded a few interesting items. I don't care if the American dream is doomed to fail. I do care that Jay Jackson has been indicted for reasons of convenience rather than likelihood. He may not have an alibi for an event that happened two years ago. His character may be decidedly unsavory and his manner over-bold. But he has no motive. He is too wily a customer to commit so blatant a crime. He earns a good living somehow, by sweat, scam or trickery perhaps, but not by thieving on his own patch, and not by violence. He's never been arrested, not in this county anyway.

"As I see it, the man who did away with Gertrude Hover had motive enough to beat that poor woman to submission and then seize a kitchen knife and stab her again and again in a frenzy. Somebody in a violent rage murdered Gertrude. I would prefer to have that person tried for killing her than have this crime fobbed off on a local rascal whose chief transgression is being born with the wrong color skin."

"You begin to sound fervent, Royce. Fervor makes a good defense attorney, but only when addressing a jury. Here in my law office it will not gain you points."

The colossal front of saying that to me a moment after he finished his own passionate tirade seemed utterly lost on Whitbeck. To grant him his due, he never sounded fervent. That keen-edged voice of his just raked along, penetrating the soul without ever gaining in intensity. I resolved not to let him bait me in future. I wanted, needed him to plead this case I wanted him to present a stunning defence, to be his second in what might well be a celebrated trial. Whitbeck knew the political players up here as few others did. And he knew the law. He was the only lawyer I knew who could without hesitation or reference cite precedent to refute whatever the prosecution might claim as admissible or deniable.

But I was leaping ahead. The case would only be celebrated if it came to trial, if Jackson stood fast to his plea of innocence, leaving his lunatic brother again suspect. Would he risk his life for William, who was apparently incapable of defending himself rationally? And further, I conceded but only in my inmost core of reason, Jackson's trial would not be of any public interest were he to be convicted. A negro condemned to the gallows for killing a white woman was hardly newsworthy. In that regard, John Whitbeck was crushingly correct back in 1887 when he condemned American society so acerbically. And right now, as I write this in 1933, Whitbeck's judgment is still accurate.

In that conversation, he alluded to an interesting aspect of the law as encoded in upstate New York. Since many local ordinances enacted in the two centuries and more since the Dutch first came to the Hudson Valley dealt with the status, treatment and apprehension of escaped prisoners, servants, or slaves, such laws should be invalidated by the Emancipation Proclamation and the thirteenth amendment and so forth. However, to my personal knowledge, such laws did not always specify the categories of runaway to whom they applied. I remembered from my apprenticeship in the City cases of runaway children thrust back into the custody of their parents with the marks of beating still on them. Since the ordinances did not specifically mention slaves as their target, many of them were still in force.

I didn't need to plow my way through old statute books to learn how Columbia County dealt with absconding prisoners, servants, minor truants or vagabonds. Such persons had no legal standing in the past. They could not testify nor call witnesses, nor claim cruelty or mistreatment to justify their flight or mitigate their punishment. Whitbeck would know if old town and county regulations had any continuing force. He would also figure out how Edwards perhaps and Gardenier certainly might use such laws to force Jackson's trial into the course they desired. It would not matter, I realized, if I found people who remembered Jackson as being elsewhere when Gertrude Hover died. They might be barred on some technicality from giving evidence. I needed at least one unassailably upright defense witness, preferably white. Bat's father had been correct.

As I descended the stairs from my employer's office and plodded home to Mrs. Bullock's grudging cold supper, my heart was heavy. Lillian would not approve of this doomed effort that could only delay my hoped-for acceptance into her father's firm; and Cynthia Jackson's youthful spirit would surely be destroyed as we white men fought over her husband's right even to an open trial by a jury composed also of white men. I do not credit myself with forethought, then or now. I simply deplored the way the world was arranged. I certainly did not entertain any urge to challenge the system or advocate equality of classes or races or genders or the redistribution of power. I could, however, see then, as I see more clearly now at forty years' remove, how economics and political expediency favor a kind of moral blindness that is sociopathic in its disregard to human rights in general, as distinct from personal freedoms of the powerful.

But there, I promised myself not to preach, since I write this chiefly for myself. I endured John Whitbeck's harangues with ill grace; and my students doze when I inject morality into my seminars.

As for my personal life, in the ensuing weeks my mind was a froth of conflicting ideas. Lillian's note to thank me for her weekend in the country contained no hint of her feelings. She must have realized how amazed and delighted I was that she accepted me. Could she also understand the depth of my unwillingness to leave my home ground and the progress I perceived I had made toward becoming a trial lawyer? Unlikely that she could conceive of me, or indeed any man, passing up her implied offer of wealth, ease, and social position. Was there a chance she could imagine herself the wife of a provincial lawyer and would-be scholar of the law? Would she support my personal ambitions? What an asset she would be to a career, with her poise and beauty. If she chose to marry me, how could I not do whatever was necessary to please her? Uncertain of my future, uncertain of the strength of my commitment to a life with Lillian, or a life in criminal law, I could see the incompatibility of my desires. I could see no solution to my dilemma.

Meanwhile, Whitbeck and I sought out everyone who knew Gertrude and anyone we could find who admitted to knowing Bat Jackson. It became apparent that District Attorney Gardenier had been before us at every turn. Veiled warnings had silenced possible witnesses to Jackson's presence elsewhere at the time of the murder, or to his lack of motive for attacking or robbng his landlady.

The chief witness against him, Emma Briggs, had emerged from the local negro community. Emma Briggs was the lynchpin of Gardenier's prosecution. She claimed to have seen Bat at Gertrude's kitchen door on the supposed day of the crime, Saturday the eighth of September in 1885. She had come forward with her accusation while Bat's brother William was in custody. One villager told me Emma had first identified William as the one she'd seen, and only later decided it was Bat. Somehow we had to challenge the accuracy of Emma Brigg's recollection, or cast doubt on her veracity.

As the days shortened and the weather grew more bitter with each journey, I took pity on my horse and rode the stage up to Kinderhook, arriving chilled and rattled, to plod through mud and then snow to visit one and then another of the modest houses facing the bare winter pasture. The inclement weather favored me. I could tell from the white woodsmoke rising from each chimney, which folk were at home. Since custom demanded the offer of warmth to any winter visitor, I was usually welcomed in for a chat. Eventually I found others who had been near the Hover place, or been with Battice Jackson on that fine early autumn afternoon of 1885. The two Sitcer boys, Charley and Adam, remembered asking Gertrude to let them cull apples that morning. Charley was a gangly thirteen-year old with blond hair that hung in his eyes and an air of miserable endurance. His brother Adam, of similar but smaller dimensions, remained pretty much mute during our chat in their mother's parlor, where they perched uneasily side by side on a horsehair sofa as if they'd never been allowed in the room before.

"Miz Hover, she come out with us. She didn't want us pickin' off the trees."

"She give us plums though, Charley," Adam put in, his only utterance.

"Yup, that's right. She shook that ol' plum tree so we could take the plums that fell. I near as asked her how come I couldn't just pick 'em off the branch. But I didn't say it. She was kinda scary that Miz Hover. We wouldn't go over to her place, except Momma wanted apples for a pie."

Most people had no recollection of the day Gertrude Hover was assumed to have died. One or two who lived nearby had seen or passed her house, but without noticing anything amiss. Whitbeck found a number of people who had seen Bat Jackson that day, and Cynthia too. Bat had been out and about buying and selling, though we noted some evasiveness as to the nature of his trade. More than one friend -- and Bat had numerous friends in the negro community -- recalled that Jackson had been at Powell's farm that day. I thought it curious that John Powell had barely mentioned this when he spoke to us. Cynthia remembered calling on her Aunt Margaret and later shopping in the village for shoes. A tenant in one of Gertrude's cottages recalled hearing voices from her house on that Saturday.

"They was loud, but I couldn't tell what they was sayin'. It wasn't Bat there. That I know," he admitted. But when I pressed him, he would only say that he knew it wasn't Bat at Gertrude's because he knew where Bat was on a Saturday. Not another word could I coax from him. I could see in his eyes the fear that he had already said too much.

The day I was deputed to call on the prosecution's star witness, Emma Briggs, I rode my horse, since Emma lived nearly two miles west of the village, more of a walk from the stage stop than I was ready to undertake in the cold. Emma Briggs was a woman of middle years who grew berries on a patch of land over toward Stuyvesant Landing. Mordecai 'Mo' Briggs, her husband, was considerably older than she. He was balding and grayed at the temples, very dark skinned, very dignified. I found him chopping kindling in the back yard. Emma was not at home. She had taken the cart over to Chatham, he explained. He buried his axe in the stump that was his chopping block and rested his gnarled hand on the axe handle as if it were a scepter. I helped him stack the wood he had been splitting. Afterward he invited me in for a glass of Emma's homemade wine, which we drank standing in the kitchen, Mo not wanting to track mud into the parlor, or perhaps not wanting to offer me a seat in his house.

After his initial awkwardness at this unexpected visitor, Mo Briggs proved gracious, even a bit garrulous, and pleased to talk about his wife, whom he seemed to regard with a mixture of pride and diffidence. He owned the land and the house he had built himself, owned it free and clear, he said with pride. The cart and a donkey Emma used to transport her strawberries, raspberries and blueberries to market belonged to his wife. In the winter she sold jams and preserves (and berry wine, he confided, offering me another tot) door to door. Emma was also a pillar of Bethel AME Church, leader of the choir, and untiringly devoted to good works. She baked fruit pies for every church function and fundraiser.

"She has a light hand with the pastry, Emma. Makes a good meal, too. She carries flowers over there to the church. Or she used to. Mista Oliver, he liked flowers in the church. Not so much now with Mista Philips. And Emma, she keeps order up there in the choir loft," Mo explained. "They need somebody like Emma to put a stern eye on the young ones particular. Pretty voices those chilleren have, but skittish some of them if they're not tied down with a look or a poke. We got a fine choir at the Beth-El. Three rows, women on one side and men on the other. You can always hear Emma ~ and that Cynthia, Margaret's niece from the hatshop. That Cynthia sings like an angel. High! You wouldn't believe how high and sweet she sings. Put Emma's nose out of joint a little, to tell the truth, when folks would praise young Cynthia. Emma's got the big voice, but Cynthia sets a harmony right on top of it all that's so sweet..." He smiled and shook his head, admitting the surpassing sweetness of Cynthia Van Houck Jackson's singing.

"You want to know about that time Miz Hover got killed, but I don't remember rightly just when it was. I do remember that year. That was when Mista Oliver came and preached for a while. He was one fine orator, Preacher Oliver. Emma had the choir; of course. Little Cynthia was singin'. She was just a girl, only just graduated the Academy then. And that summer young Jay Jackson come over the river, back to his father's place, just by the orchard there, and first thing you know that fella started coming to church. It was Emma coaxed him to sing in the choir.

"Pastor Oliver, now, he was from New Jersey, been to the seminary down there in Princeton. He could tell tales of the Underground Road to beat the band. He knew so many songs! He helped Emma teach them to the choir and all. That's what I remember about that year. Those were good times at the Beth-El, I can tell you. Now he didn't stay but a year at most, Pastor Oliver, but he had us set up right smart before he went on to grander places. He weren't shy of people, you see." He looked sharply at me to see if I understood that by people he meant white people. "He had easy ways for such a smart fella. Everybody liked him, even Miz Hover, she'd have him to tea at her house, right in her front parlor. Lovely days that year. Mista Oliver, he'd thunder out the gospel and then the choir would sing one of the old favorites like Hush, hush. Somebody's callin my name, or My Lord, What a Morning. They'd sing the great songs from slave times or the Underground Road and my heart would just fly up with the joy inside me." Mo shook his head, regretting a golden age past, and offered me the wine bottle before pouring himself a small measure.

"You were saying that Bat Jackson started coming to church that summer," I prompted.

"Well, so he did," Mo Briggs mused. "Never thought to see Bat Jackson himself, in a church. But there he was, ever' Sunday, all that summer. Of course he came to please the Van Houck girl. She caught his eye as soon as he came back home. That was the year they cracked down on gambling over in Albany, so I remember it well, bein' a betting man myself." He gave me a sly grin, showing the gap in his front teeth. The sweet berry wine had promoted me from white lawyer to fellow imbiber.

"Bat, now. He's a hustler, good at most things he tries. He hoists kegs in the brewery sometimes, and harnesses horses for the stage. That's in the winter. Summers he works out at Powell's, as I guess you know." His deepset eyes, not at all inebriate, regarded me keenly for a moment, making me wish I could read dark faces better.

"Well, I tell ya, when he came to church, I heard him before I saw him. He was sitting right in back of me, so I could hear him in the first hymn. He sang right out, no mistakin' that voice of his, nice high tenor. Made the hair rise on the back of my neck for sure. Then we sang Take me to the Water, just before Pastor Oliver was goin' to preach, and Bat, he took up a harmony in the refrain. One or two turned around then. Emma leaned out of the loft to see who was doin' that. Bat, he paid no attention to the ruckus he was causin'. After, he just turned to help Nellie McPherson put her hymnal in the rack. But he was smilin', Bat, that foxy smile he has, because he knew Cynthia was looking down at him. That's the attention he wanted, Cynthia's, but he got my Emma lookin' too. She wanted him in the choir."

I waited in vain for Emma Briggs to return, sipping her wine while Mo Briggs praised her virtues. He made such a meal of it, I wondered what faults of Emma he was omitting. It was as if he were convincing himself of his marital good fortune. I wondered why he needed convincing.

Later that same day I stopped in on a friend of Mo's, Rolf Farrier on Sunset, who after disclaiming any knowledge of Bat Jackson, told me, "Emma's Mo knows Bat. Mo worked on Powell's barn, the new one he built maybe three years ago now. Mo, he's a carpenter. He put the siding and the barrel roof on that barn. I remember him telling about it. Mo figgered Powell built it way down there outside the village so's he could stage them fistfights there. Powell's dairy herd pastures up here across the road with Moore's. He'd lose a lot of milk trailing 'em clear down there to that new barn. I don't think there's ever been a cow in that barn. Mo used to pass by here half froze and muddy that spring, and complain! 'That man don't need no new barn,' Mo would say. 'His old barn's just fine, only a bit far from the road.' The new one's over the village line. Barn like that, bigger than his house, that's for puttin' on fights." Rolf Farrier paused, regarding me warily, as if judging how far I could be trusted.

"I expect you know, bein' a lawyer, that there's a village law against leasing premises for vice. Protects us from brothels and saloons and gambling halls. Powell took care to keep his new barn empty for a while. But we all knew they had cracked down on the fights in Albany. And sure enough he started renting that barn of his for bloody knockdowns just about every week. Now Mo, he's a gambling man. Emma don't hold with that. There was trouble between them when Mo would lose a week's pay down there. Emma and Mo had fights as good as at Powell's, I bet. But Mo couldn't stay away. He'd be tellin me how them white men would wager fistfuls of dollars on a champion like Charley Moore ~ who's as black as me."

"So then Battice Jackson came...."

I waited through the sudden silence, but Farrier didn't go on. I had stretched his loyalty as far as it would go. I decided to see if Cynthia would tell me about Emma, whom she obviously knew from the church. It would be good to know of some peccadillo of Mrs. Proper Emma Briggs, a way to darken, or at least qualify her memory of Jay Jackson slipping the latch of Gertrude's kitchen door on that fatal Saturday afternoon.

Cynthia, ushered again into Whitbeck's office after her twice weekly visit to her husband, was at first reluctant even to repeat Emma Briggs' name.

"I can't. I can't say anything. You'll think I'm spiteful. She put Jay in prison with her talk. What can I say? Nothing I tell you will be untainted by how I feel about her."

"I know you have a deep grievance, Mrs. Jackson," Whitbeck said. She looked at him chidingly. "Cynthia, then. But if you know something that will help your Jay,- I really need to know it as well. We have little enough to support his claim of innocence. So much time has passed, such flimsy recollections are put forth against him. We need some facts in his support. Please, Cynthia, is there something about Emma that should be told? I won't reveal that you said it. I can affirm what you might tell me with others, so you won't be the source."

She was silent for a long interval, head bowed, watching her hands twist in her lap. When at last, she drew a shaky breath and let it out, and pulled off her gloves, I felt a great weight lift from me. Before she said a word I was sure that what she had to tell was vital to our case, that she had so far held it in her heart not only out of a tender sense of honor, but because to reveal it would breach her deep loyalty to her people, her church family, and the colored community which had reared and cherished her all her life. My own heart quailed as she cast this frail bridge of trust across the chasm between our races. And I saw her for the first time, saw her spirit. glowing like a prism, slicing into my own, changing my perception of her, of myself as my employer nodded encouragingly.

When I look at it now, I see that what separated us was merely trivial social convention. But as I moved into this new reality, leaning forward with my pad of foolscap forgotten, my role of notetaker abandoned, my whole perception of humanity, of rightness was undergoing a shift. I believe each of us has such a moment, in which understanding floods the mind beyond the scope of words to describe. (witness this inarticulate attempt to explain it). Afterward, there is no reverting to the dark cave of solitary unknowing that precedes it. I guess that people who never experience, or fail to credit such a revelation remain stunted in spirit, trapped in a selfmade prison of habit or obsession or tradition or bigotry or mere selfishness.

It must be granted that in Cynthia Jackson I had a most endearing guide for my rite of passage, but I find generally that understanding is sweetened by a coating of charm. Cynthia Jackson gave me a glimpse of her spirit, of something precious that glows unique in each and is common to all. After such a moment every person you encounter, every pebble in your road, shines like a jewel of complex and mystic beauty ~ or something like that. I can't clarify it. I know the transmutation I experienced as Cynthia Jackson confided in us that day has eased my way through life. For John Whitbeck the moment was not transcendent. He must have already passed that way. And, of course, he had a more rational style of encompassing revelation.

I can't remember all Cynthia said that day she began to trust us. I was dumbstruck, numb with the import of my vision. I do remember two things of practical use in her husband's defense. She said, "Everybody knows Emma can't see good, except right up close. She holds her hymnal right up to her face till she has the words to heart. If that donkey of hers didn't know the road, I bet she'd never find her way to market." She looked up with a wan smile at her small joke. "How could Emma see who was climbing over Miz Gertrude's fence that day? She could hardly tell if there was a fence there."

"If everybody knows this," Whitbeck mused, "I should be able to find one or two who will attest to it at the trial. Can you suggest anyone?"

She considered this thoughtfully. "Almost anyone at church," she ventured at last, "but they're not likely to want to confess it before a judge, or even to you, I guess. And who would believe them?" Then she raised a hand as if to deter failure. "What about her customers? They must see how Emma counts coins with her fingers. They could say how nearsighted she is. Mrs. Hardy or that Janie, Janie Williams, or Gladys Houck. Almost anyone over to Chatham who buys her jelly could say. But would they want to? Seems like most folks would be happy to see Jay blamed, no matter who did it. They just want to put that trouble and fear behind them.

"If Emma hadn't made up a story, someone would have," she urged. "They promised a reward, did you know? Right after it happened, Mr. Davis posted it in his newspaper. 'Five hundred dollars to anyone who comes forward with information leading to the capture of...' And Emma was in a boil after the way she sashayed around, simperin and preenin to catch Jay's attention. She wanted him in the choir so bad. And when Jay didn't pay her any attention ~ well!"

She paused, shy of confiding the rest, but then continued resolutely, "Emma, she set her cap for Jay the first time he came to church. He really came because he knew I would be there and he wanted to see me home." She closed her eyes to the bright memory of Jackson's probably sudden and intense courtship. "But Emma just pranced up to him after church. We are not so many at the Beth-El that you don't notice somebody new. So Emma just had to make a newcomer welcome. He had to meet Pastor Oliver. He just had to come sing in the choir, and he just must bring his daddy to the Thursday supper. It was all Jay and I could do to get away from her that day."

She chuckled at the memory, and was for a moment the young girl she had been two years before, giggling at the stupidity of old folks. "She kept at him all summer, as if Jay was her rightful prize, for her choir, for herself. She never noticed me beside him. She never cottoned to how it was with us. She'd say how frail Mo was getting. I do believe she was ready for her next husband ~ Oh, that's not nice for me to say! But Emma was married twice before, and Mo is so very old," she confided, sharing the youthful view of old age as a sorry decline past the age of thirty. "He won't be able to work much longer. I can't see Emma nursing him if he lingers. Then Jay asked me to marry him, and Emma told Aunt Margaret she mustn't allow it. I was just seventeen, you see, so we needed her consent. Emma said terrible things about Jay, that he was a drinker and a criminal and I don't know what all. Aunt Margaret didn't repeat it to me. She just warned me not to let Emma help plan our wedding, because she'd spoil it for sure.

"Well, there. I've said it. Now you know why Emma went to the police with that tale about Jay. She did that after the baby came. Emma couldn't bear to see us so happy. If you had seen her face when I first brought little Jemmy to church! Emma's never had a child, you see, not with all her husbands. It wasn't a week after Jemmy was born that she went to the police with her story."

She stopped abruptly, realizing she had said far more than she intended. "I must go now, Mr. Whitbeck. The stage will be leaving soon."

"Of course." He stood. "We mustn't delay you. But please, if I am to call you Cynthia, you must call me John. You have helped immensely today, Cynthia. I feel more hopeful than I did before you told me these things."

She left with a murmured 'goodbye then, John ... and Roy'.

She was hardly out the door when he turned to me. "I see you are already on terms of familiarity with our client. Is that wise, Roy?"

I thought of a flippant response: *Am I now to call you John as well, sir?* But did not utter it. The terms of friendship with my employer concerned me less at that moment than the epiphany of understanding I had just undergone.

Chapter Six

When the heart has bloomed by the touch of love's warm breath
Then faded as chilling snow sifts in
It still may beat but there is blast and death
To all that blooming life that might have been.

George Marion McClellan, "A January Dandelion"

I gathered up my notes and went quickly to my own desk in the outer office and began automatically to sort the mail. I had made two neat piles of it and was idly trimming the edges, my mind in quite another place, when my employer suddenly loomed over me like a hawk on a rabbit.

"Royce, wake up! You are dreaming, and it had better not be about that little poppet who just left here.! We are about to plead a trial that could shatter the peace of this county. I need you alert and rational, not harboring lustful thoughts about a client. You do see the inappropriateness, not to mention the disloyalty to your declared ~"

I had occasionally sensed Whitbeck's impatience with my shyness, my reserve, for what he would term my lack of social presence, but would mean lack of stature and good looks. Until then, however, he had never imputed to me a lack of character or responsiblity Was it possible that at that moment and at some level, he envied me my youth, my daring? For it seemed that my unassuming manner, my lack of standing, my timid gestures of sympathy, had achieved for me the friendship of this remarkable girl.

I looked up at him, completely dumbstruck. Whitbeck was not teasing. He seemed genuinely upset with me, or at least genuinely upset about something, and putting it on me. What had I missed? For a long moment we glared at one another. Then I put down the letter I held and stood to face him.

"Our client is, indeed, an attractive young woman," I concurred, with as much outraged dignity as I could muster. "You are the one drawing attention to that. My faithfulness to Lillian Roeder is not at issue here. There is no issue here to concern you," I told him, before turning back to my desk and taking up the letter. It was from my mother.

A very faint blush suffused Whitbeck's austere features, but apologies were not in his arsenal. He turned back toward his office, then stopped abruptly. "What have you been doing all day?" he demanded, as if he didn't know exactly where I had been, where he had sent me.

Halfway into his office he turned back with an afterthought. "I have found out that Gardenier plans to prevent our client from testifying in his own defense. I am counting on that flash manner of jackson's to winkle him out of the noose, so I shall need strong legal support to counter that strategy. According to the sheriff, he was fleeing arrest when he was caught. He was on the ferry to Albany. Therefore he's a runaway; and under state law a runaway cannot testify in his own behalf."

"What about his wife, sir? Will her tertimony be excluded as well? What if she is not actually married to him?"

"I have no intention of allowing the exclusion of any witness I decide to call," Whitbeck said coldly. "That statute applied only to runaway slaves; and it has been null for the past twenty years."

"Then, what is Gardenier thinking?"

"He will probably assert that the law, no matter that its purport was to expedite the capture and return of escaped slaves, does not contain the word slave. Sam Edwards is unlikely to be persuaded to judge it intended for the apprehension of runaway apprentices and minor children. I have it on good authority the prosecution plans to invoke it. That law, and whatever instances support it, could allow the exclusion of any testimony in Bat Jackson's defense from his friends or relatives. And believe me, there are clear enough precedents for suspending civil rights for particular cause to allow the privilege. Countering that tactic should concern us more than discrediting a witness who won't be allowed to testify under the same code."

He stalked into his office and shut the door, having masked his discomfiture at intruding into my personal life by citing minutiae with which I was as familiar as he.

I stared at my mother's elegant script on the envelope in my hand. It would be her invitation, summons more like, to Christmas at home in New Lebanon. A sudden picture rose before me of the comfortable white frame house where I was born, the overgrown acre surrounding it, and behind it the long, steep slope that carried our sleds in winter and our tumbling descents in summer. I tried to imagine Lillian tucked into a Canada-style flatboard sled, shrieking her way down the hill, her laugh ringing out as the toboggan gained speed and then spent its rush in the snowdrifted hollow.

Lillian might be coaxed into trying it once, I concluded with a sigh, but she'd not enjoy getting her clothes rucked and snow-sodden. My teenaged brother and sister would charge up the hill again and again to earn that moment of supreme delight and danger. And I would be chasing along with them, as I always had. If I refused now, it would mark me as irrevocably adult, no longer their indulgent playmate but a stiff, dull-spirited attorney. Better, perhaps, not to invite Lillian to visit, not until our future together was more certain, till I had decided whether or not I was to be the staid corporate lawyer she expected me to become.

My mother's letter, however, was not the reminder I was expecting.

'My dear Royce,' she began.

'Yours of 30th November received with much pleasure. I am so glad your practice of law begins to reward your ambitions, as it should. Your father and I are so proud of your success. You have fulfilled all we have hoped for you.

It is about your father I need to write, for he is not as strong as he was. You need to speak earnestly with him when you are here at the holiday. He must be persuaded to give up the business and give himself more time to recover from that last spell with his heart. He will plead poverty, wanting to assure that Robert, and perhaps even Marjorie, will complete their education, as you did.

But if you can convince him, show him your determination to take on part of those expenses, to help your brother at least as we helped you, I am sure he will see how much we need him alive among us, not grubbing his life away down at the works....'

There was more, a suggestion that it was time for the family to meet 'this Miss Roeder, whom you seem to admire,' and other news of aunts, uncles, cousins, family friends, a birth, which I skimmed through without much interest.

I put the letter down. Would I be willing to foot my brother's college bills if my father retired to ease his failing heart, his wheezing lungs? Robert, I knew, wanted to be a doctor, though I couldn't imagine him healing anyone. He had never rescued injured rabbits or mended birds' wings. He did have an inordinate curiosity about the inner workings of things, bodies or machinery, it didn't seem to matter. He had at that time delayed entrance into college while he worked a year for my father. As for my sister Marjorie, the youngest and brightest of the three of us, with any luck she'd be married before she caught the bug for higher education that was infecting women about that time.

If I undertook such a responsibility, I would have to delay marrying Lillian, even if her father did invite me to join Gould, Martin, Roeder with the prospect of a future partnership. And what of my own aspirations? My father's struggling business could not possibly support two students. My indenture with John Whitbeck had not long to run. I would have to strike out on my own My careful savings were intended to enable me to leave my cramped quarters at Mrs. Bullock's boarding house and purchase one of those ample, acred dwellings in the soft hills of Columbia County. I knew of several in receivership since the recent monetary crisis of 1883. Any one of them would be nearly within my means, if only Lillian would find one to her liking.

But Robert deserved his start, as I had been granted mine. I couldn't deny him a career in favor of my own.

No letter from Lillian. Not for the past two weeks. Writing to invite her to meet my family was not the proper tactic at this point in our courtship. I needed some sign from her father that my candidacy was at least under consideration. Lillian had been so confident, so insistent that an immediate decision was needed. Yet no buff envelope from Gould, Martin, Roeder had arrived with the expected invitation to an interview.

I set all this down, these personal distractions and indecisions, to explain to myself how I could have ignored John Whitbeck's apprehension about the Bat Jackson trial. It is difficult, now, for me to credit how wretched a twenty-three year old could make himself over torments which from this distance appear trivial and temporary. But I did lose sleep and appetite in the months before the trial, wasting my mind on insoluble problems and neglecting the undercurrent of expediency, common consent, or whatever nicety of euphemism concealed the frantic backroom maneuvers aimed at closing the case of Gertrude Hover's murder without probing its cause. Whitbeck bore it all, countered all objections, with hardly a modicum of support from me.

If I had been more diligent, could I have discerned the cause of those desperate delays and evasions and attempts at hindrance? Could I have perhaps divined whose hand wielded the knife that killed Gertrude Hover? I was not. I did not. Nor did John Whitbeck uncover more than faint traces of the real killer, so far as I know.

In mid-December I took the Chatham spur up to New Lebanon through a snowy landscape. The carriage windows were frosted over, but when I opened mine to gain a view of the mountains I was so assaulted by noise and soot and bits of cinder that I quickly closed it again to avoid looking like a chimney sweep on arrival. My brother met me with the sleigh at the station. So we swept along home to the jingle of bells and muffled hoofbeats, the snorts of the trotting pair releasing great puffs of frosty air. Robbie hardly said a word after his bearhug greeting. We were nearly home, gliding along through the Berkshire foothills, when he turned and spoke, his face ruddy from cold and wind, his voice harsh and accusing.

"You should have come, Roy! You should have been here months ago! Dad's so bad now, he can hardly get breath to speak. And Mother! This will kill her too. Why didn't you come when Margie wrote?"

"Marjorie wrote? When did Margie write me?" My voice sounded as frantic as his, the icy wind snatching our words, thinning our voices as if we shouted across a void. I had taken off my fogged spectacles, so I couldn't see his expression, but my brother sounded really angry.

"Doesn't matter now. You weren't here. Mother..." He faced ahead to mind the way, so I lost most of what he was saying as he continued, pouring out his stored up hurt and anxiety. "... trying ... the shop... can't do that and take care...." Then he turned back to me and yelled, "He's going to sell the business. Do you know that at least?"

I took the reins from him, slowing the horses. "Robbie, I don't know any of this. Are you sure Margie wrote me? I had the letter from Mother about Dad's illness, but that's all."

Robert was silent, hugging himself against the cold. He had shoved his mittened hands under his armpits and was staring at the jingling harness. I could imagine his expression, his mouth bitten shut, his eyes squinched to hold back tears.

"Look, Robbie, whatever happened, whatever I didn't know or didn't do, I'm here now. Whatever I can do to help, or fix it, or ease your heart, I will do it. Just don't despair. I will need you. Mother and Marjorie ~ Well, I need you. So don't go all Ajax on me. okay?"

Robert smiled faintly at that. We had more than once played out the siege of Troy on the dining room table on rainy Sunday afternoons, with a battered set of lead soldiers and a wooden horse Dad had carved for us. Ajax sulking in his tent had been a choice bit of comedy among the bloody scenes we enacted.

"I'm not sulking," he insisted. "I just wish ~"

"I know," and the desolation had crept into my own voice, "but maybe it's just a spell. Maybe he'll get over it this time, the way he did two years ago." Robert shook his head with slow grim conviction. "Well, anyway, we'll work out something. No matter what."

We were turning in at the gate, the horses following their own recent track to the barn. I was soon immersed in the mounting anguish and daily crises and hurried meetings that preceded my father's death a week before Christmas. My father was a good and earnest man, though he did leave a tangle of problems for us to sort. I did my best to assume the burden of what had to be done, since my mother was too distraught to make the simplest decision. The pharmacy did, indeed, have to be sold. Robert was too young to take it over, even if he had been so inclined. Mother had no wish to manage it, though she had made her presence felt in the shop that year, as my father was less and less able to leave his bed.

Marjorie had written to me, beseeching me to come home and take over as head of the family before disaster overtook them all. But she had delayed sending the letter, detecting some sign that our father was on the mend, that Mother was steeling herself to cope ~ had delayed until it was too late to warn me, until Mother wrote the letter that brought me home.

Lillian's note went first to Hudson and was forwarded to me at New Lebanon. It reached me the day of my Father's funeral. In the circumstances it struck a note of brittle and giddy glee.

'Oh, Royce Love,' she wrote,

'You simply must come down to see the City all aglow for the holiday! They have strung electric lights everywhere ~ well not every single where, but all the houses up on Park Avenue are glittering at night like diamonds. And Father has installed a speaking machine between our house and his office and ~ well I can't tell you how many of these telephonic devices are now sitting ready to receive instant word. If you had one in that dowdy old office of yours I could speak with you every day. Think of it! You must come down to the City during your holiday. I know how you love to rusticate with your family, but you have to come and see the magical lights that are banishing night from the City. Father and I are giving a party to celebrate the New Year; and I want you to be here. So do plan to come and stay for a day or two before you rush back to your thieves and murderers. Don't make excuses, Roy. I shall expect you.'

She had more to say, but I did not read it all. Of course I must go. This was the one possible route to escape our family's ruin. My father had left a sizeable insurance policy. My mother would be able to keep the house. If the business could be sold at its worth, we could emerge from Dad's untimely death with a certain amount of respectability. But no provision had been made for either Robert's college, or medical school, as he persistently reminded me. As for Marjorie, she wouldn't be a dowered deb. When she recovered from grieving for Dad, she would find that her debutante year, and any ideas she had of finishing school or college, had vanished with our father.

I explained to the three of them my urgent reasons for attending the Roeders' party on New Year's Eve. I did not mention Lillian's role in setting my application before her father, but I did raise the possibility of joining Gould, Martin, Roeder as worth a trip into the City and a new suit of formal evening clothes. Even so, I bade them goodbye with a distinct sense of guilt. Leaving that house of mourning for the glowing metropolis I was turning my back not only on my grieving loved ones, but on my own cherished dreams as well.

The Roeder mansion was bright with blue-white electrics. Indeed, that whole section of Park Avenue was dotted with white globes on cast-iron stanchions. The lightbulbs cast pale, static circles of light on the snowy street. Many people were out walking to view the spectacle of electricity dispelling the night. I didn't see how it improved on the mellow glow of gas lamps, except for the convenience. It occurred to me to wonder how the lamplighters would earn their living when electric lights became the norm throughout the City and elsewhere.

I was met at the door by a personage whose frock coat eclipsed my new swallowtails. I surrendered my stovepipe hat and my father's greatcoat to him with some reluctance, and suffered his severe inspection of Lillian's note, which I tendered in lieu of a formal invitation.. The mansion had what I remember as a ballroom, but perhaps it would be properly styled a drawing room, since the three great chandeliers and wine velvet hangings certainly drew my awed attention. The chandeliers were gaslit, but along the walls were sconces with electric bulbs in them. Robert Roeder had apparently not had time to get his ceiling fixtures electrified. Wiring for the sconces must be hidden behind the drapes.

I accepted a glass of champagne from the first waiter who approached, and did not at first see anyone likely to make me welcome. In fact, Lillian's father was the only person I could identify. I located him easily, holding forth to two sycophantic young men in velvet ~ the Harvard or Princeton juniors in his firm, I surmised. Then he turned from them, with a dismissive pat on each shoulder, and cast a master's eye around the crowd of elegantly dressed men and women, at the musicians sawing away almost unheard on a small dais in one corner, at the late-arriving guests still trickling into the spacious room, and at me, probably because I was still ruddy from the cold.

"Ah, Tilden. Lillian's friend. Of the New Lebanon Tildens I assume? How good you could come," he had strutted over and grasped my hand in a crushing grip.

"Good evening, sir. It is good to see you again."

"Ah yes, I recall you. Did your law at Columbia." This encouraged me mightily. My application must have crossed his desk, at least. "Well, you must have a number of friends here, then. I believe I saw Lillian on her way to the library. It's just across the hall." Then his face lit up with a huge smile and he strode past me to greet a man and woman who had just entered. I heard him bellow, 'Ah, Senator...' in a near-shout. Not above trumpeting his powerful acquaintances, I noted.

I set my glass down on the tray of a passing waiter, and went to find the library and Lillian. In contrast to the noise and brightness of the ballroom, the library had only murmured conversations and the soft glow of several oil lamps on small tables. A dozen or more young people were gathered near the hearth where a fire crackled. It was far warmer than in the ballroom. Some sort of game was in progress among four fellows at a card table. They had flung their coats over their chairs so that the silk linings made a colorful show in the firelight. They had also loosened their ties and seemed to be drinking spirits rather than champagne.

Lillian herself stood regally with her back to the fire. One hand curled around the edge of the mantel, as if to steady her, and the other reached up to stroke the peacock feather in her hair. She had cast aside a fringed shawl, which lay across the nearest chairback; leaving her arms and shoulders palely bare. I had never seen her so. For a moment, with the chair shielding the rest of her, I fancied she was naked. But of course she was merely displaying herself in what was then a continental fashion. Her face, in contrast to that fleshly invitation, held an expression as remote as a goddess. Below her bare shoulders what I could glimpse of her dress shimmered when she moved with the same iridescence as the feather in her hair. A loose circle of young people sat in the deep chairs or on the floor around her. Not one of them turned when she caught sight of me and said my name in that cool, unhurried way of hers.

"Royce! How clever of you to find us! We're hiding out from the establishment. I don't want my first kiss of the New Year to come from some fat old councilman. Or my tenth or twelfth kiss either. Come here and be introduced, Roy. Don't loiter about over there. Only so many kisses are on offer."

I realized that the card players were not the only ones who were drinking spirits. Lillian was drunk, thoroughly drunk, as I had never seen her. I crossed the patterned Turkey carpet, nodding to the groups I passed, indolent young men in shirtsleeves of snowy linen, brighteyed women in dresses as daringly revealing as Lillian's. It seemed they lavished yards and yards of rich goods on the skirts and left barely enough at the top to cover themselves. There were more men than women in the room; and Lillian had gathered to herself the largest adoring cluster of males. Her circle had kept their silk and velvet tailcoats on, but their faces seemed a bit flushed and their eyes slitted, liquor having reduced their poise and their focus. She introduced them to me, and they acknowledged me languidly, one by one, until she reached the man in the chair nearest her, a large, broad fellow with prominent blue eyes and hair almost as blonde as Lillian's own. Then she leaned over the chairback and placed her hand on his head like a benediction. "And this is Willard," she told me, "Willard Staunton, fresh out of Columbia Law. He's joining Gould, Martin, Roeder. Did Papa tell you? Papa has spoken of you, Royce. He expects you to have an utterly brilliant career up there in the country. He thinks the world of your prospects. Now come kiss me, dear. We can begin the New Year's festivities whenever we please. They'll not hear us from across the hall. Kissing isn't noisy."

She giggled and threw herself forward into my arms. She needed my support to stay upright, but she gave me her mouth with a kind of strenuous abandon. Astonished as I was, I took her bare shoulders and pulled her to me and kissed her with all my heart, knowing it to be the last time. Around us the others launched themselves into similar behavior. Willard Staunton dragged himself to his feet and tossed off the drink in his hand. When I released Lillian he was standing behind her, leering, waiting to claim her. Across the hall the older revellers took up a ragged chorus of "Auld Lang Syne."

That was how 1888 began, with the eclipse of my hopes and expectations. It is a moment that stays with me through all the years, much as I would prefer to cast it from my mind. In my sanguine moods I imagine Lillian desperately unhappy that night, splashing her father's best Scotch over the heart that yearned for me, that found me admirable, brilliant, even desirable. Occasionally I have wondered how I might have won her love, her hand, in spite of that clear rejection. If I had had more than a famous name to recommend me, if I had been better looking, taller, leaner, mor imposing ~ but I am not, was not. In later years Lillian seemed quite content with Willard Staunton, if somewhat overindulgent in her drinking habits. It is perhaps only vanity that fuels my notion of her as preferring me in her heart.

Her Papa made his choice; and Lillian acquiesced to it. She married Willard Staunton. Gould, Martin, Roeder eventually evolved into Martin, Roeder, Staunton. And I? I left John Whitbeck that year for a more lucrative position with a firm in Albany that enabled me to assist with Robbie's college fees until he was able to manage on his own. Marjorie? That's a story for another telling. Here I want to set down what happened to Jay Jackson in that grim February of 1888.

An Illuminating Thought

Before the electric light can become a brilliant success and not a burning shame and occupy a reserved seaat in the esteem of all law abiding people, there must .in its bright lexicon be no such word as fizzle.

Whenever the electric light is adopted because it is cheaper than gas, there will come such a weeping and a wailing by the grownup daughters,who have beaus to conquer, that the moanings of the gas companies will hardly be heard. For who could feel at all sentimental, who could hand in a proposition without blushing like a beet, or who would venture to suggest a housekeeping arrangement of the very lightest kind, for two in a cottage, in the presence of one of those buzzing, blazing, glaring, flaring, sputtering, fluttering electric lights? The blindest lover can make out to see the light of her eyes even by the candle's fitful light, and manage to express his feelings in broken English by the brighter and more odorous coal oil flame, and can quote peetry by the square yard when the gas is not very

good, and its shade is more shady by means of a paper overskirt of bewitching pattern.

However, when it comes to the electric light there is no turn-down. It must blaze away as if it did not care one cent for a fellow's feelings. The young ladies, although they may think that it is a good thing for lighthouses and street lamps, are down on it, for it gives them a sickly pallor, and it makes them look green.

Whatever shall be the final fate of the electric light, whether it shall wax to be brighter and brighter, and put our eyes out, or shall go down into total darkness from whence it sprang, 'unwept, unhonored and unsung' by the hand organs, more light will still be popular with the lovers of the true, the beautiful and the good-looking girls of the period. The moon will shine right on regardless of the electric light; and she cannot be coughed down. She fills all of her engagements, and plays only with a star company. All other contestants for the belt will have to occupy the off nights.

from an article in the *Daily Evening Register,*
Hudson, New York, August 18, 1885

Chapter Seven

Fell in love with a gal I thought was kind
She made me lose ma money
An almost lose ma mind.

Langston Hughes, "Po' Boy Blues"

When I returned to Hudson the following week, John Whitbeck did not refer to my father's death nor to my lost opportunity with Roeder's firm, which I had written to tell him. I don't believe he understood how serious I was about Lillian. Or perhaps he could not credit Lillian being serious about me. After a gruff greeting he sent me to grub through old newspapers again, this time up in Albany at the *Morning Times*.

"Jackson has a history up in Albany," he rasped. "He may be in the police files. The papers must have reported his arrest at least. I believe he was detained briefly soon after the Hover woman was killed. How did they get onto Jackson for it? He wasn't charged for two years after that. He was held in Albany jail, not for the murder, but on another charge of some sort. See what you can find out about that, and get the name of the person who reported him in connection with Gertrude Hover. It wasn't Emma Briggs. That's what the prosecution will claim. But you told me Emma didn't come forward with her tale about Bat climbing over Gertrude's fence that Saturday afternoon until long afterward. Jackson bedded your pert little Cynthia and got her with child, a child now old enough to walk. Cynthia told you Emma didn't start telling wild tales about Bat Jackson until the baby was born and brought to church. Time, Royce. Time. Work out the timeline. There are significant gaps. Our client should be detailing his every move since he was born. Instead he strings me along with that Fancy Dan grin and hints about conspiracy. You must get that wife of his to make him talk to us. But first, find out how and why he was arrested so speedily after the crime, and then let go. Even then he didn't decamp as a prudent man would have. He hung around for two years till they finally got around to indicting him a month ago. We need to sort out his reasons, Tilden, work out the times."

He waited for me to nod. It was suddenly clear to me that Whitbeck was easing my grief in the only way he knew, by giving me more responsibility in his case, by sending me on a journey to distract me. It would be futile to thank him. He'd deny it. With considerable difficulty I dragged my thoughts up from the very dark place where they had fallen on my ride down from New Lebanon. When I finally replied with a 'Yessir' in a voice nearly as brisk as his, he was already rushing onward..

"... large discrepancy there in Gardenier's version of events. With some luck we can pull Jackson out through it. Here," He fetched the strongbox from the cabinet behind him, "You'll need travel money and a decent hotel. Don't come back till you have the whole story. I reckon it won't be to Bat's credit, but it could raise some doubts. Justicia is blind, Royce. We must see. We must make sure her scales are fairly balanced."

So I repacked the bag I had just emptied and took the stage to Albany that same afternoon. As the chilly carriage rattled along the snowy track between dark stands of fir trees interspersed with skeletal maples and the massive trunks of giant sycamores, I pulled out the clippings I had obtained from county papers. The Hudson *Daily Evening Register* for 1885 reported several detentions of colored suspects, Henderson's arrest, and an arrest in Albany of a John Jackson. Was that the arrest my employer wanted to know about?

The sequence of developments carried in the local newspapers I had consulted, named most of the current participants in the case. Gardenier had handled the inquest into Gertrude Hover's murder, which was held in Kinderhook Village. Charles Davis had probably attended it, but gave it only a paragraph in the *Rough Notes*. Drs. Pruyn and Woodworth, also of Kinderhook, had been called to the scene and performed the autopsy. Coroner Waldron, up from Hudson, had adjourned the proceedings. The inquest was also reported in the Chatham *Courier*, which added an account of a second arrest, the first being Henderson's.

"Last Monday John Jackson alias Thompson was arrested in Albany for the murder (of Gertrude Hover). He lived in Kinderhook next house to Miss Hover's. He was first traced from Kinderhook to Hudson and it was learned he had disposed of some of his clothing on the way, From Hudson he went to Castleton, and then crossing to the west side of the river, boarded the steamer Lotta for Albany, where he arrived Saturday. When the prisoner was taken he gave his right name as Jackson and said he was also known as Thompson. Spots that resembled bloodstains were found on his clothing and will be subjected to a chemical analysis. A colored woman was summoned before Justice Clute last Monday, and she declared that she saw Jackson in Albany a week ago Sunday, and that his shoes were all red, as though he had been walking in paint. They were not the shoes worn by Jackson when arrested.

"The prisoner denies point blank that he knows anything about the murder, and claims he can prove an alibi by persons in Troy. He is still confined in the Albany jail on another charge, and will be held there for a time."

I looked up from the clipping. We were passing through winter-white fields now, with stubbled stretches where meltwater seeped away, and bright red barns set close to the road. The modest white farmhouses, protected by black pine windbreaks, seemed deserted except for the pale, slender pennants of woodsmoke curling up from their chimneys. The horses puffed and snorted and the driver shouted to slow them as we neared a crossing.

So why was John Jackson arrested that time? Was Jay Jackson John Jackson? John Thompson? Did Bat have other aliases I didn't know about? Was he known as Bat, or Jay, or something else among Gertrude's colored tenants and neighbors? That he lived near Gertrude's house seemed a very slim pretext to stop a ferry passenger arriving in Albany the next week. If he had changed clothes, as alleged, how could a few spots on the clothes he wore have any meaning or connection to the murder? And who was the woman who accused him? If Jackson was in Albany the day after the murder, what was he doing crossing the river again from Castleton later in the week? Why was Bat, one among several suspects, finally indicted for Gertrude Hover's murder? Our cocky, stubborn client could clear these matters ~ and possibly himself ~ if he could be brought to trust us. Cynthia seemed to trust me. Could I possibly persuade her to soften her husband's animosity toward white men?

Yes, of course. Cynthia. I smiled at my own weakness, my readiness to find yet another excuse to meet with Cynthia Jackson.

Meanwhile, I needed to chase down the circumstances of the arrest in 1885. If Jackson had a criminal past in Albany, we needed to know it, if only to forestall its use against him by the prosecution. Whitbeck had been right to suggest this trip to the state capital would not be brief.

I easily found the hotel he had recommended. Convenient to the police lockup where Jackson had been held, and reasonably near the office of the Albany *Times*, it was shabby but respectable, a haven for salesmen and petitioners to the state assembly. Whitbeck, I am sure, liked its modest rates. I would have preferred a warmer room and a softer bed.

Delaying my meal, I visited the newspaper office before it closed. In its musty back issues there was indeed a report of John Jackson's arrest two years before. He had been taken 'at the dwelling of Clarice Thompson, who had expected his visit and informed police ahead of time.' So why were the Albany police interested in him? For possible clarification, I sought out the *Evening Times* editor, a loose-limbed fellow with receding hair who did not offer his hand or even rise to greet me, but offered his name, Gus Loomis, around a stub of tobacco. I returned the disfavor by asking straight out if he knew more about the arrest of John Jackson than he had printed.

At the mention of the name Jackson Loomis chuckled. "You mean Bat Jackson? The one got arrested for killing an old woman over across the river?"

Somewhat taken aback by his familiarity with the nickname, I told him about the Chatham newspaper referring to Jackson as John at the time he was first arrested.

"Yeah? Well, John Jackson he's a bad'un. I remember Bat too; and I know who the woman is that turned John in, Clarice Thompson. She wasn't best pleased back in '85 during the cleanup, when John had to leave town. He was still up here pretty regular, I understand, makin his rounds, as it were. Collecting, d'you see?" He jerked his head toward the bank of photographs on the wall behind him. Several were of mounted jockeys. "Jackson carries money for the oddsmakers, the bookies. And collects for them, of course. That's as much as I know of him." He smiled the rueful smile of the inveterate gambler. "Clarice knew, of course, about when Jackson'd be comin' over. What I'm guessin' is that she got sore when he'd be right here in Albany and not pay her a call, so she went and told the cops, to make trouble for him. It was a gambling warrant put Jackson in the lockup in '85. That's what he was wanted for when he left town."

He shook his head at my evident ignorance and then explained. "We elected a new mayor in 1884, quite the reformer he is. Started by cleaning up on the fights down on Pearl Street. Too bad, in my opinion. The fights used to be the best entertainment in Albany." He removed his cigar to point it at me. "You could see maybe a dozen state assemblymen in the crowd on a Saturday afternoon, watchin' and yellin' for their favorites. And betting, of course. That was the sticker. All that money changin hands and none of it going into the city coffers. They went after the bookies first, like John. Easier to identify them than the promoters. But there was a warrant out for Bat as well that summer two years ago. He's a scrapper, y'know?"

Ah. That was a bit of information that my client had not provided, though it did not come as a great surprise. Jay Jackson had the stocky, muscular build of a boxer, and those scarred knuckles of his told their own story. So, he had gone back to live in his father's house when his brief career in the illegal fight game was cut short. As discreetly as I could. I waved away the stifling cloud from Loomis's cigar before leaning in to ask the crucial question.

"And who is this Clarice Thompson who turned Jackson in?"

"I believe she's his woman. He gave her name as his when they arrested him in '85."

I thanked him for his help and asked directions to the police station.

When I regained the street the early winter dusk had already leeched color from the day. Flickering gas lamps cast wavering circles of light on mounds of dirty snow. The new electric lighting had not yet extended throughout the capital. Unable to see what was underfoot, I soon foundered in slush, and postponed visiting police headquarters in favor of a meager meal in my hotel room while I dried my boots by the fire.

Fortunately I had the name of an Albany police captain Whitbeck knew, so my inquiries the next day bore fruit without too much difficulty. Captain Ouilette summoned a redfaced Officer Cohan, who seemed willing enough to share his recollections of John Jackson as he guided me to the criminal records room.

"We knew about Jackson. Didn't require Clara T to give him up. We were hoping for him to lead us to the promoters. There's plenty of illegal goings on up here. No need to gather in small fry like Jackson, if we can take down the top men. Clara, she was pretty het up and wanted him taken right then. He was supposed to call on her regular and leave her a little money, which he didn't do as steady as she liked. When she saw we weren't interested in takin' him in just then ~ that's when she told us he was the one killed the Hover woman over across the river. Said she saw him here in town the day after the murder with blood on him, red all over his shoes like paint. We took him in, but I, personally, didn't see any stains on him. He looked okay to me when we arrested him. Oh, maybe he was a little worse for wear, but he generally dressed pretty rough. Them

Jacksons like to fight. Bat Jackson got paid for it. That was before they cracked down on the fights. You know that?"

I assured him I knew about the fights on Pearl Street.

"Yeah. Well, Bat made money gettin' himself bruised and his nose bloodied coupla hours a week. We think John was bringin' in Canada hootch. Untaxed, if you see what I mean. That was only a rumor. I don't believe Bat paid attention to what the city council did. He showed up at the horse barn where they set up for the fights, came late of course, since he didn't fight the prelims. His name was on the poster for that day. That I remember. We were all over the place, more uniforms than fight fans, arrestin' bookmakers and wrestlers, taking down names in the crowd. So I guess Jackson saw what was up and just scarpered. When we took John, it was on a gambling warrant. He wasn't exactly our most wanted felon. Except by Clara T. She used to be his woman when he was here in town. She lives over on Washington with two children I guess are his. Clara warned us he was due to slip into town, give her some money to feed the pickaninnies, whatever."

"Bat had a reputation here, then."

"Oh, Bat? Yes indeed, Bat. Quick on his feet, quick with his hands, quick with his mouth, too."

This was not what I wanted to hear about my client.

"He was a comer, for a while anyway. When he was scrapping, before the crackdown, the crowd would yell Bat, Bat! Beat im, Battice! and like that. They'd yell for Stoke Hamm. Hammer, Hammer! Slug im, Stoke! We ~ that is, the fight fans ~ had some fine old times down there at the horse barn. Wild brawls and blood in the dirt, and the smell of horse dung on a hot Saturday."

"I can tell you enjoyed the fights yourself, Mr. Cohan. Are you a betting man?"

"Been known to go from time to time," he assured me with a slow wink. "As an unofficial observer. We kept Jackson in jail during a legal wrangle over his involvement in gambling. But we didn't charge him, couldn't find a single willing witness, so we had to let him go. Clara T peddled her story of the bloody shoes to anyone who'd listen, but John slipped away clear. Fact is, after he left in '85, Clara went back on the streets to earn her keep the way she did before she met him. Maybe she got upset when she found out Bat had gone and married some high brown girl over there in Kinderhook; and that set her against the Jacksons."

"Clarice Thompson was Jackson's common-law wife?"

"Common law or convenience. My sergeant told me Clarice was a fancy hooker, took up with John when he started bookmaking on the fights. Bat was hardly out of kneepants when he began to win all-outs down at the horse barn. And Clara T, she was queen of Pearl a few years back. That's what my sergeant says, anyway. He says in those days, not many colored men could afford her. She latched onto Jackson when she was just past her best and he was on the rise. That's how it was told to me." The flush had spread from his ruddy cheeks to his ears as he recounted this spicy tale of Albany's colorful recent past.

"Anyway, they lived together; and when Clarice popped out with his child Jackson set her up in a house over on Washington. She did pretty well, had another baby. Jackson, he's quite a rooster." Cohan's face was still pink, but his tone was now envious. "He treated her like family. But then we shut down the fights, and he took off. Then later he figured on slippin' over here to Albany without being seen, counting on a little sweet talk and some spending money to keep Clarice happy. Didn't work too well."

We had long since arrived at the file room. Officer Cohan helped me find the folder with Jackson's arrest record before striding off to other duties. I scanned the single sheet of paper in the folder, noting from it the one piece of information I needed, Clarice Thompson's address.

It was a white frame townhouse, one of an attached row, marching up a long, rutted hill. There was no walkway. My horse stumbled in the slushy, half-frozen mud and I was glad I had thought to hire him. Albany was considerably larger than Hudson, though it lacked the city solidity of New York. (I speak of it as it was when I first came here, not as it is now in 1933.) Clarice Thompson's unit had dark red shutters and a fenced front garden, or what might be a garden under its coat of sooty snow.

She was prompt to the door, a dark complected woman, tall and full figured with a colorful scarf wrapped around her head. She was dressed in what I took to be satin. At least it was some sort of shiny red material with flounces and black lace trimming the sleeves and billowing skirt. It was as if she had just come from the dancehall, except that she had covered her front with a stained apron and thrown a shawl around her shoulders.

Quite startled by this unexpected finery, and by the challenge in her eyes, I hesitated.

She did not. "Well, hello." She did not smile, but the voice was a rich, confident contralto. She looked past me to the horse tethered at her front gate, and then at my greatcoat, as if estimating its worth, or mine. After a long second she waved me inside. "You're a bold one, coming here in broad daylight," she told me, before taking my coat and scarf and pointing me along the hall. As we passed the parlor I looked in to see a small girl sitting on the floor surrounded by dolls. Her hair had been twisted into a dozen plaits, each with its own ribbon. The room was chilly, the child well sweatered against drafts. She looked up at me, and then stood and rushed to slam the door closed.

"My daughter doesn't like strangers," the woman said. "You have to tell her your name when you come again, so she won't be upset by you." She gave me a fleeting smile, raising beautifully arched brows in query. We had reached a farther door. She opened it and gestured for me to precede her into a room which I saw was a bedroom. I halted abruptly, causing her to step on my heels.

"Don't be shy, Mr. Smith. Go on in."

I turned around. Her face was inches from mine, her dark eyes now wide open. "You have mistaken me, missus. My name is Tilden. I am an attorney. I need to ask you a few questions about Bat Jackson."

"Oh." It was hardly a whisper. Her face emptied of surprise, of all expression, but she was quick to recover. "Let's go into the back, then." She stepped away and led me briskly along to the leanto kitchen, dominated by a sizeable woodstove that was emitting a blast of heat. I could smell bread baking in the oven. "You'll take coffee." She brought out two mugs and filled them from the pot that was steaming on a corner of the stove. "I hope you take it black," she said. "I save the milk for my children. Now what d'you want to know about Bat?"

"Well, first of all. Is Bat Jackson your legal husband?"

Her laughter pealed around the kitchen. "Bat? Oh, Bat! Well, I'd say my husband's name is Jackson. How d'you mean legal? Him and me, we been together six years come spring. My little girl there, she's four, and got a brother already in school. I am John Jackson's woman. He bought me this house. After they chased him outta town he came over, or he sent his brother to see to us when he could. That husband enough for you?"

"But perhaps he comes less often now than he used to?" I sipped my coffee. It was searing hot and thick as treacle. She must leave it bubbling all day on the woodstove which seemed to provide the only heat in the house.

"Who Bat? Bat don't come at all. He's in jail," she announced with a satisfied nod.

"Ah. Yes. You helped the police to arrest him two years ago. They took him up on a gambling charge. That would have kept him right here in Albany jail. So I wonder why you said that about seeing him up here the week before, about his red-spattered shoes and all. Saying all that put him in deep trouble. You won't get to visit him there in Hudson, unless you go down to see him hanged."

"Who you talking about now? John? He don't need me to put him in trouble. He's always in and out of trouble. Anyway Bat won't hang. he can find plenty of folks ready to say where he was when that old lady died. You white folks got it all wrong about that killin'" She put her mug down and looked up at me. Her eyes hardened and the hollows in her face deepened as her expression settled into a frightening implacability. For a moment she seemed quite alien, feral and fierce, a she-wolf protecting her cubs. "Needs some shakin' up that man o'mine. Needs to see sense, realize where he belongs, who belongs to him. This is family here." She had brought up her fisted hands but now unclasped them and tapped a forefinger sharply on the table. "Jacksons gettin' too uppity now, Bat marryin' that little yella snip." She spat, and then covered her mouth.

I have heard it said that men choose women who resemble their mothers. If so, how could two such dissimilar women suit one man's taste? You could make two of Cynthia out of Buxom Clarice Thompson, and have yards of sleazy satin left over. Clara T's fierceness would be a match for Bat. Cynthia was his opposite. There was something odd here. I tried to imagine Clara T watching fights at the horse barn on Pearl Street. Had she dazzled the youth and then kept him beside her? She must be eight or ten years Bat's senior, was now beginning to show it. Bat Jackson seemed to me a subtler and cleverer player than the man she was describing.

Dressed in her faded glory, masking despair with anger, she regarded me defiantly over the rim of her coffee mug. She must be calculating my use to her, even as I weighed her value in Bat's defense, in the case I wanted to win. She would not, could not, testify at the trial. Gardenier would not dare use a black harlot's testimony. Besides, as Whitbeck and I had learned in numerous interviews, half the village of Kinderhook had seen Bat Jackson the day Gertrude was killed; and the other half had seen him the following day. He had certainly not been in Albany that Sunday, as Clara T claimed..

If Clarice were Bat Jackson's wife, she could not be a witness against him. Even if Clarice were merely his known common-law wife, Cynthia was less than that, not married to him at all. If we could establish that, Cynthia could be Bat's best witness. I could easily imagine her melting a jury. However, for her to testify, I would have to reveal my client as a bigamist, or at any rate a complete cad. Did I want to establish in a public hearing that Cynthia Van Houck was not truly married, that her child was illegitimate? God knew, I knew, how tenuous the hold on respectability could be for negro citizens of this country. We were barely a generation out of slavery, and more than ready to turn a blind eye to massive and ingrained injustices in our legal system. I speak as if this were buried in the past of which I write, as if our legal and social systems have become fully impartial in the intervening generation. But I am aware of how little has changed, how little I have done to balance the scales, how little I do now.

At that moment I understood only that if Cynthia lost her social position as a proper wife, she and her son would be stigmatized, probably forced to leave the only place she had ever known, to earn her way unsheltered in a world indifferent to her grace and ability, where her color made her a menial. The thought of it left me weak with impotent anger as I rode back to the center of Albany. I had no taste for dinner, and slept little, thrashing out in my mind how this nasty tangle might affect the trial, how it possibly related to Gertrude Hover's murder.

Jackson was a rotter, but was he a murderer? First Clarice and then Emma had accused him. I was pretty sure Clarice had acted out of malice. And Emma? Besotted and rebuffed, had she really seen him or his brother William at Gertrude's place that Saturday? Always when I came to that question something nagged at the back of my mind, something Clarice had said.

Bat acted as if none of it mattered, as if he could snap his fingers and make the whole charade disappear. Was that the assurance of an habitual felon, or the over-confidence of a brash and doomed loser? We were little more than a month from the trial date, and I, at least, had not gotten from him any account of his movements on the day of the murder. He met every query with either stiff silence or cocky assertions that 'they'll see me right,' or 'it will all come out.' Never a hint as to who *they* might be. I fervently hoped that he was more forthcoming with Whitbeck.

Only once, in mid-January, when I visited him early in the morning, did Jackson offer anything like a courteous gesture. That day he looked as if he had slept little and eaten less. He greeted me with a baleful stare, and before I could speak asked me about Cynthia.

"My Cyndy wasn't here yesterday, nor the day before. You keeping her away from me?"

"No. Of course not. We wouldn't do that. There has been a message from her, however. Your son has come down with the whooping cough. She will not leave his side, I am sure, until he is past the worst of it. Mr. Whitbeck or I will keep you informed. It's a severe illness, but not often fatal."

"If she needs anything ~ money for the doctor, medicine, anything, I can do that much." He bent toward me, speaking rapidly. "I can pay your fee, if you'll just see she doesn't have to worry while I'm in here." I waited, hoping he would say more, but then doubt replaced his anxiety. His customary scowl returned. For the rest of my visit he was as monosyllabic as usual. I wondered if he ever said a word to John Whitbeck.

Suddenly the whole warp of it ~ my life, Jay Jackson's, Cynthia's, Clara T's, John Whitbeck's ~ swirled through my mind like the knotted grain of a burl, an eddy in a current far greater than this congruence. Whitbeck was intent on his legal sparring with the district attorney. Clarice Thompson lacked a moral compass, but her courage could not be faulted. She was willing to use a hostile system to gain her ends. Could I use her to exonerate the man she accused? Jackson was wagering his freedom ~ his life in fact ~ on the word of men who, if some of his reputed associates were any measure, could not be trusted. And Cynthia ~ an intelligent and beautiful woman, but a poor judge of men. Well, perhaps not in all cases. She had, after all, chosen me as her confidant.

And I? What did I want from this trial? Determination to succeed was all I had left now that my family fortunes were at low ebb and Lillian had put her father's wishes before her own. To what lengths was I, was John Whitbeck, willing go to gain acquittal for a man so clearly meant to hang? If it meant branding Cynthia Jackson as dupe, her marriage a sham, her child a bastard? Could we do her that harm to win this case?

Chapter Eight

All this trouble comes of telling truth
Which when it issues forth looks false
Seems to be just the thing it would supplant,
Not recognizable by whom it left –
While falsehood would have served in place of truth.

Robert Browning, in *The Ring and the Book*

Climbing the narrow stair to my employer's office I could hear voices, Whitbeck's rasp and a lower rumble I did not recognize. Whitbeck's greeting was minimal.

"Back so soon, Tilden? Found Albany not to your liking, I expect. This is Mr. Rowlings of the county surveyor's office. My assistant, Royce Tilden." Rowlings, a large rotund fellow with receding hair and swelling jowls, looked up from the county map that was covering Whitbeck's desk and gave me a perfunctory wave. "Mr. Rowlings has kindly consented to share his extensive knowledge of county history with me, Royce. We are fortunate to have him as custodian of our county registry of deeds, plats, and properties. And he, in turn, is blessed in administering a repository that extends to the earliest allotments of the Dutch settlers, who were such marvelously meticulous record keepers."

"Indeed, sir. And is this new enthusiasm in any way related to the case which occupies us at present?"

"Quick on the uptake, isn't he?" Whitbeck laid a proprietary hand on the uppermost map ~ for they were spread a dozen deep on the desk, with more scrolled in a bundle on one of the chairs. "Did you know, Royce, that the family of District Attorney Gardenier once owned a very pretty piece of this county? I have to wonder why Chittendon Falls, or even Stockport wasn't named Gardenierville or some such." He pulled an old plat map from under the pile, beautifully drawn in ink gone brown with age, it showed the broad, curving swath of the upper Hudson, with a large section of the present county indicated along it, the landings or hooks named, and Kinderhook Creek meandering through it, with lakes and smaller streams all carefully drawn. Across it lay a complex pattern of straightline surveyor's grids: land grants to Dutch settlers. The name Gardenier appeared on a score of the smaller sections. The biggest, the De Bruyn and Powell allotments were large blank spaces. The rest were miniscule, the names so small I could scarcely make them out.

"Interesting, eh, Roy? And look here, where the De Bruyn patent crosses the creek going toward Chatham, there is this stretch of good bottom land which belonged to ~ can you read it?"

I bent over the map, shifting the lamp to drag his shadow away from the section he wanted me to see. After a long moment squinting at it I looked up sharply. "Haaver. It says Jan Haaver."

Rowlings nodded, his chins wobbling. Oh, yes. The Haavers were here early, came with the Patroons, and kept their holding too, unlike some of the others. De Bruyns, for instance, had an unfortunate tendency to breed daughters in quantity. Not too many Vosburghs left now either, but other names remain evident in later patents and deeds. Haavers, Hawvers, Hovers, even Hoffers are from that family. I can show you the later maps, if you like, Mr. Tilden. They're in the pile on that chair."

Whitbeck forstalled that excursion. "No need at the moment, Mr. Rowlings. I am sure Mr. Tilden will take your word for the authenticity of current deeds. Gertrude Hover and her brothers were coheirs to what remained of the Haaver holdings. Richard and James, who live locally, own nice sections in Kinderhook Village. Richard also has a stretch over toward Stuyvesant Landing, including land near Mordecai Briggs's farm, where Emma Briggs has her berry patch. Gertrude, the elder sister, got the property that fronts on Sunset, that cottage she lived in, several smaller houses near it, and five acres of orchard. She also received a piece of farmland east of the holdings of her brothers, part of the plot that is shown here as Haaver's allotment."

"I had no idea the Hovers were wealthy landowners," I murmured.

"Landowners, yes. But hardly moneyed," Whitbeck said. "Gertrude donated generously to the anti-slavery movement, endowed an orphan home over in Chatham, and gave to other good works. In later years her chief income was from the apple orchard. She rented the houses on her land mostly to negro families. That area at the edge of the village has become darktown, with the AME church out there and all. I think the Hovers sold or donated that bit of land the Bethel is built on. Richard Hover wasn't as careful as his sister ~ or as generous. He did some speculating, lost most of his capital in the panic of '83 and pulled in his horns after that. James? I think James farms land down in Greenport."

Whitbeck had obviously been studying these maps, and other documents, I was sure. He was showing off his expertise in county history. It might be very useful to our case.

"Not all the Hovers ended up land-poor," Rowlings pointed out. "There's a Hover in the consortium that's planning the new rail line across the county from Stuyvesant Landing and through Kinderhook Village to Valatie, to eventually meet the Chatham spur. Railroads gentlemen," He straightened, supporting himself with a meaty hand on the maps. "Railroads are changing these maps faster than a war. And now with the telegraph coming in, and electricity ~ When the power they can generate at Niagara Falls gets down here ~ oh my! We'll all have light and power. Trains can run on electricity. Horse trolleys will be history! You'll be traveling to Albany without breathing coal dust, and in less time than you now spend waiting for the stage or the ferry. If they can lay track over the Berkshires to Boston, they can hang wire the same distance. Think of taking a train down to the City without arriving covered in soot! Think of light that comes through a wire at the touch of your hand. We can banish darkness, put an end to the perils of the night. Wonderful, wonderful times we are living in, gentlemen."

"Yes. Yes." Whitbeck put a calming hand on Rowlings's shoulder. "I understand your enthusiasm. But tell us more about this proposed expansion of rail lines through the county. Who are the members of the consortium? Have they acquired land for their roadbed, or is this all speculation?"

"Ah, well. It is all being kept quiet, of course." Rowlings laid a finger along his nose and cleared his throat noisily, signalling the need for discretion.. "Discussions have been underway for some time. The older Hover holdings lie along the proposed route, including the portion that was owned by Miss Gertrude Hover." He turned to me to explain, "Since she left no will, her estate has required arbitration, as Mr. Whitbeck is aware. Her brothers offered the acreage including the orchard to the village for an extension of the graveyard. That sale, however, has been challenged by other relatives, including her nephew George Van Epps, who claims title to the land and the house by reason of Miss Hover having been his guardian. It has been a tangle for the courts. But the land deeds, I am happy to say, are in order for heirs declared valid."

Whitbeck was nodding. This information was old to him. "*Cuius beneficium*," he murmured, his eyes aimed at me like bright daggers. Then he extended a long hand to the registrar of documents. "Thank you, Mr. Rowlings for your time and your expertise. You'll want to return these documents to the county registry. Help him if you will, Royce. They need to be rolled up and sleeved. I'll look for you at Vanderhagen's when you've finished." He was dismissing us.

He hadn't allowed me a word about my journey, or asked a single question about what I'd learned in Albany. He was making sure no hint of the direction of our investigations reached Gardenier's ear. I thought it overcautious of him. So far as I could tell Rowlings was a disinterested civil servant, without ties to the district attorney's office. He had given us nothing that wasn't in the public record, but that didn't necessarily mean his loyalty or sympathies lay with the prosecutor.

The first words out of Whitbeck's mouth when I found him at Vanderhagen's half an hour later were accusatory.

"All this time chasing after Jackson's past, Jackson's connections ~ which we should have had from Jackson himself months ago ~ and you still haven't tackled that brother of his. William was the first one suspected of doing away with Gertrude. There he is in plain view, another viable culprit, and you haven't even approached him. Do you even know where he is at present?"

I ignored this sally. What I had so far learned of William Jackson did not make me eager to confront him. "How about telling me what you expect to uncover in county land records." I countered. I was in no mood to suffer Whitbeck's superior attitude that day. The trip down from Albany had been beastly. I had arrived exhausted and hungry at my lodging, too late for supper. Then, to top off my misery, I had overslept breakfast that morning. I was running on nerves and resentment, ready to cross swords with anyone who treated me like a lacky. I think Whitbeck sensed how near I was to a breaking point.

"Here's the waiter, Roy. Order, and then I'll tell you."

I chose the special and a bowl of soup without taking my eyes away from his. "Well?"

"Kinderhook is the oldest settlement in this area. In early times it was the commercial hub of the county. Until fifty years ago it was a bustling town, replete with mills and factories and business of all sorts, a major stage stop between New York and Albany. Kinderhook Academy attracted students from great distances. And there was the law school ~"

"I am not unaware of the village's place in history, sir. Make your point."

"That was all changed by the railroad. Kinderhook wouldn't cede a foot of its precious, historic acreage for roadbed. The Hudson River line went straight up along the river, bypassed the village. You can pretty much discount Rowlings and his electric train, which doesn't carry goods. There'll be a trolley through the village, but not a coal burner. For purposes of trade, Kinderhook began to die with the coming, or more precisely the noncoming of the railroad. Manufacturing moved nearer the railheads. The village kept its bucolic beauty but lost its commerce. Without factories, the cotton mill, the sawmill, the brewery, the hat factory, business shrank. There was no work to generate income. The charm of the place remains, but that charm has a high cost." He leaned back to allow the waiter room to deposit his soup, and tasted it before continuing.

"Recently there have been efforts to correct this problem. The cross-county railway proposal has attracted speculators to acquire land for the roadbed. All very hush-hush, of course, so as not to alert landowners and inflate land values along the route. Mr. Rowlings has so far been the only knowledgeable person willing to talk to me about this scheme. He brought his maps to me to avoid being noticed if we studied them in the registry office."

I nodded, my mouth full, as I dipped a crust into the thick broth, savoring my first nourishment of the day. This much I had figured out, but let Whitbeck run on. I needed to eat.

"Gertrude Margaret Hover, the victim, owned several sizeable pieces of arable land in the county. Did you know that, Tilden?"

I paused and put down my spoon reluctantly. "I know she lived in the middle of an orchard which has since been acquired by the village for the purpose of extending the cemetery. The land where the cemetery now lies, over near the old sawmill, ends in a steep declivity, unsuitable for burial purposes. An alternative was to add a section across the Albany Road, Gertrude Hover's apple orchard." I picked up my spoon.

Whitbeck also picked up his spoon. "As you say. That acquisition had been discussed for years. Gertrude knew the Dutch Reformed Church consistory was reluctant to move forward with it. The village population is declining. Investment and upkeep for a larger burial ground have been hard to justify. Rowlings assured me that changes in the membership of the village council and the consistory were needed before the purchase could be assured."

"Rowlings seems uncommonly well informed." I scraped up the last of my soup.

"The land on which those cottages stand was part of the acreage acquired ~ since Gertrude's death ~ for the new graveyard. "

"So all those colored families will be moved out to make room for the next generation of dead gentry?"

"Perhaps not immediately, but eventually, yes." He finished his soup before going on.

"Rowlings was showing me where the other sections are that came into Miss Hover's possession on the death of her father. The Hover land inherited by Gertrude and her brothers lies along the proposed route of the cross-county railroad. One of Gertrude's brothers, the one up in Albany with the good lawyer, is a member of the group backing the railway. You can see where this leads us?"

"I am ahead of you, sir. I can also see that this case has now fallen under one of your favorite rubrics."

"*Cuius beneficium*, as I said earlier."

"That, of course, but more apropos: 'Up here politics is about real estate'."

"Ah. Yes. What you have to uncover, young Royce, is how our client Bat Jackson managed to run afoul of the politics of county real estate. Either he was deep into whatever was happening in regard to Gertrude Hover's land ~ in which case he is guilty and heaven help him, or he was set up by someone who wanted that woman's property desperately enough to kill her for it. Of course, he could have been shopped by one of his shady acquaintances from across the river, or right there in Guinea Hill. Bat Jackson is the sort who attracts enemies as well as fans."

"My, my, Mr. Whitbeck, those are nasty ideas. You seem to be making large assumptions about your client's character. You suggest that he hobnobs either with a select company of white men, or with some of the roughest black men around here, or that he is dangerous enough to someone who will take considerable trouble to see him hanged."

"These ideas aren't mine, Royce. Gertrude Hover was slain in a most vicious and violent way. If Oscar Beckwith weren't already in prison, I am sure our famous axe murderer would be the prime suspect in her death. He is about to hang for one murder, possibly more. Another murder would not increase his punishment. But that's not on, so another candidate has been found, a black felon we would be well rid of, according to general opinion. We don't want to be surprised midtrial by crimes in our client's history he's keeping from us. We have to get Jackson talking. I must know, in order to minimalize, every sordid chapter of his criminal past. The worst moment for an attorney is the public disclosure of detrimental facts he has allowed a client to conceal because he trusted him."

Coming from John Whitbeck, that was a sharp warning. He had heard or divined something damning in his prowling and schmoozing at the courthouse or across a stained table in the Iron Horse. Somehow one of us had to get Bat Jackson to offer an alibi, any alibi, or something that would point suspicion away from him! My senior couldn't use Bat's cocky claim that they wouldn't dare convict him. His bravado would not win over a white judge and jury ready to hang any accused black man, most certainly one this defiant.

"Well?" Whitbeck finally asked, "Anything to report?" I was busy attacking the roast on my plate. He wanted to know what I'd found in Albany, but I was suddenly aware of other ears amid the clatter and buzz of Vanderhagen's, of the all too mellow glow of gaslamps, of the genial intimacy of Hudson's legal community. He would have to contain his impatience till we were behind his office door. How he would view the news of the other Jackson family across the river, of Jackson's short-lived career in the illegal sport of boxing, or his possible connection to smuggling, transporting stolen goods, or other shady dealings, I could guess. He would see all of it as detrimental to the case. An abandoned wife might be an impugnable prosecution witness, but bigamy was a serious defect in a defendant's character. That Bat had fought public brawls on which bets were laid would just about settle the noose around our client's muscular throat.

Whitbeck would weigh the damage to our case. I was more concerned with the effect it would have on Cynthia Jackson. I needed her gentle powers of persuasion to overcome her husband's hostility. I didn't think he had met with open bigotry growing up in Kinderhook. The village seemed reasonably tolerant of its colored population, many of whom bore the Dutch names of founding families and had freeborn ancestors from back into the eighteenth century, pedigrees longer than many white citizens. However, Jay Jackson seemed to have grown up a rebel. He would have been one barefoot pickaninny who evaded or even refused Gertrude Hover's imperious charity. He had not stayed in school, though some bright colored students had even gone on to the Academy. He fled to Albany to escape the confining propriety of the village, and only returned to live with his father when the gambling crackdown in Albany put a stop to his activities there.

Apart from working on John Powell's farm, how had Jackson earned the money that kept him and his new bride well clothed, and afforded improvements to his father's house, since Jackson senior was clearly unfit for manual labor? Cynthia said the retainer she offered had been raised by Bethel's congregation, but Jackson had later offered to pay our fees himself.

I did not want to discover our client robbed banks or stole horses in his spare time.

The next day, following Whitbeck's urging that I interview Bat's brother, I rode up to Kinderhook again, on horseback, since a week of mild weather had cleared the road north. It was nearly noon when I reached the village, so I stopped at the staging inn for lunch. I had retrieved my horse from the stable and was about to mount when I felt a pull at my coat sleeve.

"Tilden? You are Royce Tilden?"

I turned to find that one of the other diners from the inn had followed me out to the stableyard, napkin in hand. "Yes. I am he. Did I forget something?" I searched the rather stern, unrevealing face of the middle-aged man who looked down at me out of ice-gray eyes.

"She did not die intestate, as they claim. Gertrude made a will and had it witnessed."

He stepped away as abruptly as he had come, and began to march back across the stableyard, picking his way to avoid horse droppings and muddy puddles left by melting snow.

"Your name, sir?" I called.

He turned back, and raised his voice just enough for me to hear him. "The village is full of lawyers. One of them drafted that will." Then he hurried inside through the scullery door.

"Your name, sir?" I repeated, calling more loudly. But he had gone. Here was another villager who knew something that might point away from Bat Jackson as Gertrude Hover's killer. He wanted to do the proper thing but not to be known for it. I swung up on the horse and trotted him past the postoffice and onto Albany Avenue, thinking of Charles Davis, the newspaper editor who employed negro printers and did not fill his empty columns with minstrel-style vignettes that poked fun at caricatures of blacks and cartoonishly silly women. I thought of Gertrude Hover, with her thorny personality and lifelong devotion to the abolitionist cause. No one I had interviewed had spoken ill of her, but no one had praised her for championing negro rights after the war, for insisting that colored children from the village and from around the county attend school, be admitted to Kinderhook Academy. Apparently very few had done so. It would take extreme courage and endurance to undertake the long distances and probable taunts of schoolmates, not to mention the costs involved for families often barely able to subsist. Education in those circumstances was a risky luxury.

I rode past the Academy, white woodsmoke pouring out of its chimneys and a row of traps waiting for the scholars soon to be released for the day. A curious settlement this village seemed to me, smug and secretive. How many of its residents, I wondered, held liberal views and supported humanitarian causes, but reserved their opinions so as not to disturb the prejudices of their neighbors, or risk censure themselves. Who was it who said all that evil needs to triumph is for wellmeaning people to be silent? Ben Franklin, perhaps? No matter. I say it anyway, then and now.

Snow still lay deep on the verges of Sunset. Powell's cattle were sheltering among a skeletal grove of maples, their backs to the bare brown meadow. At the Jackson house I was met at the door by a sturdy young fellow. He was shorter, than Bat, but with enough resemblance that he must be the brother.

"William?" I asked him.

"Who're you?" he retorted. Apparently he shared Bat's distrust of white men.

"I am your brother's lawyer, Royce Tilden." I took off my glove and offered my hand. William hesitated a long, wary moment before reaching to take it in his warm, leathery grasp.

"My sister, she's not here. She's at the hatshop today. I got the boy here, and my Daddy."

"That's fine, William. I don't need to see Cynthia," (I had only been hoping for it.) "It's you I came to see."

"Not me!" He exclaimed sharply. "I didn't do nothin'. I just come home. I come across from the tracks and through that way." He pointed distractedly in the general direction I supposed Gertrude's orchard to be, or her dooryard. Was he referring to that terrible day two years past, or to something that had happened an hour ago? He seemed uncommonly defensive. Was it me?

William was shorter than his brother, not much above my own height. His face bore a family resemblance, but his eyes were without the challenging directness of Jay's. Instead they were wild and fearful, dancing in all directions as if expecting trouble from every side. "Jemmy," he said anxiously, "I take care of Jemmy. You better leave."

"Maybe I can help you with Jemmy," I suggested brightly, pushing my way inside and following him to the kitchen where his nephew sat in a highchair. A bowl of gruel was just out of the child's reach on the table. William sat down and began to feed him. The boy Jemmy, who looked to my untutored eyes well able to feed himself, had fastened his unblinking gaze on me, though he grabbed at the spoon when William offered it. "Here," I said, taking the chair nearest Jemmy. "You watch me, young man, while your uncle gives you some of that good porridge." I stretched out a tentative finger, which the child seized in his sticky fist. William presented a spoonful of oats, and Jemmy took it in, grasping my thumb with his other hand and pulling it toward him. I could see the curiosity in that infant face, as lively as his father's. He examined my strange hand, a hand without color. He nearly had my spectacles before I could snatch them off, and then scanned my pale face with the same intensity, judging me decidedly lacking in at least one essential human aspect. I don't remember ever feeling more inadequate than I did under that one year-old's solemn regard.

"So, William," I said, tearing my eyes from Jemmy's pitying stare. "You were on your way home when you climbed over the back fence. This was two years ago, when Miss Hover died?"

"I was runnin. They was after me."

"The police? They said you were bothering women over there in Chatham by the station."

"Oh. That time. I told them to go away from there. That's my patch. It wasn't those ladies chased me. It was men," he added, his face sullen. Someone had harassed him, but he was the one accused.

"But why did they think you would hurt Miss Hover?"

"That Emma. She saw me goin over the fence. That's all it was. I was coming home!" he insisted, and was ready to repeat his whole story, but Jemmy interrupted, releasing my hand and grabbing the spoon away from him with a triumphant crow.

"William? You got company?" John Jackson Senior called from somewhere above.

"It's that white lawyer, Daddy. You want him up there?"

"I'll come. I'll come down. You just stay there, William. Stay with Jemmy."

The old man sounded anxious. Or was it merely that he was more shortwinded? His voice seemed more quavery than at my earlier visit. It was an old man's voice.

William plied his nephew with the spoon a few more times, leaving more gruel on the child's face than inside him. Afterward he wet a cloth from a kettle warming on the stove and scrubbed a protesting Jemmy's face and hands with the most exquisite care.

The elder Jackson made his painful way downstairs at the end of that ritual and motioned me into the parlor, where a Franklin stove was putting out welcome heat. "You come to see Cynthia? She's at the shop today," he told me as he eased himself into his accustomed chair.

"No, sir. I came to see William, but I am pleased to see you again, and glad to see you can manage the stairs. You were ailing the last time I was here. How is your back these days?"

"Tolerable. I manage," he said. He was plainly having some difficulty breathing now, but I didn't refer to it, as he seemed too proud to admit infirmity. "You be careful of William," he said softly, "William's very tender. You don't want to upset him. Better if I stay by while you talk with him. Here now," he raised his voice as Jemmy staggered into the room with William in tow. "Jemmy, come sit with Granddad while this fella and William visit."

William glanced at me warily before turning away to take a seat opposite the stove. I joined him in the room's cold corner. To my careful questions, he had little to add I did not already know. He had, indeed, been arrested for shouting at three women who stood chatting in his regular spot near Chatham Station, the spot where he usually sat to eat his lunch and observe the noon train coming through. "You can hear by the clicks if that bend in the tracks is off-kilter," he explained. "I told 'em nice to move off, but they paid me no mind. So then I said again the train was comin. I needed my spot. I said why, but nobody would listen. That was the first time. The other time, over at Valatie, that was something else. I don't remember what."

That must have been the arrest in Valatie that brought him to official notice, since it happened only days before Gertrude Hover was found dead. He had been released from the jailhouse in Valatie and come straight home, his father explained. He came over the creek bridge and through Miss Hover's orchard, and cut over her back fence to get home.

"That's all Emma Briggs saw," Jackson said, "just William coming home. But when a reward got offered for information leading to the killer she made a meal of it and served it up to the police to get hold of that reward. When she couldn't make it stick to William ~ we could prove where he was that day ~ Emma decided it was Jay she had seen. Jay doesn't climb over fences," he said disgustedly. "Jay comes up the road like a gentleman. And that day he and Cynthia were out somewhere. Only been married a week or two then. When they weren't working , they were never apart, Jay and his princess."

"So Cynthia could swear he was with her that day?"

"That day or the next. The Sunday I clearly remember." Jackson said. He hesitated and then added, "He was over to Powell's for a while on Saturday." He helped Jemmy scramble onto his lap and started a handgame with him.

"I seen em," William volunteered. "Cyndy and Jay. They come back from town. Cyndy cooked supper. She's a good cook, Cyndy. I like her."

"That's right, William. You remember it all. You remember what Asa said, Asa Gillet?"

William did not answer, his eyes crazily searching every part of the room.

His father spoke for him. "Asa said why'd they keep asking all about Saturday. Asa said he came over early that morning like Miss Hover said to come. He knocked and knocked but she never come to the door, and the blinds were closed and ~."

"Wait now!" I stopped him. "This wasn't in Gillet's statement to the police." Nor in what he told me, I knew. I had read Gillet's official statement along with the others collected just after Gertrude's body was found.

"Well, they didn't ask him about the morning," Mr. Jackson pointed out. "They asked everyone what they saw that afternoon. Sylvester told them he heard voices in the house when he went by on Saturday afternoon, so they figured she died after that. But Sylvester, he comes past here just about every day with a load of hay for the stage horses. He couldn't be sure it was Saturday he heard Miss Hover, or George or one of her brothers talking in there, or if it was Friday, or any other day. But Saturday afternoon was the time they decided on after they found her on Tuesday. Asa Gillet told them ~ whatever he told them ~ about Saturday afternoon. He didn't say about the morning, since he wasn't asked."

"Mr. Jackson, this could be very important. Do you know where Bat, where Jay Jackson was on the Friday night before September 5th in 1885, when Gertrude Hover is supposed to have been killed?" I couched my question formally, in case this was a deposition we'd need for the trial.

"Indeed I do." His voice was breathy still, but as intense as my own. "He was right here. He and his bride. They went up to bed early and stayed shut up there like two love birds till Cyndy came down to make breakfast next morning. That I know for a fact. I heard the two of them singing in the middle of the night, so soft, so sweet, thinking they wouldn't wake me with their love music. That's a sound I won't forget." He smiled and stroked Jemmy's head, the child half asleep in his lap.

"They was after me," William spoke up sharply from his corner. "But Jay let them take him instead. Jay, he didn't do it. I didn't do it neither." His crazed eyes settled momentarily on me. "Some white man took a knife to her, but they'll hang Jay for it!" Suddenly he was shouting. His father tried to rise from the chair; the child began to whimper. I stood and crossed the room to take the child and help the old man to his feet. William had gotten up and was shouting now, ugly, unintelligible phrases. I could see how they might sound like threats or obscenity, if an excuse were needed to arrest a nuisance and put him behind bars for a day or two.

I helped his father upstairs, and left him comforting the scared little boy. "Don't tell Cynthia about this," he pleaded. "She won't let William take care of him if she knows." I nodded. Cynthia Jackson probably knew her brother-in-law well enough to be aware of his outbursts. But as long as her husband was in prison she needed William to tend her son while she worked in her aunt's hat shop. Necessity held this little family in a tight grip. I thought of my own little family in its looser circle, dependent on my unsteady support and my young brother's reluctant help.

The final hours of Gertrude Hover's life were beginning to take on a coloration quite different from what they had seemed when I first read about them. What was it Browning wrote about the reliability of eyewitnesses? 'That all this trouble comes of telling truth, Which truth by when it reaches him, looks false, While falsehood would have done the work of truth.'

The glass through which we view reality is not merely dark, it is distorted by our own faulty understanding. As my own vision cleared, a new version of the woman's death, and her life, was emerging. In it, Bat Jackson's role was no longer significant, his unlovely past, his thorny personality, even his private passions held less interest for me than the past, personality, and passions of his supposed victim.

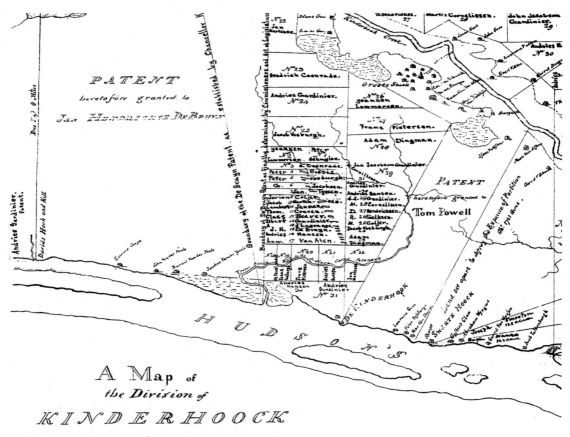

Detail of a 1656 plat map of Columbia County, New York,
reproduced from the History of Old Kinderhook, by Edward Collier, 1914

Chapter Nine

For evil to triumph it is only necessary
that good people be silent.

Edmund Burke, 1792

It was time to comply with my employer's second urging, that I pry some basic information out of Jay Jackson. The prosecution would surely want to present him as a habitual criminal, guilty of offenses not to be spoken in polite society. Our only hope of countering the sort of hints and allusions Gardenier would throw out in the course of the trial was to have the true facts of Jackson's past in hand and to minimize them as best we could. Now that I had met and spoken with Clarice Thompson, I had that bit of his past to use as a prod to get him speaking.

At eight the next morning I was following a guard through the clanking bars and barriers to that cramped room where I had visited Jackson before with indifferent results.

"You're early," he told me when they brought him in. He looked unwell that morning, his dark face pinched, the skin around his eyes purplish, as if he had not slept. But his posture was erect, almost jaunty, as he entered. I wondered if he expected to see Cynthia rather than me in the visitor's seat.

I waited while his shackles were unlocked and he settled himself at the table. "Actually, Mr. Jackson, I am late. In little more than a week's time you will be tried for murder. Yet Mr. Whitbeck and I know almost nothing more about you now than we did the first time we met. You have not offered me a reasonable account of your movements on the day your alleged victim is supposed to have died. I can only hope you have given more information to Mr. Whitbeck. You have not explained how you came to be suspected and then accused of the crime after many months had passed. Nor, indeed, have you revealed the barest facts of your life, which might be used in building a case for your innocence. It is now almost too late for us to reach an understanding of one another. But I would appreciate a modicum of candor on your part, a sense that you at least comprehend how poor your chances are in court. I urge you not to keep silent out of pride or misplaced loyalty, or to protect anyone precious to you."

Jackson waited, looking at me quizzically as if he expected me to continue. Silence hung heavy in the room for a measureless span of time. I found it difficult not to turn away from that urgent stare as I let the seconds tick away.

It was Jackson who finally spoke. "I like some of that," he said softly, "that alleged, that innocence. You being paid to explain away how I was snatched up for taking a knife to an old woman I hardly knew: I like that less. How about you pay me to tell you what I did, what I didn't do, what I know about that day?"

"Anything you tell me, Mr. Jackson, is in the strictest confidence. Nothing we say in court about you will be to your detriment. I cannot, however, control what the district attorney will put in evidence against you, or what he and his witnesses will say about you. Some of your past will undoubtedly be revealed during the trial. You might want to tell Mrs. Jackson yourself rather than have her hear it for the first time in open court from a hostile source."

"You trying to goad me? You swinging left so I will duck into your right?"

"Well, there's that for starters. Cynthia doesn't know about you engaging in allout fights for money, does she?"

He grimaced. Then a smile transformed his features, softening his feral look. "My Cyndy," his voice caressed the name. "She's like ... a shining light, like a morning star. She's so bright, and pure, she doesn't even know how dark it is outside her own brightness...." Then his voice hardened as he shut his feelings away. "And I do my best to keep it that way. If she needs new shoes or a pair of gloves, you think I want her to know I paid for them with my fists? You think I want her to look at me and see a brute, want her shrinkin' away from my hands that can pound a man down to the ground?"

"She will have to know, Bat. She may know already. How often has she bound up your battered hands and stopped your nosebleeds? Maybe she just can't admit that she knows. She loves you, Bat, you and your son Jeremiah. She'll do anything to clear you of this crime. I expect she'll want you to stop breaking the law, though, so Jemmy can grow up proud of his father."

"Bat. You call me Bat. The newspapers print that Battice Jackson's been arrested. Makes me laugh. You don't know who I am, do you? You're a soft man, Mr. Tilden sir." He curled my name slowly off his tongue, so it sounded like tele-dinnah; and sir became a parody of the southern surrah.

"Not a sporting man, are you?"

I shook my head, though I had lost enough on wagers to know what he meant.

"You need some sporting men on your jury, then. Need a few there who know my name. John Powell, he knows me. He knows to keep me on for Saturday. All week I'm in the fields. Saturday I'm in Powell's new barn." His deepset eyes had never left my face. They glittered now with suppressed fury, making him appear suddenly menacing, capable of any violence. I needed to caution him about keeping his anger in check during his trial.

He shook himself, as if aware of my thought, and continued evenly, "I do ~ what he wants done. I make his money for him. Come time to pay up, he hands me that little poke of sweaty bills and says 'Thanks, Bat. You come 'round Monday. I got some baling for you to do.' ~ like I'm just one of his hired hands. Like he doesn't know who Bat Jackson is."

"I take it your name has some notoriety, Mr. Jackson. That can be useful to your defense. Cynthia, Mrs. Jackson, will surely learn about it, if she doesn't know now. And unless you and I come to a further understanding, Cynthia will also have to know about your other family, Clarice Thompson and the children over in Albany."

"You think that's a secret? Why? Clara, she'd say anything to make trouble. She's not real kin to me, Clara T. You barkin' up the wrong tree for that. I don't even know for sure who's daddy to her children. I do help Clara out when I can. She's getting past it, Clara. That cathouse of hers got shut down by the new mayor, the one stopped the horsebarn fights. What could we do but leave town?" He shook his head, as if to rid himself of unpleasant memories. "I come back over home here, and there's Powell building his new barn, right beside the post road, so he can pull in some highclass sporting men on a Saturday. Sometimes they even get the stage to stop there! I go down to Powell's, help harvest his sorghum, and the next thing I know he's asking me will I allout box for his patrons. His patrons~" he spat the word disgustedly. "That's who will be the jury you're so concerned about. They're gonna know where I was when Miss Gertrude was supposed to be sliced up with her own carving knife. You think they got the balls to hang me for killing her, when they know exactly why I couldna done it?"

"You are telling me you have an alibi, a very public alibi for the time of Gertrude Hover's murder?"

"I am telling you where I was on Saturday the fifth of August two years ago around the middle of the day," he said angrily. "Clara T, she say Jackson across the river that day. She soon enough back off from it when she found out how the land lay. Nobody came after me when they was arresting every black man in two counties. Nobody was lookin for me about Gertrude getting killed. Not till that Emma Briggs tried it on for the re-ward.. You find out who put her up to it, you'll know who's bent on putting a noose on me. Emma doesn't like William. Maybe he scares her. Some people, they just have to hate what they fear, just have to feel superior to somebody, even when they got nothing to be superior about and plenty of people puttin' them down. You know that, Mister Lawyer? Yes you do! Emma's got it in for my brother 'cause there's few she can put herself over. She's known William since he was a boy. She knows in her heart he's harmless, just touched. My Daddy says if William lived down in Carolina ~ that's where the Jacksons came from, come up the Underground Road ~ he'd be revered. People would step near just to touch his sleeve when he jerks and shouts and talks in tongues the way he does sometimes." The chair creaked as he pulled back and took two deep breaths. When he spoke again his voice was flat. His eyes had lost their wild, staring intensity, his expression shut down into unreadable calculation.

"Emma wouldn't have made up that tale on her own, you mark me?" he growled. "She didn't even check where William was, or where I really was that day, before she nipped into the police station with her I saw him go over the fence. What kind of nonsense is that? Emma can't see the preacher from the choir loft. She can't find Mo after church till he comes up and takes her hand. She didn't see anybody climb a fence. That was somebody else's idea."

I held up my hand to stop him long enough so my notes could catch up. Witnesses. I needed witnesses to confirm what he was telling me.

Jackson ignored me. "Ask Mo Briggs, why don't you. And while you are at it, ask old Mordecai where he was that Saturday noontime. As if that matters. Saturday noontime Gertrude was long past caring. Ask anyone at the Beth-El. Ask anyone you meet on the road in Kinderhook. Ask anyone! Just don't you bother my Cynthia."

He stopped and bit his lips, sealing his mouth in a thin line. He did not speak again, or move, until I finished writing. Then he reached around to rap on the door. The warder opened it immediately. I wondered briefly how private our conversation, any of our conversations, had been. Jackson had been led away before I thought of all the questions he had not answered in his tirade. As usual, he had foxed me, had told what he wished and withheld what he chose to conceal.

Whitbeck would not be pleased with my report. It added little to what he already had gathered as he formed his idea of the defense he would mount to save our client's hide. He knew very well how difficult it would be for anyone revisiting such a gruesome event. He understood the general desire for the mystery of Gertrude Hover's violent end to be resolved and her memory set at rest. However, hanging the wrong man would not make her neighbors safer in their parlors.

What I needed ~ what Jackson needed ~ was half a dozen respectable white citizens willing to attest to his whereabouts on that fateful Saturday two years gone, if he had indeed been brawling in Powell's barn. If afterward he and his new bride had gone anywhere that day, together or separately, someone must have seen them, must know, must remember. We just needed to tie that elusive memory to a date or circumstance that would put the young bride and groom of early September of 1885 into the context of a famously terrible event.

There was another aspect of Gertrude Hover's death that bothered me. Charles Davis might be able to help clarify that. I readied myself for another trip to Kinderhook. The stage would have to take me. Late January had turned blustery and too cold for me to want to venture that far on horseback.

Davis was standing moodily behind his plate glass window. He might not have moved since the last time I saw him. As I pushed into his shop he unclasped his hands that had been knotted behind his back and reached to take one of mine. He looked pleased to see me, and I realized I liked the man.

"Mr. Tilden, is it? How nice to see you again. Come to dig among the back issues again? I'll have Daly clear a space for you." He turned toward the printshop before I could stop him.

"No, Mr. Davis. It is you I need today. I would like consult your memory, if I may, dig among the back issues of your voluminous historian's mind."

"Ah, flattery. Who can resist it? Well, come into my office then. I don't keep drink here, but there's a fire in the grate."

He cleared a chair of books for me, and poked at the fire, raising a shower of sparks. "I am amazed to see you up here so near your trial date," he remarked as he settled behind his desk. How is your case progressing?"

"Tolerably well," I told him, "A few oddities have cropped up recently that Mr. Whitbeck would very much like to have cleared away before opening arguments."

"Oddities. Is that a legal term?" He smiled at me over his two hands, which were pressed flat together under his chin.

I returned his smile. "It appears that Gertrude Hover, after dedicating her life to good causes and making promises to her tenants concerning the disposal of her property at her death, made no provision for her favorite charities, or for relatives and friends she might have wished to benefit. I find that odd. Is it true that she died intestate, that her estate had to be parceled out eventually by probate court?"

"In effect, that's what happened. Gertrude Hover's estate was distributed among her relatives about a year ago. There had been disputes and at least one appeal by a relative who had expected to be her chief heir. Essentially the matter has been closed for some time."

"You say 'in effect'. Does that mean there is, or was, some question that she might have made a will that was not found at her death?"

"Very astute, Mr. Tilden."

"You may call me Royce."

"And I am Charles," he smiled again briefly. "There are those who assumed that a will did exist at one time. Ferguson, Schuyler here in the village handled her affairs. Ross Ferguson drew up a will for her several years ago, but she never had it witnessed. I have seen an unsigned copy of it. She left bequests to the foundling home over in Chatham and to the Freedmen's Aid Society, an organization that promotes education among the colored. Depending on which person you ask, there are varying accounts of later wills Gertrude had drawn up. No one has located one that was signed and witnessed. Certainly no will was offered for probate."

"But if she did make a later will, a valid will, a lawyer would have drawn it up surely. There would be witnesses, an appointed executor. A will is an official document. It's not just a love letter to the heirs."

"I do not contest your view, Royce. However, the half dozen people who might know that such a document was prepared and signed and witnessed, cannot challenge the decision of probate if the will itself cannot be produced." He finished with a slight nod. His lips snapped shut in a thin line.

"Ah." I leaned forward a bit and lowered my voice. "Could you perhaps put names to any of the half dozen people involved in the preparation of Gertrude Hover's last will and testament?"

There was a long silence. Davis sat unmoving, regarding me narrowly, the tips of his fingers now covering his bloodless lips. I could almost hear the wheels of his mind grate across the grooves of ethics, loyalty, inclination, and begin to click along a track of possibility as a tinge of some emotion ~ pleasure? hope? ~ lit his face.

"Kinderhook has a litigation of lawyer." His voice was hardly more than a whisper. "If Gertrude drew up a will different from the unsigned one in Ferguson, Schuyler's files, I think she would have gone outside the village altogether." He paused for so long I thought he had finished. Finally he looked up, raising a speculative forefinger. "One of the Van Nesses, I believe, clerks in the Kruyder, Wilmot office in Valatie. That's near enough she could have known Jake Wilmot, at least, and at a distance she might have thought insured some discretion. The Van Nesses are colored, but they don't live out by the Bethel. They attend the Dutch Reformed Church, like the white people. If you'll allow me, I'll see the elder Van Nesses at church on Sunday, and ask which nephew is the law clerk. Law clerks sometimes know of things buried in a firm's inactive files that their employers have put completely out of mind."

"You are offering to assist in this matter? I am most grateful, Charles."

"An innocent social exchange is hardly assistance, Royce. I shall write you if I gain any information you might find useful."

"Assistance or not, your willingness to inquire is appreciated. There are circumstances in which conscience does not allow continued silence in the face of ~ what shall I call it? Not evil exactly, but acquiescence to a wrong. Silence in such instances becomes collusion, not only in the acquiescence, but in the wrong itself."

"Oh my. Is that a legal opinion, sir, or just another oddity?"

At that point I thought it wise to change the subject "Do you know the recent tale by that Englishman, Stevenson, Dr. Jekyll and Mr. Hyde? Not a political statement, on the face of it, not a commentary on our public views and acts, as opposed to our private opinions and urges is it? But all the same, it could be construed as a description of how politics is conducted in our fair land. And in politics, Charles, private opinions and urges are a powerful force. A tacit, agreed mindset can drive change, or prevent it, more surely than an election ~ than the law itself."

"My, my, Royce. I do believe you are preaching. I feel I should say amen, amen, as they do over at the Bethel. A lawyer with a political stance? Now there's an oddity."

I laughed, and so did he. What else could we do?

Chapter Ten

Between 1882 and 1890 there were 619 recorded lynchings
(execution by mob action without legal sanction) of Black people
in the United States.

source: The New York Public Library
African American Desk Reference

    I don't remember much about the last week before the Jackson trial, most of which I spent in the office helping prepare for it. Whitbeck and I were in court every day for one reason or another. My employer had filed so many demissits Judge Edwards had a clerk doing nothing but researching citations for denial. I sat or stood beside him, or watched meekly in the judge's chambers as Whitbeck and Aaron Gardenier wrangled over precedents from before I was born. It was a depressing tour of the catacombs of state and county laws designed to impose inequality on the citizens of a nation founded on egalitarian principles. Outraged again and again by the oppressive intent of bland legal language, I shut my mind and simply watched the two genial adversaries bandy words, as they had been doing since just after the Civil War.

    I learned the compass of Gardenier's oratory, and every nuance of expression on Judge Samuel Edwards' seamy face, every impatient gesture. I still have an indelible memory of his convulsive tic that seemed to mock every pleading, the way he grasped the gavel to hammer down his denials, his voice echoing down the empty courtroom with high-handed judgments on low-level exceptions. A lot of what they debated seemed very far removed from the violent death of an old woman two years since in a village that seemed so placid as to make such an act unthinkable. It was easy to understand how local people thought in those days, when Queen Victoria's severe mourning veiled polite society on two continents:

We are too proper here for such an event to have occurred. Therefore this unthinkable impropriety had to have been committed by a stranger. Strangers come among us daily, but their differences are not apparent, except for the dark strangers who have been with us for generations, living in our midst but set apart by color. They, the visibly other, forever strangers ~ they must be the source of this atrocity.

How can we count each other strangers whose long and bitter history is so twined that we must forever be defined by our divided kinship?

Whitbeck had reached far afield to battle the district attorney's determination to end this case before it ever came to trial. The issue of equality before the law was fundamental to his outlook. He was dredging up every abstruse legal obscurity he could find, establishing a space in which to claim mistrial or to appeal in the event of Jackson's conviction. Most of the time I could see where he was aiming. Several times it seemed to me he was just ruffling the judge's feathers out of mischief, trying how far he could push that massive self-importance before Judge Edwards lost any semblance of judicial impartiality and lashed out at his adversary.

They were well matched in such a battle. John Whitbeck could easily swing into his set pieces of oratory on legal malfeasance, prior intent, and the limitations of judicial prerogative, but his passionate flights of rhetoric never revealed the depth of his anger. His blade of a voice was well suited to cutting sarcasm and pointed query, but he controlled its edge. Aaron Gardenier parried with citations of his own, spiced with veiled insults and allusions to pitched battles in their past. He did not bother to conceal the animosity that fueled his irritation. I took notes as fast as I could write, but found when I read them later that they made little sense.

Who was Hollingsworth? Schuyler deposition? Wentworth codicil applicable? Wife-servant- chattel? If I asked Whitbeck about any of it, he put me off with his usual imperious 'You're the highpowered Columbia Law graduate. Look it up.' Once he sent me to the County Clerk's Office to find records of trial dates for cases like Waters vs Lemuel (C), or Johnson vs Johnson (C), none of which I ever found. I thought at the time he made them up to get me out of his hair. He must have thoroughly regretted becoming engaged in this hopeless defense. From his manner I could tell he contemplated the coming trial with distaste.

Each day of that last week we would emerge from a wasted morning in court to find Warren Street a seething boil of idlers. By afternoon, in spite of bitter cold, leaden skies and piles of stained snow that blocked half the roadway, there would be shouts and scuffles in the crowd. It seemed that every rascal in the county had walked or ridden or sailed into Hudson on the chance of some excitement. Columbia County had little to offer in the way of spectacle. Unlike Albany, or like the City, where riots in the seventies had left grisly remains strung up in trees, where smoking ruins and gutted buildings offered grim testimony to the mindless fury of mobs, rural New York didn't countenance unrest. Local poor laws were designed to keep drifters moving. There was no entitlement of jobless families to 'welfare' in those days. Columbia County's almshouses and shelters were temporary, meager, and grim. The poor were not, as Christ suggested, always with us. They were marginalized and hidden, except for that week, when Hudson became their gathering place.

February had arrived with a blast of entrenched northern winter. The forested hills lay lifeless under an icy mantle. The omnipresent stands of evergreen had turned black and brooding. There was no promise of planting or harvesting, no building, no mending: no jobs for transients or seasonal workers in that bleak landscape. The ice-houses were full, the fishing boats beached, the railroad dormant. When the trial of Bat Jackson ended in a hanging, it would be the best entertainment the young year afforded.

The trial was to open on Monday the sixth of February. On the Friday before, as Whitbeck and I shoved our way through knots of gruff, shifty-eyed strangers, bundled to their ears, hugging themselves for warmth or thrusting their hands in their coat pockets, I felt as if a hostile spirit had crept over the town, weighting the air with malice, chilling us more than the icy breath of winter. The slow-moving groups of idlers didn't exactly block us, but impeded our progress, making our walk to Vanderhagen's for our midday meal each day a test of our determined stoicism. We were marked men to them, the defending counsel, enemies of their impatience. Guilt or justice did not count for them. They nursed an unfocused fury they would vent in brutality given a chance. In idlers such as these I perceived a true threat to whatever genuine order our nation might attempt.

Pursuing that train of thought, I arrived inevitably at a place of disdain I had not intended. If one of these men were arrested and came to us for counsel, I would have to reverse myself to help defend his case, or own to bigotry as unreasoning as this mob's. I was chiding myself for an attitude unworthy of my egalitarian upbringing, when Whitbeck suddenly poked me in the arm.

"Look sharp, look sharp," he hissed and raised his stick to break through a knot of men huddled with their backs to us. They were muttering, passing something from hand to hand, a tarry piece of rope, I thought, but could not be sure. John was shoving me ahead of him, making me his buffer as he thrust among them and hustled us the last few yards to the eatery.

"What was that about?" I asked as we wove our way to his usual booth at the rear.

"Didn't you see them?"

"The crowd?" I scoffed, annoyed at being shoved along like a wheelbarrow. "They have been here all week." I hung my greatcoat and muffler on the rack and joined him in the booth as he turned up the lamp. I plucked a napkin from the folded pile and used it to polish my eyeglasses.

"Not them. The others. Across the way, loitering in Pulcher's stable door."

Now I was curious. Whitbeck had seemed oblivious to anything but the bodies interfering with his progress up the street. Apparently he had caught sight of a new element in town for the trial. I shook my head, and then smiled at the waiter who took our order for the day's special without writing it down. It was Friday, so it must be baked shad.

"Someone you know, sir?"

"No, you idiot! They were darkies, half a dozen or more. Unless the livery stable has hired on a crew of roustabouts, they must be Jackson's friends from Guinea Hill. He is rumored to be their donkeyman."

"Donkeyman?" Our waiter returned with a pot of coffee and two of Vanderhagen's thick mugs. I poured us each a steaming drink and added milk and sugar to mine. Whitbeck drew his mug close and wrapped his hands around its heat, letting the steam drift up to warm his face.

"That's what they call the fellow who transports stolen goods to a distant locality where it can be safely offered for sale."

"And Guinea Hill?"

"Your ignorance continues to astound me, Royce. Guinea Hill is an outlaw settlement in the forest above Kinderhook. It's a tract left wild by the Dutch. It was too steep, too many gullies, not worth farming with so much superior cropland to be had. The Indians hunted there. Runaway slaves hid there as well, I suppose. Who lives on Guinea Hill now, or farms some of it, or hunts the deer, I have no idea. Nor has the county sheriff. Since we put such formidable barriers in the way of darkie children getting any education, and do our best to prevent their fathers from entering useful trades, it is not surprising that they occasionally resort to crime to feed and shelter themselves and their families. I am surprised there are not more outlaws among the colored."

"If they farm the land on Guinea Hill, why do you call them outlaws?"

He chuckled, a dry and unmirthful sound. "Because they pay no taxes, Royce. They live outside our proper and customary regulations. So they must be outlaws. If a stage is attacked, or a goods train stopped and ransacked, we assume it was a raid from Guinea Hill. No matter if the robbers were blue-eyed behind their masks. They must be darkies, since all those fellows we just passed in the street are upstanding white citizens. Guinea Hill is our bit of wild country, right here in staid Columbia County in the sovereign state of New York. Everyone knows about it ~ everyone but you, it seems. You should be shaking in your buffalo boots right now, knowing that such menace resides within a couple of hours' ride of your safe, warm bed."

"I am certainly intrigued," I assured him. The waiter brought our soup and a basket of bread, which effectively stopped our conversation. When my spoon scraped the bottom of my soup bowl I took it up again. "So, Guinea Hill is black outlaw territory. I never would have guessed that we harbor a bit of uncharted frontier so near us."

"Not quite," he dipped a crust of bread in the last of his broth, and popped it into his mouth. "For the most part Guinea Hill is as dull as Valatie on a Tuesday morning. There are reputed to be black thieves living up there. There are reputed to be thieves, white thieves, right here in Hudson, if you can credit it. Can you tell them from the upstanding citizens filling their faces at the tables around us? Or are they one and the same? We attorneys only mount a defense for the ones who are arrested."

"Yes, sir. I know that. You have expounded on it before in my presence. But as to the men you saw standing about in Pulcher's doorway ~ they could have been laborers from the ice-house, or roustabouts, as you said, from the river barges. Pulcher's stable may be the only place on Warren Street where negroes can shelter without being told to move on."

"Pulcher is no humanitarian. He employs coloreds to tend his horses, but that's just good sense. They make excellent grooms, as they are the best jockeys."

I found myself annoyed at his offhand generality. "They make excellent pleaders, as well," I told him, "But we do not encounter many black lawyers." Recent memorable public speeches of Frederick Douglass and John Roy Lynch, which Whitbeck and I had attended together, rang in the air between us for a moment.

He stopped chewing, the heel of bread poised in his hand. Had the memory of Samuel Tilden's Free Soil initiative come back to him? Slowly he dipped the bread in his bowl before looking up at me, his face somber. "In another life, Roy, in another time and place, you and I might have been more content."

"But for now, Mr. Whitbeck, do you think there will be brawls on Warren Street over this trial?"

"I think there are people quite near us who would not protest if our client were to be taken forcibly from his cell and done away with."

"Done away with." I repeated. "You mean lynched?"

"Oh no, not lynched. He will meet an unfortunate accident while escaping from custody." Whitbeck savored his crust as he watched me digest this grisly prospect. The waiter took our bowls away.

"Are they so desperate?"

"The they you refer to ~you mean the prosecution?"

"I'm not sure whom I mean, sir. But you seem to imply that the men who have been gathering outside in the street all week have been encouraged to come here in the expectation ~ the hope ~ of violence. These are not friends of friends of Gertrude Hover. I doubt that anyone among the men outside ever encountered the old lady, or even knew her name before they made their way here this week. Are they friends of the prosecution?"

"Unlikely. And now we have an opposing presence, some friends of friends of Bat Jackson ~ ~ if indeed Jackson has any actual connection to Guinea Hill. We could have a nasty situation here, whichever way this trial goes or even before it opens, if Edwards allows it to proceed. I shall have had much labor in vain if our client does not live to be tried."

"Surely the sheriff can keep order over the weekend." I toyed with my knife and fork, unwilling to face Whitbeck's cynical expression. Whatever the outcome, I was passionately committed now to Jackson's defense. For every reason, political, legal, ethical and personal, I wanted Jay Jackson to have his day in court. In his more reserved way, my employer also seemed determind to lay this flimsy charge open to public scrutiny. We wanted to free the bastard, whether or not he deserved it, whether or not he had used his lethal fists to subdue Gertrude Hover and then taken her own carving knife to slit her throat. I believe we were both prepared to battle the insidious complacency that allowed the whole shabby travesty to continue.

"I shall not allow a mere riot to deter me from Jackson's defense."

Absorbed in my own burgeoning obsession, I almost missed the steel that had entered Whitbeck's voice. Always before he had maintained his detachment from the case, as if he had no personal stake in it, as if his battle were the purely legal duel over obsolete laws and the status *sub judicia* of our newly enfranchised colored citizens. Now, at last, he was intensely involved. Had the case acquired enough celebrity that his hallowed principles entered into it? I dismissed this thought as unworthy of our relationship. John Whitbeck encompassed more than the aloof dispassion for which he was publicly known. I thought then ~ and I still believe ~ he was at heart as much a humanist as old Tom Paine.

We were four days from the opening of the trial. My notes and every scrap of testimony from interviews and my bumbling investigations lay in scattered piles on my desk in John Whitbeck's outer office. I had gleaned from them whatever I thought he might need in his opening remarks. We had a list of the probable points District Attorney Gardenier would set forth in his prosecution, the expected testimony of his witnesses, and how John would counter it. The Jackson trial was held more than forty years ago, but I can call up that brief in greater detail than cases I have pleaded or examined with my students much more recently. Bat Jackson's trial came at the beginning of my career. It has colored everything I have done since as an attorney and as a scholar of the law. Small wonder that I now choose to write about it. We Americans have struggled through two wars since then, and are now suffering an economic crisis that has plunged the whole world into desperate want and hunger. But no threat from abroad or rot from within seems to have any effect on our peculiar and central snarl of racial distrust and animosity. If anything, I have seen understanding among us deteriorate during my lifetime. The mindless fury of the Ku Klux Klan, which had nearly disappeared a generation ago, has again become a public menace in this time of massive unemployment and economic disarray. I hold little hope of seeing any meaningful improvement in relations between the races during my lifetime. We are still mired in primitive, simplistic concepts of race that perpetuate the worst aspects of clan mentality and prevent us from recognizing and honoring the wonder that dwells within every individual. I am as guilty as anyone, choosing my friends for the comfort of their similar backgrounds more than the stimulation of their differing outlooks or origins. But I am growing old, and I was never a leader or a prophet. Surely the younger generation can afford to be more adventurous than I.

Ha! How I do enjoy my pulpit though. Students have been known to parody me at length in bars and cafes near the university. Old Professor Tilden, still battling Jim Crow in this modern world, when those nasty laws have been recast in much slicker versions. Samsonite has replaced carpetbags. Jim Crow is now James Jackdaw. You don't see him till he snatches your dinner.

I remember visiting Bat Jackson at the jail that week. The closer we came to his trial, the less he had to say to me. He had never responded to my reasoned and earnest pleas for any but the most superficial explanation of his actions and movements in the period during which Gertrude Hover was attacked and killed. I didn't try to see Cynthia Jackson in those final days before the trial. I was, in fact, startled when she appeared in my office late on Friday afternoon.

"Mrs. Jackson!" I was on my feet, emptying a chair of papers for her, offering to take her cloak. I was dismayingly flustered at her sudden appearance. It had been weeks since we last met. I had managed in the interim to discount her effect on my precarious emotional balance. Her sudden presence was like the touch of a match to tinder on the raw surface of my unhealed emotions, my overstretched apprehensions. Out of a wayward impulse of gallantry to this eerily attractive child I had urged on Whitbeck the defense of her arrogant, possibly murderous husband. Then I had remained to assist in the case rather than pursue my chance at a gilded career in the City and marriage to a...

Now she stood, barely a yard away from me, clutching a dark blue man's ulster about her, regarding me with those enormous eyes, finding my weariness and dread and desolation, gathering my distress to her heart. My face felt hot. I avoided her gaze.

"Please. Cynthia. Sit. What brings you down ~ well, up here on such a raw day?"

She settled herself on the flimsy ladderback chair, removing the coat, spreading the folds of a gray woolen dress carefully about her, as if she were about to be tintyped. One booted foot showed at the banded hem of her skirt. It was darkly wet from walking in the slush of Warren Street. I realized that she was giving me time to regain some calm. My discomfiture must have been painfully apparent to her. I felt as if my whole sordid life, my crushed dreams, my inadequacies, my very soul lay bare under her keen, unbearable scrutiny.

When she spoke, her voice was soft as flutes in a distant room. This must seem too whimsical a notion to be entertained by a crusty old law professor. But I feel compelled to set down, or at least hint at, the extraordinary effect of this woman's presence, which I can still call to mind at will after all these years. Until I knew Cynthia Van Houck Jackson I could never understand how Joan of Arc drew an army to follow her.

"You and Mr. Whitbeck must be very busy just now," she said. "I won't keep you long from your preparations." She indicated the inkpot and sheets of foolscap on my desk with a gloved hand.

"If this is about court costs ~ " I began.

"No. Not at all, sir. We'll manage to pay you somehow. It might take some time." She looked up at me then, her face hollow, her eyes huge, dark pits in the lamplight. "I came to warn you." She spoke just above a whisper, her voice taut. "There is going to be trouble. Jay is in danger. He knows. I just visited with him. And so are you and Mr. Whitbeck, John that is, but you must know that. You can hardly walk down the street without knowing. If there is ... trouble, you and he could be attacked as well. Some of those men outside, they are hoping for trouble. You should tell the sheriff to be ready. If they get started it won't be easy to stop. Some of my people are down there too." She nodded toward the darkness of Warren Street outside the shuttered window. "They won't stand by and let Jay be taken down."

"And you, Cynthia? You aren't safe in the street either. I will certainly warn the sheriff. But for now, you must let me see you to shelter. Did you ride the stage down?"

"I borrowed a trap in the village. It's just over at the livery stable. I'll be fine." She dismissed my concern, but I could tell that her trip down the post road had been full of terror for her, a lone woman on the road in the winter dusk, passing strange, rough men tramping to Hudson to join a riot. Going back to Kinderhook through the dark would be even worse. My decision was made before I considered its ramifications.

"You can't go alone, not with all this ... unrest. I'll ride along with you, for what little protection that might afford."

"Oh, no, Roy! You can't do that," she began, but I was already pulling on my greatcoat and fumbling for my scarf and gloves. I helped her bundle up, doused the lights, locked the office behind me and clattered down the stairs behind her. I remember feeling extremely bold as we hurried over to Pulcher's, for I took her by the elbow and held her firmly at my side, avoiding the piles of shoveled show, aware of her furtive regard as we passed under the mellow glow of the gas lamps. It was not more than a hundred yards or so to the livery stable. The bare little trap she had brought down from Kinderhook stood untended in the yard. My chief usefulness of the evening was to see to its prompt reharnessing while my horse was saddled. I trotted along beside her until we were well on the road north. Then I looped my horse's reins over the tailboard and joined Cynthia in the trap, gratefully pulling the buffalo robe over my knees for the long ride to Kinderhook.

I don't remember that we spoke very much on that ride. She was clearly anxious to be home again, where she had left William to care for little Jemmy. My mind was so crammed with threads of argument from Whitbeck's opening statement for Monday, that sensible conversation was beyond me. Our frosty breaths mingled in the darkness as the horses trotted along, their hoofbeats muffled on the snowy road, the creak and jingle of their harness cutting into the night silence under the cold glitter of winter stars.

Cynthia Jackson must have been exhausted, for she dozed part of the way. I took the reins from her unresisting hands and urged the carthorse to greater speed until the lights of Kinderhook began to show in the distance ahead of us. Cynthia roused then, and we made polite comments about the cold and the beauty of the night, until we reached the straight stretch of road just below the village. She took the reins again and shook them to encourage the horse.

"Seems so deep, the cold just now," she said. I turned to reply, but she was looking straight ahead into the darkness. "Hard to believe there will ever be flowers again. Sometimes the bad comes down like winter, full of bluster and fury, till you think you'll never see the end of it, never see gentleness rise up like the spring." She spoke as if to herself, musingly, her words puffing out into the night as visible breaths. "But you know in your heart some good has to come of all this. You just have to hang on. Do your best, and a bit more." She turned then, and met my eyes. I wondered which of us she was trying to convince. I wondered if this was a plea for the defense of her husband, or a desperate attempt to summon her own courage. Or had she in some arcane manner divined the ruined state of my life just then and offered this frail, illusory hope to carry me through my slough of despond? I withdrew my gloved hands from under the fur and closed them around her fist that held the reins. But I did not trust myself to speak.

We rode that way into the village. Then at last she turned and insisted that I dismount at the staging inn. "Are you sure? It's half a mile to your house. I should see you safe home. It's late. If anything happened to you ~ "

"We are right in the village, Roy. What could happen? You can get a good night's rest here at the inn. But you must promise to ride back to Hudson first thing tomorrow to alert the sheriff. I'm so worried ..."

"Yes. Yes. I'll do it first thing. Be careful now! Goodnight, Cynthia."

I slipped my horse's reins from behind the trap and watched her turn onto Albany Avenue, the lantern swinging from the tailboard. Soon the fading glow of the lantern was all that showed her progress down the dark street. That night's journey had been my chance to learn more of Cynthia Van Houck Jackson, to deepen our acquaintance into a kind of friendship. I had just spent several hours in company with an extraordinary and beautiful woman. Tongue-tied by feelings I could not express or even name, I had done little more than mumble. The only sensible thoughts had come from Cynthia. We had shared the warmth of a moth-eaten fur robe, were consumed by the same anxieties, perhaps even shared a tinge of the primal attraction that draws a man and a woman close in a moment of danger. I had called her by name, tasting Cynthia on my hesitant tongue. She had called me Roy.

That night as I drifted into sleep at the staging inn, I felt the tingle of forbidden lust that pulsed across the racial divide. I would deny, do deny that my attraction to Cynthia Van Houck Jackson, Battice Jackson's wife, arose out of some warped desire for dominance or the lure of miscegenation. I believe, instead, that Charles Davis was correct, that everyone who ever met her fell a bit in love with Cynthia Jackson. She was ~ may still be ~ a woman with remarkable empathy. I will always regret that I never had another opportunity, like that one I failed to seize, to converse alone with her.

Albany Avenue in Kindsrhook Village around 1880 (detail)
used by permission, Columbia County Historical Society, Kinderhook, New York

Chapter Eleven

The peremptory challenge allowed the prosecution ... must be viewed
as an incarnation of the anti-democratic impulse to keep juries all-white.

Douglas L. Colbert,
Race, Law, and American History, Vol. 8

I remember snow that morning, the morning Bat Jackson's trial was to begin. It was very cold, cold enough to make your eyes tear, make every inhalation a sharp, icy stab. A grainy, windless snowfall the night before had feathered Warren Street in a fresh white coating. All the busy, normal sounds of Hudson on a Monday morning were subdued into a soft silence in which the muffled crunch of our footsteps was gradually lost in a buzzing murmur of voices as John Whitbeck and I crossed the square in front of the courthouse. A crowd had already gathered there, milling about, stamping their feet, hoping for seats at the trial or a glimpse of the prisoner as he was brought over from the jail. Inside, a more orderly group of prospective jurors was reporting to the bailiff or seeking to be excused. Many more were in the latter category. As we pushed through their ranks to reach the stairs, Whitbeck scanned the veniremen's faces, assessing for hostility, for the ones he would want excused from the jury panel.

By eight o'clock we were settled with our notes and briefs at the defense table in the empty courtroom. Spectators, a good number of them colored, began to fill the benches. After an hour with no sign yet of the prosecutor, Whitbeck grew impatient, knocking his stick on the floor and muttering that we should have stayed at Vanderhagen's for another pot of coffee. I studied my notes and tried to ignore him. At ten we attempted to leave, since it was evident that Edwards was delaying the opening of the trial to cause us as much discomfort as possible. At least, that was how I saw it. But there was by that time no hope of getting through the jampacked ranks of idlers who had forced their way into the courthouse and filled the halls and lobby with a high pitched roar of excitement. I hoped the marshalls would bring Jackson in from Petition Street and through the alley. I didn't hold much hope for his survival if this crowd sighted him. We returned to our seats and waited another hour before Aaron Gardenier strode in. Then the bailiff called us to our feet as Samuel Edwards settled his massive bulk on the judge's banc and gaveled the room to silence.

The rest of the day was even more tedious, as each of forty-two prospective jurors was queried. We heard opinions, pro and con, on the death penalty. We watched conscientious, and weaseling appeals to be excused. There were few citizens actually eager to serve on this jury. A number wished only to be released to go about their lives. Judge Edwards questioned each one and excused several for cause, two for having possible connection to the case. Lemual Phelps lived in Kinderhook, and Martin Hover of Livingston was related to the victim. The two negroes who came as veniremen, Ezra Johnson and Grandy Van Alstyne, were of course dismissed early on peremptory challenge by the prosecution. We were for excluding from the jury all journeymen and laborers, men who might resent Bat as a competitor for their unskilled jobs. We challenged every name from Canaan, Gallatin, and the villages around Chatham that were all-white. Gardenier excused anyone from wealthy Claverack and the few tradesmen who had the look of sporting men. As Whitbeck explained to me over our hurried lunch, Jackson's near neighbors, residents of Kinderhook, Stuyvesant Falls or Valatie, were most likely to have personal connections to local colored families. Or they might have firsthand reasons to doubt the people's evidence, what Whitbeck would to call flimsy guesses. So Gardenier wanted none of them. We, of course, wanted to eliminate young bucks who saw every colored man as their enemy. Although there were by that time, colored voters on the rolls from which jury panels were selected (we were then seven national elections past emancipation), the two colored veniremen would have been astonished to find themselves impaneled. In my legal career, I never pled before a single colored juror.

By late in the afternoon eleven chairs had been filled in the jury box. Nine of the jurymen were small farmers. No major landowning family (or political dynasty for that matter) was represented. One juror was an innkeeper up in Copake. The eleventh man was a butcher's helper from Taghkanic. Whitbeck had wanted to excuse this last choice, but I pointed out that we were running short of challenges with several places to fill. The butcher in question was young, my own age or even younger, with an appearance of earnest intelligence about him that I thought could be addressed by the arguments Whitbeck hoped to present. He was skeptical, but he let me have my way that once.

At four o'clock Judge Edwards rapped his gavel, raked the recorders with a scathing two-minute condemnation of their 'culpable negligence in allowing names unfit, ineligible, abroad, or deceased' to be included in panels from which his court must draw juries, and recessed the court until the following day.

Tuesday morning began with the situation little improved. Edwards and Gardenier wrangled over arcana of selectmen's filings. Whitbeck was restless in the seat beside me, alternately watching the two confederates slice each other in acid tones that did not carry past the judge's bench, and perusing the hastily compiled additional panel of names. When he stood and strode forward, I was expecting a pro forma objection to the needless delay in jury selection. Instead, he raised his copy of the list so Edwards could see what it was, and read out the dates under its heading. The talesmen's list had not been drawn from a current list of voters but from the tax rolls of 1884. It was, as Whitbeck declared, not a valid pool of peers for a murder trial.

The judge and the D.A. turned to him, openmouthed, their faces pale and then rosy with discomfiture. Defending counsel, whose interest it was to get this trial underway before some nasty incident struck tinder to the ruffians milling outside, had just forced a further delay in jury selection. The panel presented that morning, after last night's raid on county voting lists, had to be disqualified as out of date. I kept myself from shouting my senior down, but only with difficulty.

It was then nearly eleven. We had wasted half of the second day of trial to no purpose whatever.

At that point Samuel Edwards showed his mastery of the process by plucking a veniremen's list from the day before out of his pile of documents, and reading out three names from it ~ seemingly at random.

"Objection to any of these, Mr. Gardenier? Mr. Jacobs? Mr. Whitbeck? Mr. Tilden?" He cast his good eye on us one by one, the tic working so rapidly that his other eye seemed to flutter piratically, daring us to question one of his choices. "We have an Adkins, a Wyck, a Miller." He paused. "Is Newton J. Miller present in the courtroom?"

A small, neatly dressed man of middle years, with a dark, taciturn countenance, rose from among the panelists dismissed earlier, few of whom had actually left. The judge had already vetted him, so he merely inquired as to his current status as a voter. He did not allow any of us attorneys a chance to question or challenge. He just pointed his gavel at the startled man and rumbled, "Are you prepared to serve this court as a juryman for the course of this trial to the best of your ability? So help you God?"

"I am. I will, Your Honor."

It was done. Edwards called a recess for lunch. When we returned, the spectator's benches, and even the aisles, were packed. Crowded at the rear stood a gaggle of news reporters. The editor of the Hudson *Daily Evening Register* was there, of course, and Charles Davis for Kinderhook's *Rough Notes*. The Chatham *Courier* and its rival, the Chatham *Republican* were represented, and two of the Albany papers along with one or two others I didn't recognize.

Soon after Whitbeck and I and Gardenier and his second took our places, there was a pause, a sort of ripple, like a collective intake of breath, while Jackson was led into the courtroom. According to the Hudson *Register* report of that moment, Bat looked "as miserable as it is possible for one of his race to appear." If that was true he must have recovered his poise before I saw him. In my memory his expression, while somber and determined, was one of unruffled assurance..

He was freshly scrubbed and shaven and wore a suit of somber gray with a checked waistcoat. His linen flashed as white as his teeth and his boots were polished till they gleamed, Cynthia's doing I knew. As he passed the defense table he halted, in spite of the urging of his guards, and nodded to me and then to Whitbeck before settling smoothly into the seat beside mine. Aware of the stares from everywhere in that momentarily hushed room, he seemed intensely calm, almost relaxed. The man absorbed public scrutiny as a prism draws light.

You've been here before, Bat. You take this attention as your due.

Then, in a fleeting gesture I nearly missed, his right hand lifted to his left shoulder and tapped twice with a long brown forefinger. I had been careful to face front, ignoring the crowded spectators' benches, so until that moment I had not seen the figure directly behind the defense table. Cynthia Jackson sat very straight and stiff, in dark blue, a shawl around her narrow shoulders, a veiled black bonnet concealing her face. But I knew she was smiling. Bat's gesture had been a message to her, containing volumes of encouragement, gratitude, reassurance.

For a blinding moment I was filled with a black coil of envy at that evidence of their intimacy, their hidden life of mutual references and private signals. I wanted Jackson to be the crude ruffian depicted in caricatures, incapable of such subtleties as could capture and keep the heart of a woman like Cynthia Van Houck. I wanted ~ was that it? ~ that I wanted her myself? Had I become a caricature as well, the white man ravening with dark lust? Was I too a beast, the vile dog in the manger, unable to bear the thought of this bright, courageous, innocent girl yielding him the crown of her beauty and youth, surrendering her heart to his lawless spirit, his dark passion?

My hands clenched at my sides at that sudden glimpse of evil in me, a bitter envy through which all tender emotions once centered in Lillian Roeder had erupted from my despair to attach themselves to Cynthia Jackson as lust. Bat Jackson was my rival for the impossible prize of his wife. Even as I saw my invidious, hopeless desire for what it was, I wanted Jackson out of Cynthia's life. At that moment, seeing the sign pass between them, I wanted him dead.

I literally shook myself free of such an idea, as I felt the knob of Whitbeck's cane pressing against my ribs. The court had fallen silent. After what seemed an eternity the bailiff called 'All rise' and announced the docket. Judge Edwards entered, gaveled us down, settled his bulk above us all and looked queryingly at District Attorney Gardenier, who drew his own estimable and dignified presence around him and stood to address the jury.

The Jackson trial was underway.

Gardenier began with a recital of the circumstances of Gertrude Hover's ghastly death. He reminded his listeners of the terror that crept through the village of Kinderhook when her body was found, days after she died, the buzz of excitemenet throughout the vicinity. He described the devastation of her tidy home, the broken lamp, overturned furniture, spilled contents of her cupboards and drawers, evidence that every room had been ransacked. He dwelt on the horrific trail of blood that, he said, led at last to the finding of her assailant, her ruthless killer, the soulless animal who took the innocent Christian life of a frail old woman for some banknotes and coins, the price of a few drinks (his nod to the prohibitionist faction) and a pair of shoes. (We had been expecting that).

He did not refer to the circumstance that, according to the Hudson Register of September 12, 1885, "only black men have been suspected, detained, or questioned in connection with the murder." He did refer to the location of Gertrude Hover's house "in the midst of Kinderhook's colored settlement, near the colored church and next door to bat Jackson's father's house," though the surveyor's map showed a distance of 175 feet between the two houses. He skipped over the frantic manhunt led by Albany Police Chief WIllard, which led to the apprehension of colored men up and down the Hudson Valley. He ignored the detail that private detectives from Albany and Nassau were hired in a fruitless attempt to identify the elusive murderer who had managed to escape covered in gore and carrying a sack of valuables that were never itemized, let alone recovered.

"I shall show," he told the jury, "that this crime can be inexorably fixed upon the sneering miscreant you see now before you." Jackson, at the moment was neither sneering nor in any way improper. He sat, mild and impassive, a black Buddha. A flicker of amusement told me he had noticed, as I did, that the sneering beast, now pacing before the jury, was actually Aaron Gardenier.

There was a lot more of the same. I have blessedly forgotten most of it over the years. Gardenier's voice was a supple baritone, an orator's voice, and he used it to good effect, had done so recently in his most famous prosecution, the Beckwith trial, which had crowned his career. Oscar Beckwith was convicted, on circumstantial evidence, of hacking apart and hiding the body of one or more annoying neighbors, and perhaps also his wife. He was lodged at that moment in the same jail where Bat Jackson was held. In fact, Beckwith would finally be hanged within a month of the Jackson trial. Gardenier was obviously planning to sail through this prosecution riding on that triumph. Canaan, where Beckwith had lived, was a village like Kinderhook, small, rural, off the main rail line. It is difficult to conceal motives and misdoings in such small, stable communities.

That difficulty made me all the more curious about the near universal, stony silence that had met my efforts to bring to light any aspects of Gertrude Hover's life beyond what was generally known. She was liberal, even radical in her politics. She was stingy and authoritarian, goodhearted, perhaps, but testy and sharp tongued. Had that sharp tongue infuriated somebody? Had she enraged one of her relatives enough to attack her in her own parlor? If was clear to me that her killer was someone she knew well enough to invite him into her house. Did she allow her colored neighbors in? It would have been more customary to keep them standing outside the kitchen door. Would she have let Bat Jackson into her house?

She knew Bat, had probably known him as a defiant, unbiddable child. He'd run off across the river as a youth, perhaps to escape the sort of tonguelashing Gertrude dished out along with her favors. Black boy! You stealin' windfalls outa my orchard again? I told your daddy he could come gather. I didn't say you could, or that crazy brother of yours. You git now, hear? Think you're too big to take the switch to? Big enough to run off from school is big enough to be workin. Don't you turn away when I'm talking to you! I got a dime for any big boy can split a box of kindling for me. You come knock on my back door when you're done, hear?

John Whitbeck knew, as I did, how it would have gone, from similar harangues we had endured as boys. Stealing apples was a sport for boys of all races. Chopping kindling was the chore of choice for us.

Gardenier reached his peroration at last, and called his first witness. There was little sport that afternoon. Whitbeck let pass the account of finding Gertrude Hover's mutilated body that September morning in 1885, how runners went for relatives, for the sheriff's men, for the coroner. I made a note to try to find the washerwoman who was not called as a witness, the one who had actually found Gertrude on the Tuesday after her death. I never found her.

The day's titillation was provided by Dr. Woodworth, who with Dr. Pruyn had done the post mortem examination of Gertrude's body. Woodworth leaned forward in the witness chair and confided to his friend Aaron Gardenier, as if they were chatting over coffee, gory details better left to the imagination, while a courtroom full of people listened with horrified fascination. He recalled how the house stank after being shut up for three days with a slowly decomposing body in it, how a buzzing swarm of flies obscured the body, how blood had spattered and pooled and finally congealed in ghastly patterns on the floors and walls. He told of the eight cuts they found on the victim's face and neck, how she had been beaten, her nose broken and lips smashed against her teeth, 'as if by a fist', how her fingers had been broken defending herself.

Whitbeck did not challenge any of it ~ better not to prolong the ghoulish recital ~ except for the evidence about the knife. He wanted to be sure the jury recalled the knife that had slit her throat, that it was Gertrude Hover's own carving knife, that it had been found near the scene of her murder. Bat Jackson, our defense witnesses would aver, owned a hunting knife. He was a fistfighter, not a slasher, but if he were planning to threaten someone, would he not have taken his own weapon?

Whitbeck did extract one bit of useful information that afternoon. Calvin Ackley, the surveyor, testified that he had drawn a map of the Hover holding. It was placed in evidence to orient the jury to the area of the murder. John asked Ackley when and why he'd made the survey; and he said he'd done it after the victim's death, pursuant to the sale of Gertrude Hover's property.

After him came Charles Sitcer. Charley, whom I had interviewed along with his parents, was cleaned up that day for his court appearance, his hair slicked-back, his voice creaky and his bony shins pale beneath his kneebritches. He told of going to Miss Hover's house for apples on the fateful Saturday. Miss Hover had shaken the plum tree in her back yard so he and his brother Adam could take plums home as well.

Charley's brother Adam, who was eleven at the time of the trial, but not much over eight when the murder happened, seemed overawed by the courtroom and the crowd. Judge Edwards couldn't get him to explain the meaning of an oath or what constituted truth as distinct from fantasy. Edwards leaned over Adam, his tic snapping, his gavel held like a menacing hammer ~ or so it seemed to me. I thought he deliberately cowed the boy into terrified confusion.

The editor of the Hudson *Register* at that time was pals with the John Ruso, the court stenographer. The *Register* account of the trial, day by day, was little more than an excerpt of Ruso's notes, in the scrappy, fragmented style I recall from his actual transcriptions of court testimony. In that day's *Register* however, there is a reportial comment added as column filler:

"A miniature Sabbath school was held in the Court room this morning, His Honor acting as teacher and an eleven-year-old witness as scholar. The boy's parents had obviously failed to inform him where bad boys go and so his evidence was disbarred."

It certainly hurt us to have Adam excluded. He had confided to me in our interview that he thought their little excursion for Hover windfalls might have been in August, before school began. Adam recalled that they had not seen Gertrude until she came to her back door to screech at them for rattling her plum tree. But that was evidence never recorded. Whitbeck did get Charley to admit that they might have gone for apples in an afternoon, rather than at ten or eleven in the morning as he had testified. Their mother had planned to bake a pie, he recalled, but the boys had eaten most of the apples she needed for it. If Gertrude was alive Saturday afternoon (or if the boys saw her on Friday), the people's supposition that she had died some time between eleven and three on Saturday became questionable. Whitbeck couldn't get Charley to admit he could have mistaken the date altogether, that he and Adam had gone into Gertrude's yard a day or two earlier. When John sat down I shook my head, wrote on my pad of foolscap and passed it to him: 'Better to leave them thinking she could still be alive Saturday afternoon.'

I felt he had missed an opening for doubt, but he merely shrugged. Was that the prompting of my inner demon that would compromise our defense at every turn? Would we be complicit in Bat Jackson's conviction, in his death?

Charles Davis of the *Rough Notes* was called next. I was surprised to learn that he had been among those who forced the door and found Gertrude's body. Her brother James, and Albert Van Epps the brother-in-law were there as well, and had searched the house and yard. I wondered if they had gone in as witnesses or heirs. They certainly made a meal of her estate afterwards. Davis had given no indication that he had viewed the murder scene, either in conversation with me or in his newspaper. His testimony was brief, factual, and without bearing on the crime itself, so Whitbeck did not cross-examine him.

As Davis passed the defense counsel table to resume his place among the reporters, without pausing or looking down at me, he muttered, "See me."

He had something! My spirits leapt at the hope that this meant Davis had news of Gertrude's will. If only this could provide a clue to the real killer, could redeem my faltering loyalty to our client, present some crucial element that would allow us to come out of this case without perverting justice to an unworthy end: If only! Failures were built on if onlys. All the same, I made a note to ask my employer where newsmen gathered at the end of the day.

Sylvester Van Valkenburgh, farmer of an acreage over on Eichybush Road, testified to passing along Sunset in his haywagon at about two on the afternoon of the murder, and hearing a voice that he thought came from inside the house. Whitbeck examined him closely on his recall, and concerning the supposed voice. Male or female? Conversational or angry? Definitely from the Hover house? Definitely from inside a dwelling? Valkenburgh was a stolid and unreachable witness. What he remembered he repeated. The rest he didn't know. He assured Whitbeck with great earnestness, however, that he had no idea whose voice it was. Interesting. Was he afraid to identify the owner of that voice? Was he protecting someone?

When Emma Briggs was called, I could sense a stirring among the spectators. From among the attending colored people there came a kind of buzzing murmur, as if a hive had been disturbed. It ceased abruptly at a rap of the gavel. Emma swept proudly up to the witness box. She was a tall, well padded woman with a round face and full lips that smiled easily, a woman of middle years and somewhat imposing bearing. As a fruitseller she was well known locally. Her market cart was familiar to villages for miles around her berry patch. She was a pillar of her church and the colored community. I had been told that her family was recorded (on gravestones mostly) as freedmen in the county since before the Revolution. If Kinderhook could be said to have colored gentry, Emma Van Ost Briggs, like the Van Nesses, was a member of it. That day she wore maroon taffeta with a bustle, and a matching hat which she did not remove even to take the oath. Out of style she may have been, but formidably confident with it. Her oldfashioned dress with its lavish tucks and drapes and ruffles had likely served her for decades of Sundays. It would do for a court appearance. Like her costume, her testimony was lavish and detailed and polished by repeated use. She remembered the day Gertrude Hover died. She was on her way home from selling huckleberries, almost the last of her crop. Her cart was nearly empty, and the day was hot. She was going along Albany Avenue in the village of Kinderhook, going west, at about two o'clock. The sun still high in the sky. As she passed by the orchard behind Miss Hover's, which filled the ground through from the Sunset road to Albany Avenue she related, "I saw Bat Jackson in Miss Hover's back yard. He was low and bent down. I was eating the remains of my huckleberries. I watched him, and the last I saw of him he was in Miss Hover's back door. He was in his shirt sleeves."

John Whitbeck approached Emma with a certain amount of respectful caution, wary of that massive and unassailable dignity. She sat in the witness box with her skirt spread around her, plump hands folded across her girth, displaying rings on two fingers. She looked ready to stand up and sing, or to spend the afternoon adding to her reminiscences about a crime in the making. She must have recounted this tale to every customer who'd listen for the past two years. She was as notorious in the colored community as Bat Jackson, and now was consciously proud to be instrumental in his downfall.

His first question was put softly, gently. "You kept it quiet, didn't you, Emma, this story, this notion that you saw Jackson at the Hover place that day?"

She looked at him as if he were a bug she was about to swat. Her smile was in her rich, deep voice when she answered. "No, sir. I didn't hide it. I told Mo what I saw, him and some others, too. Mo, that's my husband, Mordecai Briggs."

"Did you tell Mo and the others that it was Bat Jackson you saw? Or did you say it was William Jackson? Or maybe you pointed the finger at William Henderson, or Chester Graham, or that drifter they arrested on suspicion of Gertrude's murder back in the fall of eighty-six?"

"I may have spec-u-lated, Mr. Whit-a-beck-ah, sir." She rolled the name around her mouth like a bite of candied apple. "I did point to Bat Jackson. That's why they took him up. That's why he's here today standin' trial."

That showed a certain amount of guile ~ or excellent coaching by Gardenier. She had been ready for the question, and managed to deflect it. No need to confront her with that yet. Perhaps she could be rattled by another tack. "You and Mordecai, Mo Briggs, you farm that piece over toward Stuyvesant Landing, is that correct?"

"Mo owns that land. He doesn't work much of it any more. Mo's got the rheumatism pretty bad now."

"Mo, he's some years older than you, I guess." Whitbeck smiled down at her. "You're a young lookin' woman, Missus Emma."

She gave a quiet chuckle. Not immune to flattery then. The encounter had turned to pleasantries. Emma's hands relaxed, settling placidly into her ample lap. "Well, I thank you kindly. Yes he is, Mo, some older than I am."

"And Mo ~ he's not your first husband either, is he, Emma?"

She looked up resentfully, seeing his blandishment for a ploy. "What you askin', bringin' up my past? You after botherin' *me*? Ain't you got enough business checkin' up on Bat over there? You want their names, those three I used be married to? Least I was only married to one of them at a time. Not like some." She sniffed angrily, thrusting her chin in Bat's direction.

"So you are an arbiter of morals in your community then, Missus Emma. I am glad to know it. Does that mean you disapprove of the Jacksons?"

"I don't disapprove of Bat Jackson. He sings in my choir, or he did, him and Cynthia both." Then, aware she had given away a redeeming quality of the man she was condemning, Emma backtracked. "Even a sinner can sing," she snapped. "But Bat Jackson, he's a... He gives colored folk a bad reputation. I don't have anything to do with Bat."

"Except for accusing him of murder. And his brother too. You accused William of being the one you saw climbing over Gertrude Hover's fence that Saturday. He was the first one you named. How come you let William off the hook?"

"William, he was somewhere else that day. It couldn't have been him I saw."

"So you couldn't get William Jackson in trouble, and went after Bat. Do you have a quarrel with the Jacksons, Emma?"

"I don't mind the Jacksons. They been livin here a while. Their grandparents came up from Carolina." She spoke with the casual disdain of county people for those who'd only been around a generation or two. Whitbeck nodded as if agreeing, sharing the superiority of old county natives to upstart newcomers. Emma seemed to soften at that. She tipped her head, unable to resist a bit of gossip. "They got some poor blood those Jacksons. Old John, well ~" she pressed her lips together and rolled her eyes. "He's got a past that one. There's Jacksons over in Guinea HIll get into all kinds of evil. And Bat, he's been idle and into mischief since he was a sprout. William's a loony. He cuts through my berry patch on his way to the railroad, trompin' and breakin the canes. No sense atall in him. Once William loosed my pig into the lettuce, just outa wildness. William's in trouble then. I sent for the constable. But Bat comes along with his sweet-talk and his soft ways, a pat on your arm; and just charmed his way out of it. He charmed me that once, and did his best to charm me again, makin' soft eyes and givin' that sly grin, askin' to sing in my choir."

She stopped suddenly, perhaps hearing the penscratch of the court stenographer, knowing there were people in this room who could attest to the opposite, that she, Emma, had set her cap for Bat Jackson, prinked and paraded to make him notice her, cooed and coaxed him into the choir from the first time he came to church. That was not something she wanted in this trial record. Beside me Bat did not move, but I heard the snort of stifled laughter he could not suppress.

"So you and the defendant have a history of animosity, Emma. Is that correct?"

She gave a reluctant nod. But even for the judge she refused to speak again. Whitbeck asked that the record be made to show that Emma Briggs had admitted to a strong dislike for the defendant.

"And you went to the police with this story of yours when you learned about the reward being offered for information about Gertrude Hover's murder, is that correct?"

At that, Emma's hand came up and covered her angry mouth. Her silence was allowing the suspicion to grow that what she had so carefully presented to incriminate Jackson was the creation of a scorned woman's rage. If Whitbeck chose, we could present witnesses to Emma's attempt to win Bat Jackson for her fifth husband, a flashy young buck to replace the aging and ailing Mo, whose nice piece of swaleland she might want to keep, for it grew the best berries in the county. Emma had not given much away. He had ruffled her, but he wanted to be sure her testimony could be turned against her when the defense had its turn to call witnesses. He had a next question ready, but his witness had gone mute.

I cleared my throat, warning him not to push it. It was the first time I had interfered with any cross. He yielded graciously and let her go.

Emma held her head high as she left the witness box, but her expression as she passed me was wary, almost confused. I risked a look at the jury box and thought I detected a flash or two of complicity and at least one slight nod. The formidable black matron, with her formidably damning evidence, had revealed a possibly unsavory past, and cast some doubt on her motive for coming forward. I inferred that I had been right to signal Whitbeck. A hint of doubt was all we could hope for just then.

This hope was proved vain when the next witness testified. His name was John Ritz. His house fronted on Albany Avenue, behind Gertrude's place. Neither Whitbeck nor I had been able to interview him. In answer to Gardenier's smooth-voiced queries, he said that he had been sitting on his back stoop in the late afternoon of the fatal day and had seen Jackson come along the fence line and climb into an apple tree and then over the fence into Miss Hover's yard. Jackson was coatless, he said.

This was new corroboration for Emma's tale, and from a witness we didn't know. Whitbeck approached him cautiously as he would a strange dog. He queried him about distances and light in a late summer afternoon, and about the difficulty of distinguishing dark faces from afar, before challenging the core of his story. "So you saw someone you thought was Mr. Jackson climb Miss Hover's fence. How well do you know him?"

"Well enough to know he's the one killed her," he muttered. John didn't ask him to repeat it.

"So you know where the Jacksons live?"

"Sure I do. They've always lived back there."

"Can you tell why Bat Jackson, whose house is off Sunset, would be coming along Albany to get home? It's clear out of his way; and he had to climb the fence in his good clothes, in his best boots and white shirt. Why would he do that?"

"Objection! Objection, your Honor. The witness is being asked to speculate on a murderer's behavior."

"The district attorney, your Honor, is speculating on the guilt of a man presumed innocent." Whitbeck retorted, hoping against hope that some juryman would catch the unlikeliness of Ritz's testimony. What criminal, planning robbery and assault, would take the long way round, the more public route, to reach his intended victim?

When pressed, Ritz stuck to his testimony, even decorated it, claiming he saw Bat come over the fence from Gertrude Hover's yard, and then go back into it.

"But Bat Jackson's own yard is in that direction, is it not?" Whitbeck asked, and had him refer to Calvin Ackley's map, which was proving very handy in cross-examinations.

Ritz grew a bit surly at that, so John let him go. He had confused his own account. That was enough, I hoped, for the moment.

Adam Finkle was the next witness. Him I did meet and question on one of my visits to Kinderhook. Adam was a farmhand, an occasional harvester and dairyman at Powell's. He did know Bat Jackson. I had no reason to doubt that he'd seen Bat, as he swore, on Albany Avenue, over by the cemetery late on that Saturday afternoon. When Whitbeck rose for cross, the witness seemed as much at ease as when I'd spoken to him back in the fall in his own parlor.

"You and Battice Jackson work together sometimes, it that correct, Mr. Finkle?"

"Sure we do. Over at Powell's."

"So you know Bat pretty well, then."

"I known him since he come back over the river, maybe two, three years now."

"So you've seen Bat many times, in all kinds of weather, all sorts of situations."

"I seen him plenty of times. We worked some long days together. I got no quarrel with Bat."

"So you would know if on that afternoon two years ago Bat Jackson was in a rage, or shaking with fear, or trying to slip away without being seen. Is that correct, Mr. Finkle?"

"He was just walkin' along the street by the cemetery, heading away from town. He gave a shout, and I answered. That was all."

"So he seemed pretty much as usual."

"I'd say so. I think he might of put up a hand to say hi. I was across the road from him and going the other way. He seemed just ~"

Gardenier's objection cut across whatever Adam Finkle would have added. Of course it would have been speculation. But then, so far, speculation was the prosecution's entire case. Bat Jackson walking on the main street of his own village on a Saturday afternoon ~ or even climbing a fence to get home or whatever he might have been doing that day ~ that was hardly evidence he'd committed a crime. It was an indication he was going about his ordinary life. Could the jury see that? I hoped so. I hoped my employer's gentle approach in questioning prosecution witnesses did not indicate that he was slacking off. I hoped he was conscientiously pursuing his defense, but I was not sure that was true. In his place I would have stung harder.

Samuel Garrison was the next witness. Whitbeck looked at me when he was called, but I only shook my head. Clearly John had not read all my reports. I ignored his raised eyebrow. Garrison was a large, gangly fellow, uncomfortable in the suit he wore for court. His testimony, elicited in a heavily jocular manner by Gardenier's second, put Battice Jackson again on the Albany Road at around four o'clock on the day of the murder. Garrison and Norton Pockman, who testified next, were at Pockman's house at the edge of the village when Battice came to the back door selling woodchuck oil. The rendered fat of woodchucks was commonly used at that time to clean guns. It may have been used for machinery too, but I knew of its use by hunters. It was an odor that didn't disturb the deer.

According to Garrison, and to Norton Pockman, 'young Battice' sold two bottles of woodchuck oil to Pockman that day for twenty cents apiece (which seemed to me a modest price for the effort involved in snaring and killing and cooking the animals down to produce it). Neither hunter could settle on a time for this encounter, putting it perhaps between three and four that afternoon. Both of them remembered that Jackson had made change of a dollar for the forty cents, taking a roll of bills from his pocket "about the size of his finger," Garrison said. Pockman averred that Battice brought out some change as well and remarked, "You needn't think I'm broke." Whitbeck tried to get from them what remarks of theirs had preceded that curious statement by the defendant, but couldn't get either of them to admit to baiting their colored neighbor for earning small change peddling what his father or his brother had toiled to produce. It was not easy to imagine Bat himself trapping woodchucks or standing over a cauldron of their simmering remains to gather the oil. He seemed far too mercurial to undertake anything requiring that kind of patience.

Whitbeck pressed Garrison on the little roll of bills he had seen Bat take from his pocket. He allowed that a roll the size of a finger could have been no more than a few dollar bills. The prosecutor hadn't asked about the state of Bat's clothing, so John asked Pockman what the defendant had been wearing that day. He was at first vague: 'Just regular clothes, like now, I guess.' But when pushed little, 'Had his good suit on, did he? Had a stiff collar and tie? Wore a vest that day?' he gave up that it was hot, that Jackson didn't have a jacket, that his white shirt, so far as Pockman remembered, had no grass stains or apple bark or dirt of any kind. 'No bloodstains?' 'Not that I saw.' It was a small victory, which Gardenier immediately plowed under by getting Pockman to point out that Jackson had his shirtsleeves rolled up, so any stain would have been hidden.

By then it was after four, later than the hour in the day of Gertrude Hover's murder which the district attorney had chosen, somewhat arbitrarily, as the time of her death. Judge Edwards consulted his big pocket watch and declared us adjourned until the next morning.

As we were preparing to leave, I asked Whitbeck where I could find reporters after a day in court. He jinked his eyebrows at me and frowned severely. "The Iron Horse," he grunted. "Is it wise for you to be seen drinking with the press, Royce? Think how your landlady will react when she hears of it."

"And who at the Iron Horse would inform Mrs. Bullock?" I asked him sharply, as I struggled into my coat. He shook his head and waved me off, intent on starting for home. He had had little enough time in recent weeks to spend with his wife and children.

A hidden sun had hardly warmed the day, and now the light was leeching away from a pewter sky. Most of the courthouse crowd had dispersed. It was not a time of day, nor a weather for loitering. I walked briskly up Warren Street. The roadway had been swept clear, so I used that rather than the footpath, and saved my boots. A closed carriage, a shay with a blanketed bay in the shafts, waited at the edge of the common. Before I could turn off Warren Street toward the Iron Horse, the carriage door opened a crack and Davis called to me.

"Over here!"

He didn't raise his voice or use my name, but the sound carried easily across to me on the icy air of the quiet evening. I climbed into the carriage and settled myself on the seat beside him before I spoke. "I feel like a conspirator, Mr. Davis ~ Charles. Have you something sinister to tell me, or is your historian's sense of import working overtime?"

"Neither, Royce. I merely wish to protect my source, as you must protect me. You cannot offer any provenance for what I am about to tell you. Nor can it appear in print." His hand lay heavily on my coat sleeve. In front of the mica shield the horse stirred in the traces and snorted impatiently.

"I'd offer you a drink at the tavern, if I thought you would accept it," I ventured. His furtive manner made me uncomfortable. I had not asked him to steal state secrets after all. A will should be on public record somewhere at least.

"We in Definitely Dry Kinderhook are pledged not to enter establishments that serve liquor," he recited primly. In the darkness I could not tell if he was serious or joking.

"I assume you have discovered the reason Gertrude Hover died intestate."

"I have ascertained, from an unimpeachable, undisclosable source that in the summer of 1885 Gertrude Hover had a will drafted, that it was signed and witnessed, and at the time of her death was believed to be in her possession. It does not seem to exist now."

"No copy remains in the hands of her attorney?"

"No signed copy. A draft only. It has no legality. It is a dead issue, Royce, as dead at its testator."

"Can you tell me who would have been the executor of this will?"

"Jake was. Jacob Wilmot. That's the only reason there's an unsigned version in his files."

"Are you willing to divulge the terms of this no longer existent will?"

"That's the reason I didn't write you, as I hoped to do. Under no circumstances could I commit to paper what I am about to tell you."

I laughed briefly, making the shay bounce on its springs. "Spare me the melodrama, Charles. The document has surely been destroyed. Anything you tell me about it cannot affect the outcome of Jackson's trial. It's highly unlikely Bat even knew such a will existed. And I can't imagine how destroying it would benefit him."

"No. That's quite true," he said, unmoved at my amusement. "Your defendant wouldn't destroy the will. He was actually a beneficiary, in a way."

"Would you explain that?"

"Gertrude Hover, according to Jacob Wilmot's copy of her will, prepared in July of 1885, left her house to her brothers. She left a piece of property to the foundling home in Chatham. She left some shares of railroad stock to her suffragist friends up in Seneca Falls. She left her orchard, including that nice plot with the houses on it that she rented to her colored neighbors, as well as a parcel over behind the AME church, to the congregation of Bethel AME."

I gasped, and tried to halt him at that point, but he went on, reciting from memory a series of smaller bequests to relatives and friends, all that Wilmot's clerk divulged about a document that was now without validity. I wondered briefly if Davis had actually seen a copy of the will, or merely had it described, or even read to him.

"Did Jacob Wilmot add any notes of his own to the file?" I asked without much hope.

"Only that he was present at Miss Hover's home on August twenty-third of that year when she signed the will drawn by Jake Wilmot in the presence of two witnesses."

"Did his note include the witnesses' names?" If I knew who they were, I could find them, have them afford corroboration that the will had existed, that it had been signed only two weeks before her death.

"Yes, Royce, Jake noted the names of two witnesses: Harlan W. Miller, farm equipment salesman now deceased. I wrote his obituary. And the Rev. Thomas C. Oliver, who was then, I am told, pastor at the Bethel."

"Wasn't that a conflict of interest? If Oliver was the preacher, wouldn't he be considered a beneficiary?"

"Apparently not, since he was only there on a temporary posting. Something of a star among the AME brethren is this Thomas Oliver. Not long before that he had graduated from Princeton Seminary, and after less than a year at the Bethel in Kinderhook he went onward and upward to a more prestigious posting. My own pastor over at Kinderhook Dutch Reformed tells me that Oliver made quite an impression in his short time in the village. During his stay there that little church was packed on a Sunday morning. He was a rarity, an educated black clergyman, very respectable, had white folks inviting him to tea. Had Gertrude Hover summoning him down the road to witness her will." He sighed. "So there it is, Royce, there was a will. It disappeared. Jake Wilmot won't admit it ever existed; and of the two witnesses one's long gone and the other dead. If Gertrude was murdered because of her will, you'll never be able to establish it. You certainly can't use what I've just told you. I can't see how it would help your client if you tried. How would Bat Jackson know about the will? Can Bat even read? He might just steal papers and destroy them out of spite or whatever."

"You have a very skewed idea of my client's character, Charles."

"Got past you with his famous charm, has he?"

"Maybe he has. Maybe his charm will be his defense. If Battice Jackson came to her door, Gertrude wouldn't have let him in. She would never let her colored neighbors in, except to scrub the floors. But she would have listened to his blather. She was not above being flattered by a snarky young fellow like Bat. If he needed money, he could have charmed her out of her spare change. He'd promise to paint her window frames or trim her roses back or whatever. With that glib tongue of his, he wouldn't need to kill her, now would he?"

Davis was still pondering that salvo as I climbed down from his carriage onto the snowy road. I watched the shay roll away into the darkness before making my way home to Mrs. Bullock's bland and ample supper.

I was in possession of an important piece of information. It should illumine the mystery behind Gertrude Hover's murder. But as I trudged through the icy night to Union Street, I couldn't for the life of me make sense of it, or see how I could use it in Jay Jackson's defense.

Chapter Twelve

No man is safe, his property and all that he holds dear are in the hands of the mob, which may come upon him at any moment, at midnight or mid-day, and deprive him of his all.

Frederick Douglass, speaking before Congress in 1867

I didn't rush to give John Whitbeck my interesting discovery that night. For one thing, it was cold and getting colder. I relished the hot meal that waited for me at home, and spent the evening reviewing testimony of defense witnesses for the next day. Also, I wanted to let the significance of Gertrude's will work itself out in my mind before I told Whitbeck about it.

He seemed quite unsurprised the next morning when I did report what Davis had given me. Of course, we were in Vanderhagen's for our brief morning conference before the day's session. In that public venue he would mute any reaction, in case some friend of Gardenier might be watching. But it seemed to me he had expected the existence of a will.

"Royce, we can't take that anywhere useful. If it's true, and if it would help our client, there is still no way to connect Gertrude Hover's death to a will she took pains to conceal from her family. There were a dozen people in and out of that house after she died. Any of her relatives could have taken or destroyed it, or bundled it up with the rest of her papers and burnt it in ignorance after her death. They were pretty quick to clear out the house. They wanted to sell it. Your trail ends with that dispersal."

"But who ~"

"Doesn't matter now who could have destroyed it, or why. Leave it, Roy. You need to think how we can counter what the prosecution is piling up against young Jackson. You also need to caution our man, Royce. He's like a hellhound on a leash, the way he looks at witnesses. Get him to calm down. He sits there like a volcano. He has to keep that ferociousness out of his face, out of his eyes." He scowled at me and rapped his cane on the floor. I had been unaware that he noted, let alone gauged Jackson's expressions in court. The jury must notice also. It was a lesson I meant to take to heart.

When we had resumed our places in the courtroom and Jackson was beside me, I scrawled a note on my pad and slid it in front of him. He looked down briefly, and then nodded. Afterward he turned around, quite deliberately, but Cynthia was not in her usual spot behind us. She was to testify that day. My note of warning accomplished two things. It had the effect of toning down whatever reactions Bat might reveal from then on, and it showed him to be literate. He had read my sloppy cursive without difficulty or hesitation. That nugget, like the matter of the will, I tucked away, hoping it might be useful at some point.

Then the session began and Gardenier called his first witness, Martin P. Hawver. Hawver might be a distant relative of the Hover family, and of Gertrude, but nothing he said gave that away. There were Haavers too, and Havers, who lived locally. The Dutch were not sticklers about spelling in the early days. Martin Hawver sold fish at the Saturday market in Kinderhook. According to his testimony, Bat Jackson had come to his stall on the day of Gertrude Hover's death and paid him thirty-five cents owed from a purchase Jackson's wife had made the week before. This transaction occurred near the time Hawver closed up his stand, between five and six in the evening in the village square. Hawver remembered that he had made change of a two-dollar bill for the defendant. Hawver described Jackson as 'dressed in his Sunday clothes' and that he saw blood on Jackson's shirtsleeve, which the prisoner said was due to a wrestling match.

Even when pressed hard about why and how he had retained these odd and clashing bits, (how could he see a bloodstain if the man wore a suitcoat?) Hawver stuck to his amazingly detailed story. I was sure he'd been coached, but Whitbeck couldn't shake him.

Then Gardenier called a colored witness, Leonard Collins, to corroborate the incident with Hawver. Hawver had not recollected Jackson being in company when he paid the bill, so Whitbeck in cross took the opportunity to explore with Collins what else he remembered of that day in 1885. He readily stated that Bat had told him about fighting in Powell's barn, being hit on the nose and getting a nosebleed. I thought that Bat's tender nose had sufficient exposure by then. So did Whitbeck, apparently. He asked what else Collins and Jackson had done that Saturday. They had gone to Chatham together, Collins confided, guileless as a puppy. There they had 'stopped around at some places and had some drinks.'

"You mean hard liquor drinks?"

"Well, Battice, he's a beer man. I drank some mash."

Gardenier also called the liveryman at the Kinderhook stable, James Michael, who told of renting a horse to Jackson and Collins to go to Chatham. Collins had paid him the two dollar rental, he said. He also remembered noticing blood on Jackson's shirt front.

In cross examination, Whitbeck asked him if both men had come into the stable, or just Collins. He recollected that Jackson had gone back to saddle the horse while Collins settled the fee. "So in the darkness of your stable, with his back to you, saddling a horse, you noticed the state of Mr. Jackson's shirt?"

"I'm saying what I saw," he snarled, but I thought we had him there, and John him go.

Nelson Eaton, who worked at Powell's, testified that they had been threshing at Powell's the week before the Hover murder, up until the Thursday, when Jackson left. When Whitbeck queried him, he admitted readily that Jackson had cut his fingers on the Thursday while binding sheaves behind the beater. We got this in the record, though it didn't seem to have any significance for the case. Bat would not have worn his white shirt working Powell's fields. He wore a white shirt on Saturday because he was a boxer, not a fieldhand. But we couldn't risk using that.

Another Powell hand, Lorenzo Decker, was called to testify that he had wrestled with Battice Jackson on that Thursday, but didn't see his nose bleed. William Haggerty was called to back up Decker's statement. Gardenier had not added one fact to his case all morning. He was just boring us to death with extraneous bits of flimsy. I was tensed to stand and raise the issue of relevance, but Whitbeck tapped my hand insistently with the head of his cane, so I sank back in my chair, as the D.A. called Gertrude Hover's nephew George.

George van Epps: If I were listing suspects for this crime, he'd be near the top. A short, pudgy young fellow with a high, whiny voice and slicked-down sandy hair that rose in a cowlick on one side, van Epps clerked in the drygoods store in the village. He testified that his aunt, Gertrude Hover, had come into the store on the Thursday before she died and purchased a length of ruching to trim curtains. She had given him a five dollar bill, which he had changed, returning her a two dollar bill and some coins. This attempt by the state to lay a trail of house money was so flimsy, neither Whitbeck nor I challenged him.

John Trimper, proprietor of a shoestore in Kinderhook, came to court to tell about Battice and Cynthia Jackson buying Cynthia a pair of shoes on the Tuesday that Gertrude Hover's body was found. Trimper remembered seeing what he described as fresh blood on one of the bills Jackson had given him in payment. (Fresh? Any blood from Gertrude was then three days dry.) He also noted that Cynthia had returned the shoes that same day because they didn't fit. Trimper didn't explain this, but everyone in court knew that colored folk weren't allowed to try on their purchases before they paid for them, in case white folks wouldn't want to buy what their colored neighbors had touched. That always seemed a bit silly to me. White folks didn't hesitate to wear what colored washerwomen scrubbed and ironed for them. They ate the good food prepared by colored cooks, gave their newborn babies into the care of colored nursemaids. But we didn't touch that bit of local custom. Gardenier's presentation was putting the jury to sleep without any help from us.

We recessed for lunch, after which Gertrude Hover's brother, James Hover of Stockport, was called. He was a dapper old man, surely older than the victim had been, with palsied hands and a voice like dry leaves. He seemed ill at ease, or maybe just unused to being in front of so many people. He told the court of calling on his sister on Sunday the sixth of September in '85. He found the house locked up and supposed that she was out for the day. Whitbeck asked him if his sister customarily locked her house when she went away, if he had ever found her house locked before that day. He thought about it so long I wondered if he had fallen asleep. Finally, he shook his head, unable to recall a locked door. His sister was mostly home when he called, he said. "How about when Miss Hover made her long summer visits to Seneca Falls? Did she lock up then?"

He looked puzzled at the question. "Well, she'd have the cleaning woman come and water her fern and the aspadistra and so forth if she was going to be gone for a week or more."

"Did the cleaning woman have a key?"

"Guess not. She said the house was locked, or on the latch anyway, that Tuesday we found my sister's body. She called Trimper and the constable. They went inside."

"So, you would say that finding Miss Hover's house shut up tight was unusual?"

"I don't believe my sister even owned a key. The door latched on the outside, as I recall."

So why, if it latched on the outside, did the washerwoman not enter on the Tuesday?

Except for that small curiosity, I felt the afternoon was going pretty well, until Gardenier called his next witness. The name Otis Birge was new to me, a last minute inclusion in the prosecution list. Birge stomped to the box in workboots, looking as if he'd just come from the icehouse or the tannery. He identified himself as a 'linesman from Chatham' and said he'd been in the county jail there in Hudson until a few days previously, awaiting trial for assault. That explained the scruffy, slightly unsavory appearance. I glanced over at Bat to see if he knew what Birge might have to say. Bat was following my advice to the letter. He sat as if drowsing in his chair, his hands curled loosely on his thighs. His half closed eyes gleamed alertly, however.

Birge said he'd been Bat Jackson's cellmate during his stay in prison and that Jackson and he had talked some. "Once," he recalled, "I suggested we were both in a bad fix. Jackson said 'I know we are.' So I asked him how he planned to get out. He said, 'If they squeeze me too tight they'll know more about it.' Then I got free on bail, and Jackson asked me to go and see his father. He said to tell the old man unless he got him out he would give the whole business away."

Whatever the business was, I objected, and got it expunged as hearsay. But it was still in the minds of the jurors. Whitbeck was on his feet before Gardenier sat down, and went after Birge hammer and tongs. He admitted that his case had been summarily dismissed by Judge Edwards in special session just the night before. He described the assault charge as arising from a misunderstanding. He denied that his remarkable evasion of a prison sentence had anything to do with his appearance at this trial. John made him repeat his story. It was an odd tale and, if it was true, perhaps indicative of some shady doings in the Jackson family. But there was nothing in it that pointed to Jackson's guilt, or even any connection to the death of Gertrude Hover. I hoped his retelling made that clear.

When Whitbeck sat down I slid a note over to me. "Calm down," it read, giving him the advice I had earlier given Jackson.

Gardenier then recalled the nephew George, who described the fastening on his aunt's door as an old fashioned latch. The kitchen door, he stated, was hooked on the inside, the front door latched on the outside. Ah! Another bit of village custom. The (colored) washerwoman would have gone to the back door, of course, and found it latched from the inside. So she wouldn't have gone in. The front door was for whites. That little matter settled, the prosecution rested its case.

I presented our formal application for dismissal of the indictment against Jackson on grounds of insufficient evidence. Judge Edwards denied the motion. John Whitbeck took exception, to get it on record for an appeal. ~ all pro forma.

Gardenier had ended his prosecution evidence a bit after three; and our little dance of documents had taken another quarter hour. It seemed to me far too late in the day for Whitbeck's opening speech to the jury. For one thing, it would have taken us past the judge's usual four o'clock adjournment. My employer looked over at me; and I laid my hand on the carefully prepared draft of his opening statement and pushed it across the table away from him. He looked at me and sighed. Then he stood, and without preliminary called the first defense witness.

Albert Van Epps of Kinderhook, George's father, said that when he entered his sister-in-law's house on Tuesday the eighth of September in 1885, he found the window of her bedroom unfastened. This indication of a quite different sort of entry than what the prosecution posited for Bat, couldn't be let stand. On cross, Gardenier pulled out of Van Epps that John Jackson, Bat's father, was the one told him that morning Gertrude Hover had not been seen for days. Van Epps also mentioned, in response to Gardenier's questioning, that Gertrude's reading lamp was on the mantelpiece, filled and trimmed (a sign she had died during the day) and potatoes, some peeled, were on her kitchen table.

The day. Why would she be killed during the day? Why this insistence that the crime had been committed on a sunny afternoon, when any movement around the house was likely to have been observed by someone? And the argument, the angry words, the beating, the stabbing, the overturned furniture and smashed crockery ~ how could all that have gone on in the middle of a Saturday afternoon and no one be aware of it? Neither the police investigation nor our repeated efforts had turned up a single witness who'd observed anyone actually enter Gertrude's house that afternoon. No one had been found who recalled hearing noises of the struggle that must have occurred. How easy the achievement of secret evil appears to be, while ordinary life proceeds heedlessly all around it. Discounting the testimony of Emma and Ritz, neither of whom had much probity to my mind, there was nothing to connect Bat to Gertrude's house on the day she died.

Whitbeck next called Asa Gillet. Asa, Gertrude's disgruntled tenant farmer, had been interviewed by the prosecution, and by several reporters, after he and I had had our conversation. He was reluctant to testify, but very willing to air his grievance against his dead landlady. "She swore to me she had it wrote down I was to have my land while I lived," he asserted. "Not just my house, the field too. I worked all those years, puttin' up with her whining. 'Help me with this, Asa. Mend this. Build that.' Then she dies, and I'm out on the road. Nothing. Not One Thing is left to me."

It was his anger, I think, made him forgetful of what he had said to various people. Two years had passed while he nursed his grudge against a dead woman, fearing any day to be evicted, though it hadn't happened yet so far as I knew. I believe he no longer knew the truth of what he had witnessed at the time of Gertrude Hover's death. Whitbeck got from him the crucial testimony that he had gone to see Miss Hover at around seven on that Saturday morning, but found her door latched, her curtains closed, and the blinds down. Except for that ~ which should have been a deciding factor in establishing Bat's innocence ~ Gillet let us down terribly. At first somewhat vague, and then truculent, and finally as shtum as he had been when I first met him, he denied what he had earlier told Coronor Waldron and Justice Cook. Even when his depositions were brought out, he disowned them and denied his own signature on the documents. It was the comic relief of the day, and a disaster for us. But there was nothing to do but soldier on.

James Ritz's wife testified to seeing a light in Gertrude Hover's south window on the Friday night before she died. Nellie McPherson, housekeeper to the Wendovers of Kinderhook in 1885, testified that on the Tuesday the murder was discovered she had paid Cynthia Jackson for helping her make and hang a new set of drapes in the Wendovers' parlor. She had given Cynthia two one dollar bills and fifty cents in change.

Whitbeck then called Cynthia Jackson to complete that account. She wore dark green wool that day, and a tiny black hat with green velvet leaves around the brim. It may have been only in my imagination that under the fall of her skirt her slender form trembled as she came forward. But it was not imagination that she turned to smile timidly at her husband as she passed the defense table. When she took the oath in that flute-like voice and sat primly in the witness box, I could almost hear the collective sigh in the courtroom, as every man drank in her ethereal beauty, mated it to the prisoner's intensity, and indulged in envious speculation. As if to fend off the stares, Cynthia kept her worn shawl clutched tight around her as she gave her full name and avowed she was the wife of the prisoner, that their home was in Valatie, that in 1885 they lived with Jay's father in Kinderhook.

"Bat also has a brother who lives at home, does he not?" John asked.

"Bat has three brothers grown," This was news! "Bat's the best of them. He wouldn't harm anybody a lick." Except in a boxing match.

Whitbeck steered her away from that gray area and aked her about the vexed question of cash the Jacksons had in September of 1885. Cynthia told the court that she had used the money from Nellie McPherson to buy shoes at Trimper's. Before she and Bat had entered the store, she said, she had given him the bills so he could pay for the shoes. John ended her witness with this touching gesture to maintain her husband's dignity.

Gardenier, of course, tried hard to spoil it, venturing very near racial slurs when he asked about her earnings and Bat's earnings and her need for shoes that Tuesday two years before, shoes that she then returned to Trimper as ill fitting. Gardenier got from her that she already owned two pair of shoes when she bought the new ones at Trimper's. But Cynthia glided over his insinuations, explaining in her silvery voice that "boots for trudging and slippers for dancing, everybody needs. My aunty found me a pair in Stuyvesant Falls that very day. They fit me just fine, which Mr. Trimper's shoes did not."

Gardenier then challenged her on discrepancies between what she had deponed at the time of Bat's indictment and what she now claimed. Cynthia sat up straighter and looked directly at the district attorney for the first time, anger simmering in her eyes.

"I was sworn before Justice Cook," she snapped, "as I am sworn before Judge Edwards now. I know, and you know, I never said that if Bat didn't give up the alcohol I would put a halter around his neck. As for money, I didn't see Bat have any money that Saturday. Bat was away all Sunday with three others, over toward Chatham Center."

At that, Gardenier let her go, tacitly acknowledging he had been unable to shake her.

Whitbeck gave the court a moment to hold Cynthia's image in their minds before calling James Ritz's son Henry, another Powell employee, who swore to witnessing Bat's tussle with Lon Decker in Powell's barn on the Thursday before the murder. He described how during the fight Battice had suffered a nosebleed that caused blood to spatter down his clothing and onto his shirtsleeve. Henry was immovable under cross examination. I was proud of him. Even Whitbeck seemed to relax a bit at that point. Jackson leaned forward attentively with his hands laced together on the table, the picture of confident innocence. Their hopefulness made me very uneasy.

Whitbeck then called Jane Ann Williams, a very proper member of Kinderhook's colored community, and likewise a pillar of the Bethel Church. Jane Ann looked to be in her middle years, and was dressed in russet velvet, surely her finest, with an elaborate tower of a hat I would wager was a present from Cynthia's Aunt Margaret. She sat stiffly, as if posing for a tintype, and spoke deliberately, allowing the stenographer ample time to copy down her assertion that Emma Briggs was known by her friends and neighbors to be near-sighted. Emma, Jane Ann said, had to bring things close to her face to see them. "She holds her hymnal right up to her face," Jane Ann demonstrated with her own hands an inch from her nose. "And even then she can't see the words too good. She's got the tunes down just fine, though."

"So, if she were over on Albany Avenue and saw someone climbing a fence at Miss Hover's, could she have possibly known who it was?"

Gardenier was on his feet shouting, "Objection! Objection! Calls for speculation on the part of ..."

But we had gotten it said that Emma Briggs didn't know who it was climbing the fence that day, or even if she had actually seen anyone there. When Gardenier challenged Jane Ann in his cross, she dug in her heels, showing a spunky spirit under that shell of propriety. Emma, she confided, was "something vain about her looks, so she won't wear spectacles." In private, she might be more open, Jane Ann explained. "She'll likely tell the truth about it if she's just talkin' to you. She'll be quicker to lie if she has to swear and have it written down and all."

There were chuckles at that. I had to smile at the D.A. putting himself in a hole. He dismissed Jane Ann before she could do him even more damage.

After that Whitbeck called Clarence Moore, a colored neighbor who had been at Pockman's when Bat sold the woodchuck oil. Clarence said Bat had come there earlier than Garrison and Pockman remembered, more like two or three in the afternoon. That had to be, because Moore had gone up to Castleton after that, and been back home for his supper. He couldn't have done that if the incident happened late in the afternoon. .

Phineas Sitcer was called next, a shy clubfooted lad with a wide grin and an open manner. He said he was working with Battice Jackson on Powell's farm on the Saturday of the murder. They had worked from sunup till about one in the afternoon, and then went up to the village to get their pay from Mr. Powell. They waited for him until some time between two and three. Phineas remembered seeing Jackson receive two bills and some silver, after which they went to Mrs. Reed's saloon for a glass of beer each. Sitcer swore that was about three in the afternoon. Cross-examined, Phineas allowed he wasn't sure how much money Battice Jackson got from Powell, nor could he be absolutely firm about the time of day, since he didn't own a watch.

I thought we had come out of that day in fair shape, and was much relieved when Judge Edwards brought the gavel down, ending the session. Before they led him away, Whitbeck warned Bat he would be testifying the next morning. He smiled, the lazy grin I had learned to expect, and cocked his head.

"I'll be here. Wouldn't miss it," he said jauntily as they led him out.

Whitbeck and I made our way to the cloakroom and bundled up for the walk back to his office. We were both tired. I would have liked his opinion of the day's proceedings, but knew how stiff he could be with self-criticism, how pessimistic, so I saved my breath, as we used to say, to cool my porridge. I hung my greatcoat on the hook behind the office door, and was shoving my gloves into the pockets when I noticed there was already something in one of them.

With a mild frisson, I drew out a sheet of white paper, stiffer than foolscap and heavily inked in black with a drawing and a bold notice, rather like the Wanted posters tacked up in postoffices. It was the sort of handbill passed out in the downtown streets of Albany, and occasionally in the streets of Hudson down near the river. It advertised a boxing match.

I may have gasped. I certainly grinned. Someone wanted to be sure we were aware of Bat's second occupation. Since boxing was illegal in Columbia County, as in many parts of the state at that time, bouts could not be advertised in the newspapers, or posted on palings. Handbills, like the one I was holding, were the chief mode of publicizing such events. I scanned the drawing of a fighter that filled a good part of the sheet. He loomed out of the page, a fearsome figure, bare to the waist, black and dangerous, fists raised and powerful shoulders hunched, ready to strike or dodge. In large print the date September Fifth was advertised for a boxing match. No year, of course, but three names of the all-out bare-fist wrestlers were listed. Top billing went to "Thresher" Williams. Second was "Badass" Jackson. The venue for this sporting date on a Saturday of that recent year was "Powell's Barn on the Post Road up from Hudson."

In my mind, the testimony of Powell's hired hands re-echoed. Unlike other witnesses, who had referred to the accused as Jay Jackson, or Bat, they had called him 'Battice.' Or that was what I thought they said. At the time it had not registered with me. Now I saw they had been signalling the fact well known to every boxing enthusiast, every gambler, in the county. Bat Jackson, 'Badass' Jackson, had indeed been fighting in Powell's barn on the Saturday of Gertrude Hover's murder. Win or lose, he had been bloodied. And he had waited while Powell settled bets and counted the take before receiving whatever fee he'd been promised. Phineas Sitcer had come as close as he dared to telling it in court. It would be a serious offense for Jackson to be caught fighting for pay, promoting gambling. That was why Gardenier had excluded every confessed bettor from the jury. That was the hole in Jackson's alibi for the day, the reason he went to Chatham to celebrate. He'd won his fight. The sheet I held was proof of his innocence.

I looked again at the handbill, wondering who had stuffed it into the pocket of my greatcoat, and then wondering how we could best use it, wondering if a five year jail sentence was really worse than standing trial for murder.

"What's that you are reading?" John Whitbeck demanded from the doorway of his office.

"If I am not mistaken, sir, our client's acquittal," I told him.

Warren Street, Hudson, New York, 1870
used by permission of the Hudson Opera House Archive

Chapter Thirteen

In many states federal officials ... realized that eliminating discriminatory testimony did not mean an accused Black could receive a fair trial, "owing principally to the prejudice of white jurors."

Douglas L. Colbert,
Race, Law, and American History, Vol. 8

Warren Street on Thursday morning was nearly impassable. John Whitbeck was completely impassable. Having pointed out to me at length and without demur that since the defendant was concealing his actions on the day of the crime, and since the prosecution had spent two years gathering evidence of Jackson's motive for murder and robbery, it was hardly reasonable to expect to change the public (or jury's) mind in one day. He then lapsed into stony silence while we finished our coffee and bundled up for the icy trek to the courthouse.

Our client, Jay Jackson, Badass Jackson, had been less ineluctable the night before when I showed him the handbill and pressed him on what seemed to me an unassailable alibi. He had first laughed harshly. "Badass ~ That's how Powell calls out my name before the fight, when he's takin' bets. I got a name so bad it can't be printed in the newspapers. Don't you think that's funny? After the fight, I wait and wait while Powell settles up and counts his money. Then he'll come to me with a little wad of singles, sayin' that's my share. My share! He puts away ~ I don't know ~ fifty or more. I get five, six sometimes, and it's my hands raw, my nose bleedin'."

I did not move a muscle for fear he would stop as suddenly as he had begun. This was more forthcoming than Jackson had been in four months of interviews across the same pitted table on which the evidence now lay, the crudely drawn effigy of him with his nickname boldly printed, advertising a match on the same day as Gertrude Hover's murder. Incredibly, he preferred the threat of hanging for a crime he said he didn't commit to the certainty of serving time in prison for breaking one of New York's gambling laws, the 'blue' laws designed to appease the WCTU.

"You want me to say I was there fightin' that day? When Cyndy had me promise on the Bible I wouldn't do that no more? My Cynthia, she just doesn't understand how hard it is, sweatin' all week for a dollar or two, comin' home broke-back weary every night, when I can scrap for an hour one day for three times that. All she sees is boxing is against the law, could send me to jail if I'm caught. How I'm gonna take care of her and Jemmy when I'm in prison for boxing, for making money on the gambling? I didn't get caught at it over in Albany. I never been caught, not really. So I won't own to it in court. You can't make me do that. You just have to show I'm not the one killed Miss Hover. That's what we hired you for. Nobody asked you to go pokin' around raisin' trouble for me. Little Phineas, and Leonard, and Ritz and them, when they testified in court they kept saying 'Badass' this, 'Badass' that, and you never noticed did you? You thought they was callin' me 'Bat - tice' like in the prissy newspapers. I have to laugh sometimes, how dense people can be."

"Perhaps I do seem dense to you, Mr. Jackson. But Mr. Whitbeck and I are trying to prevent you from being convicted of murder. Your stubbornness could get you hanged, Jay. You are going to testify tomorrow to what you did that day in September two years ago. I have done my best to produce men who were with you for nearly all that afternoon, but if you won't affirm that the reason you were at Powell's was for an exhibition of boxing, and not to thresh hay or collect your week's wages, and that you won your fight and spent the rest of the day celebrating your victory, then I can't promise the jury will accept your version of events."

"Well then, I guess I will have do it myself, convince them how it was. She was most likely already dead, Gertrude, when I left home that morning. You know that, Mister lawyer. And you know I had nothing to do with stealin' her can of coins or smashin' up her house, or cuttin' her so she bled to death. You know that. They all know that." He shook his head, as if to dismiss the amazing ability of white folk to ignore simple truth. Then he rose to his feet in an eely, balanced motion that made me aware of his agile strength. I would have liked to see Bat Jackson wrestle, but I never had the opportunity.

He stood over me, shaping a smile below cold eyes. "If there's nothing else you want to tell me, I got supper waitin'," a politely ironic dismissal, but clear all the same. Not for the first time he had addressed me as a hireling. I reminded myself that in spite of his race, he was, indeed, in charge here. For that space of time he was the master, and knew it, and at some basic human level enjoyed the reversal of social roles. He might save this case for Whitbeck the next morning, or he might get himself executed. Either way, Bat Jackson was the one in charge of doing it.

So, in the morning, Thursday morning, the eleventh of February in 1888, John Whitbeck and I forced our way down Warren Street, threading the line of buggies and wagons, one or two sleighs, and an overflow of blanketed saddle horses which could not be accommodated at Pulcher's Livery. We pushed slowly through the jostling throng waiting in the courthouse square to get in to see Jackson himself testify on what was expected to be the last day of his trial.

No one was calling it the Hover murder trial. Gertrude Hover's terrified struggle and bloody death had been forgotten during two years of endless, inconclusive investigation and abortive arrests without a conviction. A curious official blindness had excluded from consideration the logical suspects for her murder, those close to her whom her missing final will excluded from inheriting. To me it seemed more expediency than logic to concentrate suspicion on local colored workmen. What Whitbeck thought seemed less clear to me. In our discussions he always stressed the primacy of principle over social climate or public opinion. At that moment, with racial hostility mounting toward violence in the county seat, it was clear that official strategy, as well as my employer's confidence in the aloof scales of justice, had miscalculated. The Bat Jackson trial had become a test of white attitudes toward a people less than a generation up from slavery and only grudgingly integrated into New York State citizenship. The possiblity that discriminaton's barriers might be permeable caused uneasiness not only in the ranks of the privileged, but among the poor who vied most fiercely for meager gains. In that contested area lay the threat of violence.

There were few women among the spectators that day. I recollect seeing more men of the rough sort, who had mostly stayed outside the courthouse earlier in the week. On many faces there was a grim purposefulness not noticeable earlier. Passing one knot of scowling blackamoors, I wondered if this was a delegation of Bat's friends from Guinea Hill. In my timidness I imagined weapons concealed under the heavy boatmen's jackets, what are now called peacoats, that were much in evidence. A ferocious intent had burgeoned overnight, either to implement or usurp the public will. No matter what was decided inside the courthouse, this was a surly crowd, ready to break heads. Hostile gangs had assembled, tribes on the brink of battle. Or so it seemed to me as we struggled through their ranks. My apprehension was causing me to be melodramatic. Hudson was hardly a typical venue for a race riot or a lynching. There were, indeed, 137 lynchings in the United States that year, 1888, but none of them happened in New York State. John Whitbeck would attribute that to our advanced state of civilization. I took a far less optimistic view. We just had too little hot weather for evil to boil up. Our vigilantes were few for they had to be winter-hardy.

"Our client will never live to mount the gallows," I murmured, as we settled ourselves at the defense table.

Whitbeck did not reply until the quiet courtroom began to fill with people. Then he took pity on me, or perhaps simply couldn't resist showing off his insider's view. Breaking his adamantine aloofness he leaned so close to my ear his breath warmed my temple and confided "I must agree with you. They don't want to risk an appeal. Gardenier has wasted the last two years rehashing Oscar Beckwith's conviction. He has no intention of allowing that to happen with this case. They'll convict Jackson tomorrow, and after dark he'll be out the back door and his head bashed in. There is no way, no way at all for me to win this, Royce. Not now, and not later on appeal or technicality. They want it over and forgotten. Getting rid of a troublesome Black is a bonus, but the important thing is to have the Hover case closed. We won't have another Fall River here. It wouldn't suit the perceived character of Columbia County."

"Why not, sir?" I leaned away from him, feeling uncustomarily bold. "The perceived character of Columbia County includes Henrik Hudson's unruly crew, the Dutch who conned the Mohicans out of some prime real estate, and a certain notorious prank involving a hapless schoolmaster and a pumpkin. Then you have the birthplace of one of our less than glorious presidents, one who allowed the development of oppressive policies we are still trying to overcome." My voice had risen, as the level of conversation rose around us. Whitbeck responded just as sharply.

"That's your skewed perception, Royce. This is an idyllic area, a great valley, spread like the land of Canaan between the Catskills and the Berkshires, flanked by the royal Hudson River and watered by a dozen sweet streams like Kinderhook Creek and the Skatter Kill. We pride ourselves on the honesty and sobriety of our laborers, the prosperity of our landholders. the soundness of our banks. Don't for a moment think to make a career here on scandal or miscarriage of justice."

Was he in earnest or merely having his little jest with me? I did not know John Whitbeck well enough to read his moods or detect irony in his tone.

"I wouldn't dream of attempting such a thing, sir," I said coldly. Let him make of that what he would. We turned away from one another and lapsed again into silence until Jackson was led in, trailing a sudden hush in his wake that precluded further conversation.

I had not turned round to see if Cynthia Jackson was present this morning. But before Bat took his seat he turned to face the spectators and smiled and bowed, so I knew she must be in her usual place behind us. Probably his father and William were there as well. They would be among the few not crowded to discomfort that day, for people were crammed into the benches like church on Easter morning.

Whitbeck had no compunction about heightening their suspense. Instead of calling the defendant right off, he first called a jailmate of Bat's, one John Cesar, a colored transient of indeterminate years and irregular occupation. Cesar readily described his own brief detention in the Hudson lockup, where he'd been privy to conversations in the cell adjoining his, talk that went on between Bat Jackson and Otis Birge. Bat Jackson, Cesar said, chided Birge for accusing him of statements about 'squeezing,' and sending Birge to threaten Bat's father. Cesar remembered Bat insisting he had only asked Birge to have his brother visit the jail, knowing, as Birge did not, that Bat's father was unable to come. Cesar attested, that Bat had accused Birge of making up a tale 'out of air and evil'. Whitbeck had Cesar explain that Birge was back in jail because his bail had been rescinded. He wanted the impression affirmed that Birge was an unreliable witness. After a few derisive questions Jacobs, Gardenier's second, let Cesar go.

The Hudson *Register* for that day remarked on the defendant's poise. "Jackson is certainly gifted with steady nerves. Not a tremor of a muscle has been detected at any time during his trial." When I looked at Jackson that moment, he had the deceptive stillness about him of a panther stretched on a tree limb, seeming to doze, but ready to attack. Then Whitbeck raised an eyebrow in query. Bat nodded. Whitbeck rose and called him to testify.

The Chatham *Republican* for the following Tuesday reported that Bat "kissed the book with a smile" before taking the oath. I don't remember any such theatric. What I do recall is his presence afterward, when he turned and slowly surveyed the courtroom, nodding to Judge Edwards and then to the jury, the prosecutor, and finally the spectators.

Standing there, he seemed to expand in size, to fill the room with latent energy. He was not smiling. On the contrary, his face was a warrior's face, implacably fierce, with menace incised in deep grooves around his mouth and in hollows under his cheekbones. I would never have the courage to enter a wrestling ground and face an opponent looking as Jackson did then.

John Whitbeck stood easily, not using his full height, seeming almost to defer to Jackson, giving him a moment to settle in the chair before prompting him to state his full name, "Jacob Battice Jackson," and occupation, "farm laborer," for the record.

Jackson was so completely braced for combat that his voice seemed squeezed out of him. Judge Edwards leaned forward to catch his replies as Whitbeck led him through his actions on the supposed day of Gertrude Hover's death. The jury seemed hardly to breathe. Silence spread through the courtroom so that any sound, a shifting foot, a muffled cough, burst like a gunshot. Bat sat at ease, the only relaxed person there, as he ruefully admitted his unfortunate proneness to nosebleeds. He told of wrestling with Lon Decker that week in September of 1885, "just a scuffle for fun." Afterward, he had gone to the baling machine to extract a last bundle of straw and caught a straw up his nose that made it bleed. "I wiped my nose on my shirtsleeve. My dear wife doesn't like me to do that. So I'm sorry about it, but I don't believe there was any dripping down my front. That would have been too much of a mess. I would have had to take my shirt off right there." He was alluding to the boxing match, of course, for which both fighters would have stripped to the waist.

The whole of Saturday, from helping load the threshing machine in the morning, to the afternoon spent with his friends and the night of drinking, he recalled wearing his shirt. "I had a bath and put on clean for Sunday," he finished. Whitbeck led him through the wait until John Powell finally paid him at the market, "at about three in the afternoon. He gave me a two-dollar bill, a one-dollar bill, and the rest in silver." Jay did not indicate that the later trip to Chatham was unusual, a night to celebrate the besting of Williams, Bat's accession to top billing on the fight circuit.

His next testimony covered the rest of that afternoon, the supposed period of Gertrude Hover's death, so Whitbeck had Bat tell in his own words how "Phineas got paid then too, and I took him to Mrs. Reed's for a glass of beer. Then I went home for a bite and picked up two bottles of woodchuck oil for Pockman."

Jackson stood and walked over to the surveyor's map to point out his route past the Hover house and over an unmarked footpath out of the village to Pockman's house. He remembered Garrison and Pockman riding him about "niggers needin' woodpiles and woodchucks' to feed themselves," which got him riled enough to show them the money in his pocket. Afterward he had caught a ride back to Asa Gillet's place and crossed Gillet's patch and over the fence to his father's woodshed and into his house to "clean up a bit and put on some cuffs to go down into the village."

Bat's account of the evening was essentially the same as what Collins and Martin Hawver had given earlier. He could not recall exactly how much money changed hands that day at the fish stall, at Herrick's Saloon, at Ball's for a new shirt. He gave Collins a dollar for horse hire to Chatham. "I recall we drank and I got full. We got back to Kinderhook at about two on Sunday morning. I still had fifty cents in my pocket." Bat said that Mrs. Powell had paid him a dollar and a quarter on the Thursday before that fateful Saturday, "for work I did for Johnny Powell." That came dangerously close to admitting John Powell had paid him on Saturday not for farm work but for fighting at wagers, the very felony Bat wanted kept out of it.

At the end, Bat sat forward in the witness chair, the very embodiment of outraged innocence, and denied with intense and reasonable earnestness that he had any knowledge of Gertrude Hover's murder. He assured us all that he had not been near her house on the last two days of her life, nor had he confided in Otis Birge while he was held in prison awaiting his trial. He added that he had no idea who might have done the "terrible deed that put an end to a fine lady who was my neighbor all my life."

All of which made me wonder if someone present in that courtroom might need assurance of Bat's ignorance of events in the Hover house on those crucial days. His 'saw nothing, heard nothing, know nothing' declared a total lack of knowledge about the identity of her killer. Although he spoke with the confidence that had made all of his testimony so enthralling, those last sentences had the effect of pleading (or so it seemed to me). Did Bat actually know, or suspect, who the killer was? I wasn't given time to ruminate, as Aaron Gardenier leapt to counter everything Bat had said that morning.

He turned first to the supposed day of Gertrude's murder. "You claim, Mr. Jackson, that you were at Powell's on that Saturday. Is that true?"

"Yes sir."

"And changed to your Sunday best at your father's house?"

"My clothes were all there," Bat told him earnestly. "My father's house was searched at the time of Miss Hover's murder. I know they found all my clothes. They didn't find no bloody ones."

"Who was living there at that time?"

"My father and my wife Cynthia. We were new married then."

"No brothers, Mr. Jackson? Don't you have a brother?"

Gardenier had asked that question expecting one answer. He received quite a different one.

"I have five brothers, three of them are grown. John is about my build and height. The others are shorter ~"

The D.A. broke in harshly to put a stop to this revelation, and took Bat again through the period of the murder. "I went to Powell's Tuesday morning. I worked until Friday night. I was there Saturday morning about seven o'clock and stayed until the machine was moved (the massive steam powered thresher that moved from farm to farm). I got $3.75 from Powell..."

But I wasn't listening. Great chunks of understanding were tumbling into place in my mind. What I had thought to be an error in the report of John Jackson's arrest in 1885 in Albany, Clarice Thompson's sly hints and evasions, that jailhouse reference to 'squeezing' now had an object. Bat Jackson had an older brother John, the John Jackson, perhaps, who lived over in Guinea Hill, who had fathered Clarice Thompson's children, who might be much more of an outlaw than his brother Jacob now on trial, who might be involved in Gertrude Hover's violent demise ~ John Jackson had just been described by his brother Jacob as 'the same height and build as me.'

Gardenier, recovered from the shock of the accused offering a totally unexpected response, took on his best insinuating sneer, scoffing at Bat's pretended innocence, prodding him to admit a criminal past that had begun, according to the D.A., when he was hardly out of nappies. Bat acceded to boyhood pranks and thievery. He admitted that as a little lad he once stole a five dollar bill from Gertrude Hover's bureau drawer. At Gardenier's insistence he described the downstairs rooms as he remembered them.

"There is a trapdoor leading to the cellar," he recalled, but he insisted that "I haven't been in Miss Hover's house in a long time." He added, "I was only home that Saturday about fifteen minutes. I saw Pitts picking potatoes as I went through Pockman's lot. When I went past the Hover house I didn't notice the house. It was about four o'clock when I got to Pockman's and a little after five when I got to the village."

Gardenier worried away at every aspect of Bat's story, but I could see his questions had become a bit warier after that one surprise. He got Bat to agree that he had told Birge to ask his brother to visit him in jail, and to admit that he had received Three Dollars and Seventy-Five Cents from John Powell (an amount already established in our own examination, so why was Gardenier making it a capital offense?). After conceding this known fact, Bat smoothly added, "I had no money until I got that money." I could tell from his frown that Gardenier hadn't thought of that fact emerging.

Gardenier then tried to show Bat had lied to Collins about the blood on his sleeve. But Bat said that he didn't want Collins to doubt his ability as a 'tumbler.' It was not an elegant duel. The D.A. growled and spat like a mongrel dog worrying a wolf. He was coming close to accusing Bat of the skills used to beat Gertrude senseless, that he was an experienced prizefighter.

Judge Edwards interrupted at that point to ask precisely what Bat had said to his friend. about the blood on his sleeve. Jackson looked up at the judge in amazement, as if a portrait had spoken.

"Ah, another party heard from," he said, straightfaced. "Well, sir, I did tell Mr. Collins that I was in a tussle. I just didn't say it was that very morning. That morning I was at Powell's about seven o'clock and stayed until the machine was moved."

That morning? Ah. The boxing match was advertised for ten in the morning. Bat had just slipped into the court record a reference to what he had been doing that morning, not sweating at a threshing machine, but battling in front of ranks of witnesses. If Bat went down, he intended to take John Powell with him. I felt my heart quicken at that, for the prosecution had now come close to danger for themselves. It was not in the their interest to have it publicly known that forty or fifty upstanding local residents, including John Powell, a major property holder and political contributor, knew exactly where Bat Jackson had been that day, since they had likely been there as well, breaking the law as surely as Jackson and Williams and Powell had. Judge Edwards had poked a fox den and found it harbored instead a mountain lion. Gardenier literally backed off three paces before continuing. His rich, orator's voice was lower by half an octave when he asked about amounts Jackson spent at Mrs. Reed's, and whether he gave Hawver a dollar bill to pay for fish, or what he had in his pocket when he came home in the small hours of Sunday morning. Trying to identify Bat's expenditures as bought with Gertrude Hover's house money was like sorting well water with a dipper.

I continued to be amazed at our client's resolute and icy reserve. Questioned about the utmost trivia of his actions on a day more than two years earlier, he never threw up his hands in exasperation or pleaded loss of memory. He denied that he had told Justice Cook a different version of the transaction for fish, or that he had told George Harder the sum of money Powell had paid him that day was not three dollars but less: "a dollar in paper and a quarter in silver I got from Johnny Powell on Saturday."

At the reference to Harder, I was struggling to my feet before Whitbeck objected, "How dare you, sir! How dare you bring in extraneous hearsay to impugn this witness! You have made what case you could. Do not attempt to obfuscate ..."

The judge brought his gavel down with the force of an axe. But Whitbeck had gotten his view into the open. He was coming close to accusing the prosecution of deliberately clouding facts to make their case. Unfortunately the prosecution had also gotten into the record Bat's conflicting statements about the day of the crime.

Jackson, however, went on with his reply, as if ithe dustup among othe lawyers was of no concern to him. "I know George Harder," he confided. "He's not too reliable about sums of money." Laughter erupted at that. George Harder was reputed to run a dicing den.

Gardenier continued to worry at Jackson's movements on the day of Gertrude Hover's murder, each question an accusation, trying to rattle Bat's impenetrable calm. "Tell me, Bat," he urged at last, "how often did you hire a horse on a Saturday afternoon and ride over to Chatham to get drunk?"

I stood to object. Jay Jackson's leisure pursuits were not at issue in the case. And Bat had reddened at the insinuation. A broken promise to his wife seemed to fluster him more than being accused of murder. Gardenier pleaded that the question was intended to elicit evidence of a pattern of behavior, or a departure from a usual pattern. The judge allowed it, and pointed the gavel at Bat, ordering him to answer the question.

Bat proceeded adroitly, sidestepping his gambling and his drinking. "Well, sir," he seemed to search his memory. I hoped my objection had given him time to consider his response.

"I didn't take the pledge yet." That brought more chuckles and guffaws from hearers who knew his thirsty ways. "All the same, drinkin' so much was not what I usually did. I don't believe I was drunken that time neither. But if I had a mind to drink some, it was easier to do over to Chatham than in Kinderhook. Everybody knows that." Bat glanced toward the jury for acknowledgment of what just about everyone in the room knew, that the Temperance movement in the county was centered in his earnestly and militantly sober village.

"Yes. Yes. But aside from the fifth of September that year, what other times did you go off to the saloons of Chatham?" Gardenier was reaching again, committing the tactical error of asking a question without knowing the answer to it.

"I was over toward Chatham Center that Sunday." Jay began, "and put my money in a pot for whiskey. We went around to Houck's woods. I didn't see any cards played that Sunday. I didn't play penny smithers, nor did I put anything on the game. They went for whiskey twice, but we never drank free. I got my fifty cents worth of whiskey in a bottle. I didn't have any more money. I didn't play cards, only gave my money to buy whiskey."

Gardenier stepped forward, seeming to loom over the seated prisoner, swoopng for the kill. "Did you say to George Brown that you killed Gertrude Hover?"

Bat's eyes widened. He leaned back in the witness box and gazed at the D.A. as if astounded.

"I never said any such a thing. I never admitted to anyone I killed Miss Hover. I did not say to George Brown on Tuesday, 'I had to kill her; I could not help myself'. Birge and I were in the same cell for three months, but we never got close. I did not say that if they squeezed me too hard they would know more about it. What I told Birge was that if he went to Kinderhook he should see my brother, not my father."

Perhaps it was that calm denial, delivered seemingly without rancor, that elicited the *Register*'s praise for Jay's steady nerves. There was also an added column filler in that day's *Register*: "Why not deputize Jackson and clear up the mystery once and for all? Birge said squeezing would do it. No ladies need apply, as he is married." The next day's Hudson paper also alluded to Jackson's embarrassment when he was asked about his carousing. "The D.A. made handsome Jacob the mark for dusky glances yesterday afternoon. Jake blushed in great shape, but owing to their color, it was impossible to note the effect on the females."

Until he had stated his full name at the start of his testimony, I don't believe any newspaper had printed Jackson's first name as Jacob. It is possible he had been generally thought to be his brother John. It is even possible that he was arrested, indicted, and brought to trial under that misapprehension.

"That year," Bat returned to Gardenier's earlier question, "in eighteen and eighty-five? I lived in Albany that year till the summer. And after I met Cyndy, that's my dear wife there," and he pointed guilelessly at Cynthia, who first smiled sweetly back at him and then ducked her head as every eye in the courtroom sought her out, the bolder spectators standing for a better view. Edwards rapped for order, but he had been the first to look over to where she sat.

"After I met Miss Cynthia Van Houck, I began attending the Beth-El. That's the AME Church on my road. Mr. Oliver was there preaching then; and he soon sorted me out of my previous sinful ways." He spoke without emphasis, but I caught the gleam of unrepentant amusement in his eyes. "Cyn and I, we were only just married at the end of that summer. Only time

I went to Chatham around then was that one Saturday, and that was unusual. That was a celebration." Jay stopped suddenly, his face went utterly blank. His brief eye contact with Cynthia had distracted him, caused him to slip in this deadly fencing match with the district attorney. He had revealed something unintended.

Gardenier was quick to take advantage of it. "So that night's carousing was a celebration? What were you celebrating, Bat? Were you celebrating the death of your old tormentor, the woman who knew your evil ways and wasn't afraid to report your crimes? Was that it? Were you celebrating the terrible crime you committed that day?"

"No, sir. I didn't commit any crime that day. Nor Miss Hover, she didn't torment me. She didn't hold any grudge against me. I could always make her laugh. That's what she'd say when she caught me funnin'. There was never bad blood between me and that lady, except if she was hard on William. I don't allow folks to be mean to my brother.

"As for celebrating, a man will want to enjoy an evenin' with his friends after he's wed. We finished the harvest that day. I wouldn't be seeing my friends much after that weekend."

Bat turned his serene and benevolent gaze on his wife again, showing us all why he no longer sought the company of his erstwhile companions. It was a masterful finesse. He had avoided the dangerous reason for that celebration, his triumph over Thresher Williams, his accession to top billing among the battlers in Powell's barn. And, of course, the five dollars (or whatever Powell paid him for winning) was money he could not account for to his new bride, so he had been free with it until it was spent. He had neatly avoided that pitfall, sprung a prosecution trap, and incidentally met the D.A.'s implied accusation head on and plowed it under. A wily and agile mind ~ I hoped he'd live long enough for us to congratulate his poise under fire.

Gardenier ended his cross-examination soon after that, tacitly conceding he had failed to shatter the defendant's coolness. The judge then called a brief recess to let us all settle down.

When we returned, Whitbeck requested the defense privilege of re-direct, without any real hope of achieving it, but Edwards simply nodded. The bailiff reminded Jackson that he was still under oath; and Jackson nodded in what I think was a conscious parody of the judge. He knew Whitbeck couldn't do worse to him than the D.A. had, but he was sitting very still and alert. This was territory not gone over previously. I smiled to reassure him, but he did not respond. His expression was not quite hostile, but his dark eyes were wary and intent on his attorney.

Whitbeck began in a voice as still and dry as ashes. "My colleague has drawn from you an admission about a juvenile prank of yours, Mr. Jackson, an incident involving the theft of a five dollar bill from Gertrude Hover's kitchen cookie jar, was that it?"

Jay smiled. "Now, how could you know that, Lawyer Whitbeck? How could you know that I snuck in while Miss Hover was gone to the market, just wantin' a cookie, and there she had put a bit of paper money in that crock?"

"I didn't really know, Mr. Jackson. I just guessed what a motherless boy might be up to. You have a reputation for mischief, for flimflam; and you probably earned it back then. But your Daddy made you return that money, didn't he?"

Bat chuckled softly. "He surely did. But first he whupped me good, so I wouldn't forget his teachin'. Miss Hover, she was goin' to take a stick to me too. But her brother, he was there, and he rode off and got the constable. That's how the other lawyer he knew about it. The constable said he wouldn't take me in. Bein' I was so small I could probably skinny right between the bars of the jail. But he said he'd put it down, so I would have a criminal record. I do believe that's the only criminal record I have up to now."

"So, that time you went into Miss Hover's house to snatch a cookie, and found that five dollar bill in the cookie jar that your Daddy made you return, how did you get into the house, Mr. Jackson?"

"That was easy. Everyone knew, that is, all of us who lived there and did work for her, how Miss Hover kept her back door latched from the inside. Hook was on the screen door. Come to ask Miss Hover does she want her grass cut or kindling chopped, or like that, you tap on the screen. She'd open the door, but the screen stayed latched. That was how it was. When she went away she'd latch the front door on the outside. It was the front door you could get in by when she wasn't there. It had a latch, not a key."

"So any neighbor wanting access to Miss Hover's house could just wait until she was not at home and go right in through the front door."

"Yes, sir. That's what I just told you."

"So if you, now, no longer a scamp of a boy, but a grown up flimflam man, wanted to get inside Miss Hover's house for any reason, all you had to do was wait until she went off to market and then go in by unlatching the front door. Is that correct?"

"If I wanted to do that. If there was any reason to go in there. That would have been how to do it. But I'm not a robber. Nor a flimflam man neither, Mister Whitbeck, sir. So that's not what

I did. I never went near Miss Hover or her house after I came back home to live with my Daddy."
He sounded indignant, but laughter flickered in his eyes and softened the lines around his mouth.
Jackson knew what his lawyer was doing.

"So, since you had no contact with Gertrude Hover, did no chores for her, paid her no
calls in the months after you returned to Kinderhook from Albany, it is unlikely in the extreme
that you would have gone to Miss Hover's back door on the Saturday afternoon of September fifth
in 1885. Is that correct?"

"I wouldn't have gone there. I didn't go there. I told you. I told all these people, what I did
that day."

"Thank you, Mr. Jackson. Your Honor, I have no more questions for the defendant."

The judge called a recess then. As Jackson was led away, Whitbeck looked up and nodded
to him. For John that was blatant admiration. I don't believe he had ever seen a defendant
withstand a prosecution assault more adroitly.

Columbia County Courthouse, Hudson, New York, site of the Jackson trial
used by permission, Columbia County Historical Society, Kinderhook, New York.

Chapter Fourteen

It is the proud boast of our nation ... that we have altered the very structure of our Constitution to assure that all persons in the United States of America are equal before the law...

John V. Whitbeck,
quoted in the Chatham *Republican* of February 14, 1888

The afternoon had turned bitterly cold. Few in the crowd of spectators chose to venture out into the day during the recess. In fact, it was apparent that we would have great difficulty forcing our way out of the building. Instead we paced the back hall between the court and the judges' chambers for a quarter of an hour. Whitbeck alternately relished the fine points of Bat's testimony and chuckled at Gardenier being outwitted by Jackson's adroit responses.

"He's gained a victory, that young fella," he concluded. "And an enemy too. He sealed his fate by besting Aaron, but at this moment, I bet he's crowing."

As we re-entered the courtroom, Cynthia Jackson came up beside us and touched John's sleeve. "Oh, Mr. Whitbeck, thank you." Then she smiled at me. "I knew Jay would be fine once he had a chance to tell how it was. He was brilliant, wasn't he?"

"Yes, my dear. He was truly brilliant," I whispered. "But you must take care to be away from here tonight." Then we were swept up the aisle by the press of spectators behind us, and I couldn't even see her as we took our places. My employer lanced me with a sharp, disapproving stare, but said nothing.

Mrs. Jane Reid was our next witness. A plump and jolly woman of forty or so, in a quite stylish russet colored costume and a crushed silk hat that could have been made by Cynthia's Aunt Margaret, Jane Reid kept a little grocery store on Albany Avenue that was frequented by both white and colored villagers. She was fussily careful in her testimony, counting off events on her fingers, as if totting up items in a shopping bag. Item Emma Briggs was a customer in her store. Item Emma came by every few days for item a poke of sugar or item a bunch of celery, or item some carrots. "They don't grow spuds or carrots, her and Mo. The roots take too long to fill out, you see. But I do like Emma's berries (item). Sometimes she leaves some for me to sell."

Whitbeck steered her to tell how Emma had trouble finding cornstarch or tapioca on Jane's shelves. In the month or so since we had interviewed her, Jane had grown cagey.

"Well," she confided, raising both hands to fend off such an admission. "I do recall her needing help when she first came into my store. That was five, maybe six years ago now, when she married Mo Briggs. I thought at first she just couldn't read. But that's not it. She manages pretty well nowadays. She knows where everything is, you see." That was so inconclusive Gardenier didn't deign to challenge it.

Then Mrs. Nancy Van Ness was called, a very proper member of Kinderhook's colored elite. Colored Van Nesses had lived in the village before there was an AME church there. They lived over on William Street in the village proper, rather than out on Sunset. As Charles Davis had told me, they attended the Dutch Reformed Church. Mrs. Van Ness was a spare, diminutive woman, with a smooth brown face that gave away nothing, not her age, not her emotions, and not a complete sentence, for the most part. Yes, she was acquainted with Emma Briggs, and yes, she had known Emma for some years. Emma was indeed hard of seeing, had been so as long as Nancy Van Ness had known her. Yes, Emma Briggs had in Nancy's hearing described herself as being so nearsighted she picked her berries by feel and had trouble sewing on a button.

Gardenier's attempt to fluster Mrs. Van Ness backfired when he pressed her as to whether she knew from observation that Emma had poor eyesight, or simply believed what she had been told about it. His questioning got from her the longest string of words in her testimony. "Oh, I do believe what Emma Briggs says," Nancy assured him. "You can trust her word about when berries ripen. Emma has complained to me about being hard of seeing. No reason to doubt it. She won't say it out in court though. She wouldn't want that wrote down about her. Emma's a bit vain. Aren't we all? She'd sooner lie under oath than in private. I believe Emma when she tells me she can't see good. I believe Clarence Moore too, when he says Jay Jackson was over to Pockman's that afternoon when Emma thought she saw him climbing Gertrude Hover's fence." And she smiled serenely up at him, having made her point effortlessly.

Gardenier let her go before she tangled him up any further with her soft politeness.

Whitbeck then entered in evidence a copy of the Hudson newspaper of August 10, 1885, that contained the announcement of a reward of $500.00 for information leading to the conviction of Gertrude Hover's murderer. Emma had come forward with the first of her several accusations in the weeks following that notice. She could truthfully claim she had not been paid to shop Bat Jackson, since there would be no payment until he was convicted. But she would certainly be richer if Jackson went down. He put this at the end, not so much to further discredit Emma Briggs, as to show the desperation with which the prosecution sought to put a name to Gertrude Hover's killer ~ any name, any killer ~ and so bring about closure to a sordid chapter in county history.

Whitbeck first showed the folded newspaper to Judge Edwards, who allowed it in as Defense Exhibit A. Then he approached the jury box as he opened it to let them view the prominent reward notice. As he did so, a slip of paper fell from between the pages and drifted to the floor in front of the jury. It was the fight handbill with the drawing of Jackson on it, his sobriquet 'Badass Jackson' in bold type, along with 'Thresher Williams' and a third fighter called 'Hacker Jack'. I had slipped it inside the newspaper, my little jest of the day. John reacted quickly, bending to scoop it up and thrust it into his pocket as if it were of no consequence. The judge was too far away to have seen what it was. Nor did the prosecution register any awareness of what had just happened. How many jurors had seen it? No matter. All of them would know about it as soon as they spoke together.

I thought we were in pretty good shape just then. But John clutched my elbow as he settled back into his chair. Look sharp, his grasp was telling me. Sure enough, Gardenier asked for the court's indulgence to call rebuttal witnesses.

An old acquaintance, the very first person we had interviewed after Cynthia Jackson hired us, Mrs. John Powell, was the first rebuttal witness called. Like other women who appeared as witnesses, she had armored herself in her best outfit for court. She made an impressive figure as she sailed up the aisle like a battleship among dories. She attested to having paid Bat Jackson his week's wages on the Thursday, or perhaps the Friday, before Gertrude Hover's murder.

"That Bat, he's a good worker," she added, "but he don't need payin' twice in one week. I gave him meat, too, when we butchered. More than once, three times, I think, I gave Bat meat to take home to his pa, who was ailing." She did not think Bat had been at the market on that Saturday.

When Whitbeck challenged her about whether she actually gave the meat away, or sold it, she allowed that she had charged some for it. "I didn't ask much for it, seventy-five cents once, sixty cents another time, and then maybe just a quarter. If he didn't have coins in his pocket, he just worked it off."

"So, Mrs. Powell, you charged Mr. Jackson at retail for meat he had butchered and dressed on your place?"

She was indignant that he would interpret her kindness as exploitation. "You don't understand. It was charity. I thought you were a nice man! I was wrong." He had made his point, but it cost him all hope of another go at her coffee and sugared buns.

Gardenier then re-called Dr. Woodworth, who had examined Gertrude's body. This time he came as a medical expert, to say he had treated Emma Briggs for difficulty with her eyes, but it had been three or four years ago. He averred that a person who can't see nearby objects can often see long distances. From what he remembered of Emma Briggs's problem, he thought it likely she could see at a distance. Whitbeck let me cross-examine Dr. Woodworth, partly because the doctor was from my part of the county, and partly because he knew I'd enjoy taking the doctor's puddle of supposition and generality apart, like kicking over an anthill.

Deputy Sheriff Theo Nixdorf took the stand to swear, as a customer of Emma Briggs, that he trusted her weights and measures and had never noticed her having trouble seeing. "She knows to count the money I give her and make change. She seems pretty sharp to me." Whitbeck asked him if he had ever seen Emma Briggs except for buying berries from her.

"Well, I buy a rabbit if she's got one."

Whitbeck let him go. It was not in our interest to impugn the word of an officer of the law.

Charles Davis of the Kinderhook *Rough Notes* came on to agree with the prosecutor that Emma Briggs was, as far as he knew, an honest tradeswoman, with sufficient sight to carry on her business. When he had finished this toadying recital, Whitbeck in cross asked him how often he dealt with Emma Briggs. He smiled, as if he had been hoping for rescue. - "My dear wife Frances is the one who usually does the grocery shopping for our family." Then he added, "But one cannot live in a village as small as Kinderhook without knowing the people in it. Emma Briggs is well thought of by all who have commerce with her." He was uneasy sitting the fence. He had put himself out to help us, against his professed dislike of Bat. No need to make him an antagonist.

Gardenier then called John Powell, Bat's erstwhile employer. Powell, it emerged, was not in court. He had to be summoned from the farm, a dozen miles away. Remembering his aversion to talking about that fateful week of 1885, I wondered how the district attorney thought Powell could help his case. Judge Edwards declared a three hour recess to enable the witness to be brought in. Whitbeck had just enough time to go home. I struggled through the surly, milling throng to reach Vanderhagen's, where I had a wonderful, leisurely dinner, my first pleasant meal of that week. The trial was nearly over. Whitbeck's closing address to the jury was well prepared. Nothing I could do would influence the case now. I put it out of mind, wondering instead about my uncertain future. John Whitbeck was unlikely to take on a law partner. If he did, I was not the man. He would not want as a partner anyone so young, nor a democrat, nor anyone named Tilden. He'd prefer an NYU law degree to my Columbia pigskin. He'd want someone taller, bolder, more confidant. Likely, since he had all those qualifications himself, he needed no partner at all.

When I came out onto Warren Street, wine-warm and sated, night had fallen. The gas lamps made soft, wavering pools of light that bled unevenly onto piled snow in the dark troughs between the storefronts and rowhouses. Sensible people, pretty much everyone in fact, had gone inside. Perhaps only a few diehards would return to hear John Powell's reluctant testimony.

At seven o'clock Edwards declared court again in session. John Powell tramped to the witness chair with the same heavybooted tread I remembered from our visit to his house. He wore pretty much the same sort of rough garb, except for a loose woolen surcoat that did not completely hide his braces or his belly or the big square buckle of his belt. He did not look pleased to be among us. He seemed, unless I was projecting my own angst upon him, extremely apprehensive.

Aaron Gardenier led him through the establishing facts, his occupation, the location of his several pieces of farmland, the period Bat Jackson had worked for him ("From that summer the Hover woman died, till you put him in jail," he snarled.). When Gardenier divined that his witness was p-ast his outrage at being haled from his warm hearth into a long ride on a harsh winter evening to swear to God knew what lies and half truths, he asked about events of the first week of September in 1885. Powell hardly paused to shift his glare from the jury to Gardenier before denying any memory of that time. He was not sure Jackson worked for him that -week at all.

"How can I know after all this time whether Bat was still on that harvest? If he worked I paid him, unless my wife did."

He could not remember being at the village market that Saturday. He could not remember what Bat wore when he was working the fields, or when he came to collect his wages. John Powell's recall was as leaky as Sitcer's, who had provided such amusement to the court. But this was not a befuddled laborer. This was one of the county's more successful and prominent citizens, scion of an old county family, and a potentially generous donor to the next election campaign. No one dared laugh at John Powell. Nor did Gardenier press or ride him.

Neither did Whitbeck. If he let on that we knew what had gone on in Powell's barn that day, Powell and Jackson would both be at risk. But not for murder! A public boxing victory at noon did not constitute an alibi for Bat. What it did was set up the character of a long, celebratory day and evening in which a stopoff for petty robbery and incidental murder became ludicrously unlikely.

We had long despaired of making Jackson accept that his life was truly in danger, though my heart quailed for him. Now it became evident, from the way John Powell's hand had trembled as he was sworn in, and from the scythelike rasp of his voice, that he, at least, was sensible of peril. Whatever was at stake for him must include a warning that sealed his mouth and threatened to open his sphincter.

When Powell stood and left the courtroom in a sort of lurching run, I expected Judge Edwards to adjourn us for the night. It was a quarter past seven, long after the lamps had been turned up. The wind had stiffened and was rattling at the windows. Home fires and blessed sleep beckoned. Edwards glared in the direction of the prosecution table and asked if their rebuttal was complete. When Gardenier agreed he was done, the judge pointed his gavel at us, his tic screwing up half his face, as if he were sharing a private joke with someone behind my left shoulder, and said "Do you have closing remarks to share with the jury and this court, counselor?"

I was stunned by this sudden leap into an unheard of extension- of an already late court session. So was Whitbeck. (I later looked and did not find another instance when Judge Edwards had kept a trial going past supper, past dark, past eight hours. The Hudson *Register* next day printed a mild protest at the inconvenience to newsmen.) My employer untangled his length and allowed himself to be urged to his feet, with Jackson offering a sharp nod of encouragement, and me responding for him that the defense did indeed wish to address the jury on behalf of the accused.

He shuffled needlessly through- the notes he had not expected to use until the next morning, and grasped the table edge with white-knuckled fingers. I poured him a glass of wate, which he sipped sparingly, looking down at me as from a great distance. His chair scraped loudly as he stepped away from the defense table.

"Your Honor," he began hoarsely, "Gentlemen of the jury." There. That was a better sound. Whitbeck's voice, while rather high in range, was commanding and quite flexible. He had no trouble being heard in court, and enjoyed public speaking. Certainly he held his audience without effort that night. His reputation as a pleader was well earned. I would like to be able to claim that my whole mind was on what he said to demonstrate Jay Jackson's innocence, to save his life if he could. I took notes, as I had all during the trial. Without them I could not be setting down this record. But what I actually remember was watching him pace down the row of jurymen, knowing how he was gathering his strength, counting breaths until his pounding heart slowed, until he reached that place actors find, where revelation and substance lie to hand, as the opening bars of a sonata draw the musician into the sure unfolding of ideas and inevitable flights of expression. I also rejoiced for him that he had worn his old boots, the ones that did not squeak.

He glanced once toward the defense table, where Jackson and I sat, still as effigies, watchful and expectant. Then his eyes went to the seats behind us where his wife sat. Cynthia Jackson was not in her usual place. She was standing at the rear where pressmen prepared to take notes of Whitbeck's eloquent summation and constables held their nightsticks ready to quell any disturbance. She was holding a sleeping child in her arms. She'd brought little Jemmy to see his father on the last day of his trial. Jackson must be aware of her, of that serene benediction.

Whitbeck's gaze swept back to the jurymen; and as he cleared his throat to begin, I glanced behind me and caught sight of an unexpected, familiar face in the crowd. My sister, my young Marjorie, sat in one of the front benches, tucked beside Mrs. Bullock like a pinnace beside a steamer. When had she arrived? Why had she not let me know she would be here? The answers came as swiftly as the questions. I had hardly been home this past week to sleep, let alone open mail or sit down to a proper meal. If she had written to announce her coming, I would not have picked up the letter. Marjorie, little Margie, had come to see the end of our notorious murder trial. Well, for this community it was notorious. Marjorie had come so that she could report it all to my mother, of course. What an adventure for her, a mere schoolgirl: to go a day's journey by herself, to brave cold and snow and strangers, and find her way to my rooming house in an unfamiliar town. I was touched to the heart by her courage and loyalty.

Dear Marjorie. That bright face with its merry brown eyes, that hatless mop of dark curls, was exactly the sight I needed to put a smile on my face as Whitbeck began to speak, querying the jury in a conversational tone.

"Can you recall just what you did on any given Saturday two years and more in the past? I cannot. Unless the day can be tied to a memorable event, it will have long since passed into the pleasant oblivion of our precious days of weekend relaxation or family pursuits or travel. If we learn of an event that clouded one of those days, we more readily remember where and when we heard of it than where we were, what we were doing in the usual way, before such news came to us.

"However, when the event is a deed of extreme cruelty, we want the perpetrator found. We want justice for the unfortunate victim. We want the horror and fear removed, the normal pace of our lives restored. We want to know everything that led to the evil deed, what the victim's relatives and friends were doing, where anyone suspected of the crime could have been on a particular day, at a particular time. That's what we have required of each and every witness who came before you this week, including the defendant. Where were you on a particular Saturday in the early autumn of 1885? Unless you were involved in something you'll never forget, your wedding, or the birth of a child, or your once-in-a-lifetime trip to see the great falls of Niagara ~ you are unlikely to have a precise recollection.

"So, we have gleaned from the several accounts presented to us in this trial, a somewhat confused and contradictory notion of what happened in or near Gertrude Hover's house on the day of her murder which was not discovered until the following week." He gave them a moment to consider those lapses of time before offering some examples of the various accounts of the day of Gertrude's death. John Jackson senior, and James Sitcer, and indeed Bat himself, looked back on that day and remembered an ominous silence at the Hover house from the early morning onward. One or two thought it was on that day, rather than some other day, they had spoken with Miss Hover. Others put the sound of voices they had heard from the house together with that afternoon. Still others told of seeing someone in the Hover yard, or at her door.

"One witness," he smiled, "claims to have seen the defendant climbing Gertrude Hover's fence that afternoon. That witness, Emma Briggs, has been described by reliable sources as unable to descry her own husband from the length of the Bethel Church. How could she know whom she saw, or if indeed she saw anyone near the Hover property that fateful afternoon, when Gertrude Hover in all likelihood was lying in the charnel house where her life had bled away several hours earlier?

"When Emma Briggs, after falsely accusing three other colored men of being the mysterious and apocryphal Kinderhook fence climber, says she saw Mr. Jackson committing the Fence Offense, as it were, he was, as has been demonstrated by both prosecution and defense witnesses, pursuing a normal Saturday's errands, finishing a week's labor, collecting his wages, keeping an appointment with a buyer of woodchuck oil, and settling debts with one or two tradesmen. After which he spent the rest of his free day with his friends.

"Isn't that more or less what each of us can remember of our actions on a pleasant, sunny Saturday afternoon at harvest time of any year, last year, the year before, or the year before that? There was an attempt to show Mr. Jackson as a fleeing felon on the day after Gertrude Hover was murdered. You may not be aware of it, aware that he was accused of running off to Albany on Sunday the sixth of September in 1885. Since the route he was supposed to have taken in his flight was roundabout, leisurely, and quite public, since his supposed flight would have interfered with his usual attendance at the Bethel Church where he sang in the choir, and since he is known to have been in Chatham Center that day, even the prosecution has omitted any mention of it throughout this trial. The district attorney in his cross examination of Mr. Jackson elicited a full and circumstantial account of the defendant's movements on that Sunday. He was certainly not in Albany spattered in red paint. As for the previous day, the supposed day of the murder, my client cannot be identifiedi as the man at Gertrude Hover's back door, if such a person was actually seen. Emma Briggs attempted to pin the crime on William Jackson, or on William Henderson before settling on Jay Jackson, a young fellow quite without motive for any controversy or confrontation with the victim of this crime. Bat Jackson ~ Jacob Badass Jackson ~" Whitbeck tasted the syllables of Bat's nickname with considerable relish: let them cringe who resorted to the euphemism. "~ works hard and earns every penny of his pay. He keeps his family from want, and contributes both his labor and his commerce to this community. As much as any man here, he belongs to this valley and deserves the understanding and fair treatment due to every citizen."

According to my notes, that was more or less how the summation began. I did not attempt to put it all down. The court stenographer is supposed to take down everything that is said in a trial, the official transcript of which should be available for anyone who wishes to consult it later. Whitbeck went on to review the conflicting threads of testimony, showing as well as he could how time had worn away details and could have transferred moments from nearby days into that one. He had the jury smiling at the operetta played out that summer in the choir loft of the Bethel, when Emma Briggs set her middle aged heart on a likely young buck, unaware that he was then quietly and earnestly wooing the lovely Cynthia Van Houck. Unaware, that is, until their wedding was announced, only weeks before Gertrude Hover's death. How, Whitbeck's argument implied, could a man with the companionship of that marvelous creature, waste an hour attacking and robbing an old woman for a bit of house money? He'd just wearied himself all week to earn his wife's keep honorably. Why risk a peerless woman's scorn by doing needless violence, breaking the law, taking a life?

He described Gertrude Hover's known habit of latching her front door on the outside when she left home, pointing out that any of her neighbors who wanted or needed to get inside could simply wait until she was away and nip in whenever they pleased. He referred to Bat's reputation as a tease who could have coaxed Gertude Hover out of a loan if he chose. Bat had been cajoling her out of whippings since he was a boy, but at that moment he was a grown man, newly married, and a hard-working citizen. He had neither need nor motive to commit robbery or violence.

Whitbeck had them laughing at Otis Birge's drunken fantasy, and at the desperation of the prosecution that allowed such bathos into a trial for murder. He demonstrated the weight of recollected facts and material evidence that pointed to the crime as a deed of fury and darkness that had to have been committed before dawn on that Saturday ~ at a time Jacob Jackson was asleep beside his new bride in his father's house.

He never glanced at me until he had finished laying out every fact of the case for the jury's inspection. When he did look in my direction, I had my watch out, signaling him to end it while they were still awake. Remembering how his chums had made fun of my prolixity, I was cautioning him to drop the rest of his pleading, all his rhetorical flourishes about the majesty of the law, his delicate hints about issues of property and politics in our fair valley.

Whitbeck was quick to take my suggestion. He threw in a grand phrase or two about forbearance, to soften any juror bent on hanging, and then skipped to his peroration.

"Gentlemen," Whitbeck told the jury, softening his voice as if speaking to them in confidence. "There are aspects of this terrible crime which will remain unresolved no matter how carefully you sift what has been brought to light in this trial. The death of Gertrude Hover leaves behind a grievous remorse in this community. The true reason for her death will remain a mystery, even if you condemn Bat Jackson and consign him to the gallows. All the silent secrets of that bloodstained house will still cry out her anguish, and will still not be known. Who was heard to talk within that house at two o'clock on Saturday? We know where Bat Jackson was then. We don't know who or where the murderer was by that time.

"My colleague and I," (at his nod to me I was as startled as if he had just produced a hen from his sleeve) "have not dared to suggest another culprit for this evil deed. It is not the duty of defending counsel to present an alternative reality to the one postulated by the prosecution. If I were to fasten this crime on another individual, I would be doing the same arbitrary destruction of character that has been committed against Jacob Jackson."

He paused to let other names rise unbidden to the jurymen's minds, one of Gertrude's relatives perhaps, or Bat's elusive and sinister brother John.

"I believe you can see that brute in your mind. The perpetrator of this horrible murder, at whatever time he actually did beat and stab Gertrude Hover to death, must have finished his fiendish work so mired in gore, so besmeared with the blood of his victim, that he must hide himself, go somewhere he could be alone and scrub himself from head to foot to remove the evidence of his atrocity, and regain enough composure to appear in public with at least a semblance of some small equilibrium of mind.

"Yet, if this murder was committed when the prosecution has averred it occurred, Bat Jackson, within almost that same moment he is supposed to have been at Gertrude Hover's door, was also observed, in the same clothes he wore all that day, with his white shirt and white hat, greeting friends in his usual jolly manner, trudging over to Pockman's with his woodchuck oil, settling up the week's grocery bill, hiring a horse to ride to Chatham ~ all in public in that very village where everyone knew him, and knew his customary manner. I ask you, as his peers and neighbors, to consider how this could be. Could you do such a thing? Could he carry it off among folks who knew him well, had known him all his life?"

Whitbeck straightened to his full height and took a deep breath before going on, slowing the pace of his words to give his conclusion space and weight. "Gentlemen," he slowly surveyed all twelve of them, meeting each pair of eyes in turn, "It is the proud boast of our nation, which some of us here present have fought honorably to establish and maintain, that we have altered the very structure of our Constitution to assure that all persons in the United State of America are equal before the law. All persons. Of any creed, color or stripe. Without exception. If in this instance the proof offered for your judgment is such that would cause you to acquit the most exalted citizen, be he an official or captain of industry or scion of an ancient line, then you are equally bound to acquit a common man, such as the prisoner now before this court. Trusting in your considered judgment, and in your capability to bear the mortal burden that has been placed on your shoulders, I leave Jacob Jackon's fate in your hands."

Bethel African Methodist Episcopal Church, Kinderhook, New York as it appeared in 1887
used by permission, Columbia County Historical Society, Kinderhook, New York

Chapter Fifteen

When I get to be a composer I'm gonna write me some music...
Of black and white black white black people
And I'm gonna put white hands and black hands
And brown and yellow hands and red clay earth hands in it
Touching everybody with kind fingers
And touching each other natural as dew
In that dawn of music
When I get to be a composer.

Langston Hughes, "Daybreak in Alabama"

John Whitbeck sat down, taking the linen towel I offered to wipe the sweat from his face. He seemed to collapse into himself. For myself I wanted to be gone from there, to join my sister, and seek home and bed. I thought Whitbeck had done as well as could be done. He had answered all doubts, made a plausible bid at persuading the jury to our way of thinking. He had possibly tipped the balance of hope in our favor. I would have welcomed other opinions, preferably opinions that supported my own, but just to be out of that room would do.

I poured water for him and drank half a glass myself, wishing it were something stronger. Whitbeck carefully squared the papers on the table, anticipating the adjournment that would send us home for the night. I could see the weariness that assailed him as soon as he finished speaking. When I showed him the time he was shocked to see he had spoken for two and a half hours. It was going on ten o'clock.

Edwards brought the gavel down, squelching a low murmur of commentary that had risen from the spectators. Then, instead of using it to adjourn the trial as everyone expected, he pointed it menacingly at the district attorney.

"Is the prosecution ready," he boomed, his tic spasming furiously, "to make its closing address?"

"We are. I am. Yes, Your Honor." Aaron Gardenier spoke before standing. He had no more anticipated this that we had. Lawyers prefer to present their summations by daylight, to clear-eyed listeners and to a press corps alert enough to take copious notes to quote in the next day's news. Getting this case into the jury's hands by tonight, however, would gain a day, make a verdict possible before the end of the court's week. That's what Judge Edwards had in mind. Summations on Thursday and verdict by Friday, while the mob outside still threatened riot. He was expecting, I thought sourly, counting on mob rule, vigilante action. Anything to prevent an appeal, a dragging out of the investigation. That, at least, was my interpretion of this move.

"He's setting up a midnight lynching," I hissed, as Gardenier gathered his notes with understandable reluctance and asked for the lamps to be trimmed. He was buying himself a few minutes of preparation; but in any case he wanted plenty of light for his final statement. He needed an attentive jury to hear his closing address for the People. .

There we were, already up past bedtime, fatigued by a long day of testimony and harangue, and doomed to a long night of it. Gardenier did not spare his captive audience a single scrap of his argument, from the broadest claim and tiniest detail to the boldest conclusion. Gertrude Hover, he decreed, was killed on Saturday, September fifth of eighteen and eighty-five between the hours of twelve and three o'clock. The prisoner in the dock, Bat Jackson, he avowed to be the man who killed her. He recapitulated at length and ad nauseam the words of every witness he had called to support his contention, gathering them into a tight circle of accusation that surrounded Jackson in a net. He ridiculed Bat's testimony as "so full of inconsistencies as to appear utterly unreliable."

In his view, the accused had invariably corroborated the account of each prosecution witness to a point where his guilt became evident. Beyond that point he made them all out to be liars, perjurers. "Now perjury, gentlemen, is a serious accusation. If it were to be proved against any of the people's witnesses, severe punishment would be the result. For perjury by the defendant, the punishment would be added to his already horrible crimes. He could not be hanged twice, but surely deserves to experience a single instance of final justice at the people's hands.

"I believe, gentlemen," he intoned grandly, rising to his climax, "that you are prepared to mete out that justice, to deal fairly and finally with this unrepentant prisoner who has flagrantly transgressed against common decency and the peace and safety of this community for far... too... long!. I am therefore confident and satisfied to leave judgment in the hands of twelve honest, thinking men, to you, my friends and neighbors who now occupy this jury box as representatives of us all."

I was impressed with his brevity, at least. He'd taken only an hour or so to dissect and cast doubt on every one of Whitbeck's arguments and pour tar over Jay Jackson's character as thoroughly as possible. I took few notes, as this would all be in the court record, the ad hominem argument (Bat was black, ergo Bat was a miscreant), the eloquent damnation, the character assassination. I thought about the possibility of a libel suit as a recourse for Cynthia when this was over. With Bat dead, she'd have need of whatever monetary redress that could be obtained for her. This idea flitted through my mind as Judge Edwards gaveled us into silence one more time and began his own summation and charge to the jury.

He spoke for nearly another hour, fifty minutes, according to the Chatham *Republican* recounting of the trial. He spoke from his high seat, laying his gavel aside for the first time all week. While he was intent on setting out the responsibilities and restrictions of jury deliberation, his tic was much less in evidence. I wondered if having to sit there without speaking, without lending his personal slant to the proceedings, exacerbated the spasms. The courtroom held a thoughtful silence throughout his charge. The twelve jurors seemed hardly to breathe as they listened raptly to his cautions and instructions on the limits and requirements of a jury's power and authority.

Nor did Bat move for that last hour. He had not seemed to stir at all after the great, shuddering sigh that engulfed him when he resumed his chair after his testimony and cross-examination. He received Whitbeck's final pleading without any sign of emotion; and throughout Gardenier's summation he held himself tense and still. His piercing gaze never left Edwards' face while the judge set forth the minutiae of the juridical process.

By my pocket watch, it was lacking midnight by a quarter of an hour when Judge Edwards sent the jury out to deliberate. I thought it pretty likely that they would be quick to agree on a night's sleep before trying a first vote on my client's guilt or innocence.

As soon as the judge adjourned us and shifted his bulk from his high seat, the courtroom burst into bedlam. They had been mute for an unconscionably long period. Everyone had an urgent opinion or observation or complaint to share with the person next to him. I tried to make my way to Marjorie, but the aisle was so jammed with knots of shouting and gesticulating spectators, it was all I could do to keep my feet under me. Whitbeck's cane was of little avail, but he did manage to join his wife, and sat quietly with her while the crowd pressed around them. From the little I could see, the hall outside the courtroom door appeared equally crowded. Newsmen were shouting at colleagues outside and forming temporary alliances with their rivals to wedge their way through an unmoving mass of humanity. One bailiff, attempting to unlatch the second leaf of the door, got his hand stepped on and abandoned his ineffectual effort to relieve the congestion.

For several minutes we had the makings of a small riot right there. I saw panicked faces as some individuals began to choke and squirm and claw against the stasis that allowed no one to exit, or even to move for the most part. Then word was passed back to us through the crowd that the square outside the courthouse had filled with rowdies determined to seize Jackson as he was taken to the jail. I heard the words 'armed' and 'barred the door' in a cacophony of versions of what prevented us from leaving the building. Surely the marshalls will handle it, I thought, and then I thought

The marshalls are inside with us. Someone must let the sheriff know.

Then, with bedlam rising all around me, my mind shrank away from confusion and achieved an obvious connection. The sheriff already knew. I had warned him myself. Someone with greater influence than I must have advised him not to interfere with citizens who took action. The sheriff was also an elected official who would suffer the weight of public will. I could not expect him to do anything against the armed might of vigilantes whose support at the polls he was soon to cultivate.

Jackson dead, the case of Gertrude Hover's murder closed and forgotten: That was the aim of all this of course. To forget poor Gertrude Hover, to forget the barbarity of her death ~ that's what they all wanted. If the conduct of this trial were to be challenged, if Whitbeck appealed the verdict, it could drag on for another two years. In that period Edwards, Gardenier, the sheriff, even the mayors of Hudson and Kinderhook, would stand for re-election. So how had the judge, or the mayor or the district attorney, advised the sheriff to deal with this violence the People had encouraged, if not fomented? Was that why the judge had continued the trial so it would end this night? Had they set up this confrontation fully expecting an outcome to the trial that would lead to Jackson's death?

It was so noisy in the courtroom I could not think past that one grim conclusion. The sound of angry and frightened voices was bouncing off the hardwood floor and unpadded oaken benches. It ricocheted from the barreled tin ceiling, filling every bit of air space in a solid, writhing mass of noise. I felt drowned in it, unable to breathe. The racket itself seemed to prevent me from moving. Like those around me, I began to tremble, to panic.

It was then, even as hysteria threatened to turn us from lawful citizens into a penned bedlam of wild creatures, that a different sound began to infuse the ugly roar of confined and furious citizenry. Soft at first, but persistent, a kind of sustained buzz grew in the room, until I eventually recognized it as humming. Some negroes among us had begun to hum, gathering an undertone of insistent vibrancy into a sonorous presence that slowly replaced the shouting. It was as if an avalanche gradually spilled into a still pool of water. By the time words emerged from that vibrating unison, the raucous chitter of the hysterical crowd was lessening slightly, gradually dying away until one voice poured a kind of sweet benediction over the soft, insistent humming. *Steal away*. Just the two words gave meaning to the tone that settled and hung in a clear diapason. *Steal away*. Firmer that time, some voices holding, some rising into harmony.

Directly behind me a deep bass led the plagal shift. I could feel it vibrate in the floor under my feet. From all over the room others joined in to tune and round the chord that now swelled to fill every atom of air, till it hung like a live presence in the shallow vault above us. This could not be only the dozen or so who would have come down from the congregation of the Bethel in Kinderhook. I surmised that singers from AME and Baptist churches all over the county were joining that old hymn they all knew, that pulled the soul back to the days of slavery, to desperate yearning and secret promise of freedom. *Steal away* home. Treble voices soared for a moment. *I ain't got long to stay here*. I could hear in one or two voices near me a southern cadence that made the words *I hanta gotta long ta stah hyar*.

When the verse was lined out, I heard what I imagined to be Cynthia Jackson's voice, high and clear, with a carrying quality not there when she spoke. *My Lord, he calls me...* And then all the high voices continued. I felt a hand take mine, and looked down to see my sister Marjorie, reaching slender fingers to grasp and push her way to my side.

As the singing ended, I sensed a slight relaxation in the mass of people, a collective exhalation of pleasure. Some few, perhaps, had shoved through the door. Out in the hall, too, they were singing. Behind me now, the same rich bass took up *Didn't my Lord Deliver Daniel*. I wondered if they had planned this, if the colored community had heard or divined the violent intent growing in the street all week, and had called on members of every negro congregation in the county to comfort Bat on this long night before judgment, and possibly prevent the barbarity of a summary execution.

From somewhere in the distant reaches of the building a tenor voice lined out the plaintive, minor strains of *One more river to cross*. That, I knew, most of us there knew, was a song from the Underground Railroad, from night tracks and weary plodding with the big dipper and the north star for guide. Some of the older people in that room must have personal knowledge of the perils and desperate hopes of such a journey.

Was it Jacob Jackson's voice raising that song of yearning? I never actually heard him sing, as I never heard Cynthia to put a name to her voice. I wanted it to be Bat singing, wanted him trapped in the back hall of the courthouse, safe from the vigilantes who would assail the side door through which prisoners were taken back to the jail. The larger mob must be charging the courthouse steps and ramming the main entrance. If the sheriff, if the constables ~ if they sought the help of every reasoning man in the street ... We could not know what was happening outside. I did my best to reassure Marjorie, who clung to me as we stood immobile, surrounded by the rich swell of singing voices.

They sang us past our panic. I don't remember all the songs they gave us. Eventually everyone was singing, or mumbling the words at least, as the strains of Tenting Tonight, and the Battle hymn of the Republic, and other ballads familiar to all of us, filled the space. I remember grasping Marjorie's hand and pulling her along as we finally shoved out into the hallway, where news was spreading that lawmen had at last arrived in force to disperse the mob. The Whitbecks slipped out by the Judge's exit and were away before us.

Knowing how meager the official law force was in the county, I guessed the sheriff had resorted to deputizing the roughest idlers to disperse their fellows. He'd offer a night's wage to men who otherwise would be fashioning a noose for the lynching. Cold, and a bitter February wind, would do the rest. There would be no riot tonight in Hudson.

When Marjorie and I, with my landlady in tow, finally emerged from the courthouse, the crowd had scattered as if blown away by the wind from the river that whipped us up Union Street and into the welcome warmth of Mrs. Bullock's premises. Mrs. Bullock made us a cup of cocoa before urging us to bed. Marjorie was flushed with excitement and would have stayed up all night, I think. My landlady was unused to young people, and in my case seemed to think it inappropriate for an aspiring lawyer to be connected by blood to a sprightly child who might at any time say or do something to cause embarrassment or scandal to the detriment of a budding career. But who am I to criticize Mrs. Bullock? I have arrived at this point in my life with habits as rigid and conventional as hers were in the year of the Jackson trial.

I said goodnight to Marjorie I assured her that the next day would be far less perilous.

"They've put a lid on it for tonight," I urged in a creaky whisper, for we were only ten paces from the parlor door. "Every constable in the county will be out tomorrow. Our musical friends saved us from a nasty moment. We could have been trampled to death, but it's all fair sailing now."

That was my hope at least. A quick verdict could stir it all up again. The sheriff had made a tactical error, appointing deputies from the crowd, giving them authority they didn't have before. I noticed that he'd also let them keep their weapons, which was worse.

"You don't think Mr. Whitbeck's summation had any effect on the jury then," Marjorie asked timidly. I murmured some encouragement to take to bed with her. For myself I expected little sleep in the few, anxious hours left of the night. Then Mrs. Bullock called out, complaining of the lateness of the hour and ordering me to lock up.

I rose when the sluggish winter daylight paled my window, and hurried out before breakfast, in case there was a report from the jury room. Whitbeck found me at Vanderhagen's and insisted on a substantial meal before facing another boring wait in court. Warren Street was strangely empty. All week we had been delayed by milling ruffians, but that day they seemed to have found shelter elsewhere. Granted, a sunless, icy morning, the coldest yet, made standing about outside an unpleasant prospect.

As we started up the broad courthouse steps Whitbeck observed, "They'll be round the back today, waiting for him to be taken away. It may be safe for us law-abiding sorts to use the front entrance. Have you arranged an escort for your little sister?"

"Mrs. Bullock and another lodger will be with her. If it ends today, I'll make sure she gets back to the house without harm."

He grunted a reply, and then we were in the echoing lobby and struggling up to the courtroom through a phalanx of excited citizenry and shoving ranks of newsmen. The Press. That's why they are called the Press.

Judge Edwards convened court at nine-thirty, and asked the bailiff to summon the jury. However, Whitbeck's opinion of their stolidity was borne out when they sent word that they were not yet agreed on a verdict. After some conferral, the judge called a recess until after lunch. We made a meal out of a late coffee hour, Whitbeck and I and Jennings the lodger, with Marjorie and Mrs. Bullock. Marjorie was apprehensive about the aftermath of the verdict.

"Will we be imprisoned in the courthouse again, Roy, like last night?" she asked me, her eyes huge with wonder at this amazing adventure.

"Won't that be a fine tale to tell Mother when you get home! Would you settle for a verdict that frees our client? I'd like you to have that feather to take home to her and Robbie."

"Now, Mr. Tilden, don't have the child hoping for what can't be."

At that moment I could have throttled Mrs. Bullock. With every heartbeat, every pulse of conscience I was signalling that half-acre of farmers and their leaven of three tradesmen to see sense, to see justice, to see past the bigotry that made only dark men suspect in Gertrude Hover's death, that precluded other possible killers with deeper and darker motives than the People had set forth.

"You may be underestimating the wisdom of Jackson's peers, Mrs. Bullock, I chided.

Soon after that I took Marjorie on a brief walk around Hudson before seeking warmth, if not comfort, at the courthouse.

At a quarter to one that afternoon Judge Edwards entered and ordered the Sheriff to have Jackson brought into court. That was a signal for those who still loitered in the hall to scamper for seats. The jury filed in and responded one by one when their names were called. I looked from one face to another, searching for the telltale frown, the glance toward Bat that would reveal their aggregate will. They seemed not so much determined as dazed, almost pole-axed.

The judge inquired of the foreman whether they had yet reached a verdict.

"We have, sir. We have, Your Honor. We find the defendant not guilty."

He had not allowed the judge time to wedge in his usual query, or ask Jackson to stand while the verdict was read. Whitbeck rose immediately, and I struggled to my feet pulling Jay up beside me. I almost expected other words to follow, hardly believing what I had heard. Bat turned to his attorney, his brow creased with question. "Did he say me clear?"

"They have declared you not guilty, Mr. Jackson. You are free."

"Free?" He breathed the word, and then his whole face broke apart into a grin of such amazement, such delighted relief, that I smile to remember it now, nearly half a century later. He grasped Whitbeck's hand, and then my arm was round his shoulders and we were joining in a mute, congratulatory circle. Cynthia came forward, and they embraced and wept and were surrounded by a throng of well-wishers. After Jackson went over to shake hands with the two prosecuting attorneys, his friends bore him out of the room and away from the courthouse. They would use the front entrance, as befitted one exonerated of guilt in open trial. Those who would have assaulted Bat on his departure by the prisoner's door were left without a victim.

During this rather joyful disturbance, Judge Edwards managed to rap us down. He thanked the jury. I do believe he gave them credit in his discharge for their attention. carefulness, and judgment in performing their civic duty – or something like that. As soon as he pronounced us adjourned *sine die*, Whitbeck and I went to greet Aaron Gardenier and Jacobs the Assistant D.A., as Jackson had done with surprising gallantry.

According to the Chatham *Republican* of Tuesday, February fourteenth for that year, eight of the jurors felt from the start of deliberation that the state had not made its case against Bat Jackson. The four holdouts stubbornly stuck to their Guilty vote through many ballots during that Friday morning, while we, and Bat, and a gang of vigilantes, and Gertrude's murderer, whoever he was, clenched our hearts and hoped for acquittal or for conviction.

It was not so much that they thought him innocent. They thought there was room for doubt of his guilt. The shadow of a doubt: that's all it takes for twelve sober men and true to acquit. That shadow, however, falls equally on both sides of the evidence. They had not cried him innocent, just not guilty. I was sure, that raw February Friday, that I would never see Jacob Jackson again. He would remove himself from the cloud that had fallen over his character, over his life. He would take his wife and child and go where no one had ever heard of Battice Jackson or of Gertrude Hover. Nor would I ever again see Cynthia Van Houck Jackson. That too I knew, as surely as the other.

What I could not know that day, as I put my sister on the stage, tucking her in with shawls and bearskins for her long, uncomfortable ride home, was how the case of People versus Jackson would affect my reputation and my outlook in the years that followed.

Chapter Sixteen

I've known rivers: Ancient dusky rivers.
My soul has grown deep like the rivers.

Langston Hughes, "The Negro Speaks of Rivers"

    I have often thought of setting down my recollections of the Jackson trial. Why else keep my notes for all these years? It has always seemed odd to me that the case has never been cited, or even mentioned, in later civil rights pleadings. I would rather have my name connected to an instance where the right thing was done, than with my relative Samuel Tilden's famous case where the wrong thing was done, where the people's will was thwarted.

    The trial and acquittal of Jacob Jackson was featured in the local press as a worthy bit of post-Reconstruction justice. The conscience of a community was seen to be expressed in the unwillingness of a jury to condemn a negro on what the jury concluded to be insufficient grounds. For a week juridical wisdom was puffed ... the ultimate fairness ... the virtue ... the hope ... et cetera. Whoever reads my words will know how hollow all that righteous claptrap was, how empty our hope for a just and equal system of opportunity and good government. Even now, in a new century, after a war even more atrocious than the one in which John Whitbeck served gallantly, and after an economic crisis of unprecedented magnitude has plunged the whole world into want and hunger ~ even now as I write this in 1933, forty five years after the Jackson trial, seven decades after the

Emancipation Proclamation declared valid and universal the promise of our Declaration of Independence that all men are created equal ~ equality in law among us or between races and classes has not been established. Nor is it earnestly pursued or even desired by many in positions of power and authority.

But here, again, I indulge in rant, as occasionally I do from the lectern. I try to limit that proclivity, particularly when I see a hall full of law students put down their pencils and prepare to snooze. I am not the spellbinder John Whtbeck was. At the risk of belaboring my point, I list below some illustrative court cases to show our tottering progress in the years since 1865, when the Thirteenth Amendment was added to the U.S. Constitution.

These citations will be on the final exam.

One Step Forward	Two Steps Back
1865 Equal Rights Amendment adopted	*1865* Supreme Court limits application of civil rights to federal government, allowing states to limit voting rights, access, and other freedoms. *1876* Supreme Court declares equal rights not an absolute guarantee, allowing states to ignore intimidation and terrorism by the Ku Klux Klan and other vigilante organizations.
One Step Forward	**Two Steps Back**
1880 Supreme Court rules that to exclude negroes from jury lists violates the constitutional rights of a black defendant.	*1883* Bank failures and widespread unemployment lead to northern migration of negroes, exclusionary trade unions, real estate zoning, de facto segregation.

One Step Forward	Two Steps Back
	1883 Supreme Court rules that the 13th Amendment did not give Congress power to outlaw discrimination in access to public places.
1890 Michigan Supreme Court outlaws segregated sections in public places.	*1890* Supreme Court gives states control of elections, allowing discriminatory regulations to stand. *1896* Plessy vs. Ferguson gives authority for legal segregation in a case establishing the 'separate but equal' principle.

And so on and on my list could continue, until just last year, 1932, when two cases before the U.S. Supreme Court established that neither exclusionary voting qualifications, nor denial of adequate legal representation could be permitted under U.S. law. I followed these two cases through the courts and use them now as examples of both triumph and long delay toward equality in American legal process.

It can be seen from this sorry trail that the science of law does not develop progressively, as John Whitbeck averred. Further, from the several wars of aggression that have devastated the world since Whitbeck wrote that "modern wars are fought not for conquest but on principle," that postulate of his cannot be supported either. Whitbeck, like the Greek philosophers he admired, did not allow unpleasant actuality to cloud his vision of the ideal. Also, of couse, he did not live through the events that form our rather different period of human history. He died in 1907. I have experienced the nasty times since then. Still, I would not have written this history if I did not, like John Whitbeck, believe with all my heart in the possibility of human progress toward a more just and equitable social order. I would like this record to be a reminder that ordinary individuals can show extraordinary wisdom, that their example is worthy of emulation. Even so, I must concede that their action was the exception rather than the rule in the American legal system.

Jay Jackson haunts any podium I mount. He is my dark, sardonic, silent champion. My Elena tried unsuccessfully to find him She would have liked to meet him, to befriend his lovely wife Cynthia.

My Elena. You may wonder that such a graceless, inconsequential person as I, with my weak eyes, thinning hair and thickening waist, could attract and win to his side a tender beauty with twice his intellect and breeding. I wonder myself at that stroke of fortune.

Elena, I suppose, was initially drawn to me because of my connection to the Jackson trial. She was the daughter of a colleague, Arturo Benez-Carriegas, who taught Spanish literature at the university. Elena, his dutiful daughter, kept the elegant house of her widowed father, and dreamed of succoring every ill our flawed society has allowed to flourish. She was the scourge of Albany's real estate barons, the bane of a blatantly inadequate school system. She would have ~ Ah! What would she not have done had she lived her life out? I met and admired her when I came to teach at the university. Elena, of course, learned of my brief career as pleader for the disadvantaged. Eventually, overcoming the severe disapproval of her father, the proud and stiffbacked Professor Benez-Carriegas, Elena and I were married. She came into my life with such grace and quiet courage. She was ten years my junior and fifty years younger in spirit. Most of all, having given up her youth to care for her father, she wanted a child before she was too old to conceive one. She died giving birth to a tiny baby girl who outlived her only an hour.

Elena, in the brief years of our marriage, never ceased to urge me to write an account of the Jackson trial. She tirelessly pursued any small clue that might lead to the whereabouts of Jacob and Cynthia Jackson and their son Jeremiah. After she died, I abandoned all thought of resurrecting that early chapter of my life, which included the Lillian episode, my father's death, and my minor part in the defense of Bat Jackson. Jackson was assuredly a difficult client, stubborn, arrogant, sly, and evasive. He was also husband to a remarkable woman. I have never tried to sort out the conflicting feelings of envy, admiration, and distrust I felt for him, or my complex feelings for his wife. When Elena died, I put the project of writing about him aside with some relief.

After Elena's death my dear sister Marjorie came to live with me and keep my house. Marjorie had stayed at home while our mother was alive, and afterward met and married a naval officer several years older than she. They had no children. (My brother Robbie has taken care of continuing our family line with his three sons.) Marjorie's husband died of yellow fever out in the Philippines at the time of the Spanish war. There, a whole life done up in four sentences. I can be concise when I choose. John Whitbeck would be proud of me. I admit that the ability to capsulate my ideas into serviceable brevity has taken long years for me to develop. I have come to understand that after twenty minutes of lecture receptivity to any idea plunges steeply. One powerful deterrent to writing about the Jackson trial has been the memory of Whitbeck's two-and-a-half hour summation. How could I offer the case to law students as a model, with that great albatross of a speech hanging at its conclusion? Though Marjorie urged on me several times the idea of recounting the Jackson trial, I managed by various excuses to avoid it.

It has seemed to me presumptuous to capitalize on a victory for which I could claim so little merit? My involvement was marginal. Little heroism was shown. Neither the white nor the black community emerged blameless from that ordeal. Bat's white neighbors did not come forward on his behalf, although their silence and evasions and refusals did count in his favor. The chief witness against him, Emma Briggs, was colored, as were the several friends who spoke up for him. Then and afterward the shocked silence of good village people allowed Gertrude Hover's murderer, whoever he was, to elude official attention or pursuit, and finally to go unpunished. That same silence would, I believe, have allowed Bat Jackson to be hanged for the crime, or beaten to death by a mob, without serious protest.

My sister Marjorie, an avid reader, was in the habit of digesting every law journal that came into the house and giving me over dinner a digest of anything she thought worthy of my attention. She was both thorough and sprightly at this self-appointed task. We both enjoyed it. She never forgot her experience at the final day of the Jackson trial and the eerie hours of confinement that followed it. So, when she came across the name Jeremiah Jackson in the Princeton Law Review, she presented it to me as proudly as if that citation were a relic of Troy or King Tut's tomb. Naturally I wrote immediately to Jeremiah Jackson in care of Princeton. He was cited in the journal as co-author of an article on applications of the Napoleonic Code in states of the Louisiana Purchase.

I wrote Jeremiah Jackson three letters over the next year. He did not reply, not even to deny a connection to Jacob and Cynthia Jackson who had been married in Kinderhook, New York in 1885. I realize now, far too late, that I would give much to know what Jay and Cynthia Jackson did after they left Columbia County in 1888. If I had asked Bat's father before he died, or inquired at Bethel AME, or made an effort before the family moved away ~ If. If. However, like a lot of white folks then and now, I found any effort across the color line to be an uncomfortable venture. Like the haunting refrain Bat lined out the night they were planning to lynch him, that's one more river we have yet to cross. Always, always one more river to wade, to span, to leap, on the way to everybody's freedom, till we see individuals, fellow wayfarers, instead of an alien crowd on the far shore.

My sister Marjorie died six months ago, in April of 1933, as I was finishing my final teaching term at the unversity. Her health had been failing for the past several years, but I was unready for the terrible vacancy her loss has left in my life. As a sort of tribute to her, and to Elena and Cynthia Jackson and my mother ~ to all the kind and lovely women who have graced my life with their presence ~ I decided to teach a unit on civil rights laws and court cases from the period of Reconstruction and the rise of Jim Crow laws to the recent resurgence of the Klan in our 'separate but equal' present. I thought of the Jackson trial as an example of what I intended to clarify in the course. I was hoping ~ am still hoping ~ that an understanding of how slow, intermittent, and unwilling our country's progress has been in the area of civil rights and equality under the law might serve to inspire one or two students to take up the cause of equal justice in their law practice.

It is a frail hope. Graduating into this grinding Depression they will be struggling to afford a shingle and office rent. There are few enough paying customers for young lawyers in the current economy. The notion of taking on pro bono work, or even accepting clients with inadequate means and little chance of winning a case, cannot have much appeal for them. Nevertheless, I began to assemble material for a series of lectures. Among other things, I wrote to the Columbia County Clerk in Hudson, requesting a copy of the transcript of the Jackson trial. The clerk wrote back that he was unable to comply.

Thinking that a personal visit would change his mind, I traveled down to Hudson, not by stage or boat these days. I feel ancient that I can remember the stagecoach, remember horse-drawn trolleys. I could have taken the train, but my car offers more comfort at less cost. So I drove down the winding roads and over the soft hills of the Hudson Valley to the city where my career began. Hudson has not altered a great deal from the brawling river port it was forty years ago. It is a bit shrunken, quieter. Vanderhagen's is gone. Mrs. Bullock is long deceased, her boarding house fallen into dereliction. The Iron Horse is ostensibly closed now due to Prohibition. But I noticed a well worn path to its back door. Seeing it, I had to smile at the memory of John Whitbeck mocking the folly of legislating virtue by making vice illegal. I remembered, too, his scathing condemnation of our short-term approach to social engineering, tackling each complex, deepseated human failure as if it were a single dragon to be slain, one more river to cross, with utopia beckoning on the other side.

The county clerk was courteous and patient, providing me access to the records room and court dockets. However, my own search was no more successful than his had been. For the year 1888, the page that listed trials at the Third Circuit Court at Hudson was numbered without break through three sessions. No trial was listed for the week of February sixth. The docket number I remembered had been assigned to a different case. There was no record of People versus Jackson. The record was seamless; and it was incomplete, false. Certainly the later courthouse fire might have destroyed transcripts, but how had even the record of the trial's existence been obliterated?

I showed the county clerk my trial notes and the faded newspaper clippings from 1888. He was as baffled as I, though he could scarcely be expected to feel my indignation, the helpless anger I did my best to conceal till I had left the county records office. I found my way to a soda shop and sat in its cool depths while I attempted to fathom the intent of expunging a trial record. As Whitbeck pointed out very early in our handling of the case, the possibility of setting a legal precedent with the Jackson trial had disturbed Judge Edwards from the start. I had not been present for the hearing of most of the challenges Whitbeck filed, but I do remember his indignation at attempts by the district attorney to preclude or disallow any testimony favorable to the defendant.

Knowing their evidence was entirely circumstantial, and therefore weak, the prosecution tried to use old blackbird laws to stop Bat's friends testifying on his behalf. Blackbird laws were statutes drafted in the north to allow fugitive slaves to be captured in free states and returned to their owners. Slave hunters, called blackbirders, were known to apprehend freemen as well as escaped slaves. The blackbird laws prohibited testimony by either captured slaves or other negroes on their behalf, and rewarded justices for ruling in the slave catchers' favor. Some of those laws had been drafted without direct reference to negroes or slaves. On the surface they seemed to be aimed at fugitive apprentices or runaway children. The claim that Bat was a fugitive under those old laws was not upheld. Whitbeck's pleadings prevailed decisively.

As for the attempt to prevent Cynthia from testifying, using obscure old rulings prohibiting wives from speaking for husbands in court ~ or common-law wives, as Cynthia was purported to be, it was not Jacob but his brother John who had a family in Albany. Whitbeck challenged and bested a number of dodges while I was seeking white witnesses to attest to Bat's good character. He was far more successful than I. Sadly, good people can be very pusillanimous when social pressure is applied. Or not. John Powell, pushed to the wall, refused to give evidence for or against Jackson. Charles Davis kept aloof in public but offered help privately.

I count their actions as examples of the blundering dance of rapprochement in American race relations. There must be some tolerance, or even kindliness, in Kinderhook village, however. The Bethel AME still holds worship, nearly fifty years after a benefactor, Gertrude Hover, was murdered, and one of its members tried for the crime. I infer from this that colored residents remain in the village in this year of 1933.

The City of Hudson, too, has citizens of color, and lawyers, and local newsmen. Has no one of them consulted that county record in all these years? How could such an erasure have been managed without anyone noticing?. Sipping the last of my sarsaparilla and gazing out at the baked summer street, I speculated about what must have happened after Jackson was acquitted. Having exhausted the trumpery of pre-emancipation regulations, someone with authority, or merely access to county records and an eye to political repercussions in distant times and places, had managed to hide or destroy the official account of a colored defendant's trial and acquittal by a jury of white men for a brutal crime against an elderly white woman. That suppression was a form of racial bias I had never before encountered. I could not imagine Samuel Edwards conniving at it, or Aaron Gardenier. So who?

The why was patent. Without an official record, the case could not be cited in court as a precedent for dismissing purely circumstantial cases against other colored defendants. Legally it had never happened. Ostensibly the case of Gertrude Hover's murder was still open, although I knew there was no further investigation into it after Jackson's acquittal.

Then there was the allusion to Jay's brother John, the elusive elder brother who was Bat's height and build, his near double, the man with red paint on his shoes arresed in Albany after Gertrude Hover's murder. So far as I know that possiblity was not pursued later. John Jackson, Jr. was thought to frequent Guinea Hill, was reputed to be an outlaw, smuggler, purveyor of stolen goods, and guilty of other crimes handily tacked onto a runaway, particularly if he were black. Jay could have been shielding his brother John, if he thought him involved in the murder or robbery, or just far more vulnerable if accused. But John Jackson could not have had access to court records, or have possessed the ability to erase them. For all I knew, John Jackson was no more connected to Gertrude Hover's murder than Jay was.

When was the trial transcript removed and the record expunged? Did it happen while John Whitbeck was alive, while he still practised law in Hudson? Was it during Gardenier's bid for a judgeship? It could have been done later, when the colored population of Columbia County began to feel unwelcome after sundown, an attitude that grew after the turn of the century: Toil in our mills and fields, clean our houses, but don't live in our village. That sort of hostility has rendered much of rural America bland and white and isolated. Since the Great War we have retreated into Xenophobia and racism. I see it even up in Albany, which was once a center of abolitionist activity and negro activism, a shelter on the Underground Railroad.

If we burn our boats, abandon part of the crew whose skill and toil have brought us this far, how can we ever hope to cross to a better place? There is always one more river. We are on a long, long journey and cannot afford to scorn a single individual among us. Every spark of human spirit is needed. Unimaginable ventures and perils lie ahead of our infant species ~. Once again, my twenty minutes are up.

At the county records office I pressed the clerk for some other repository that might preserve the trial transcript I knew, I *knew*, must exist. I had seen John Ruso, the court stenographer, noting down every word. I had my own notes. I had the exact dates of the trial, its assigned number in the record book. I knew the name of the judge, the prosecutor, the defending counsel, the accused. I certainly knew the verdict. I showed the clerk my own notes again and a brief of the case to prove that what I was looking for did occur, did exist, must be somewhere in his purview. He remained unable to offer a solution.

Beyond that I had no recourse. Judge Samuel Edwards is dead, Aaron Gardenier is dead. John Whitbeck, who would have delighted to do battle over this, is also long dead. I am perhaps the only person still alive with knowledge and concern for the unsolved murder of a spinster back in the olden times, before electricity and gasoline and world war and global economic failure. Well, actually my concern centers more on the course of the trial of her accused killer. A white jury declared a colored man not guilty of her death. It should have been a source of pride in the county.

True, it did not further the search for justice on behalf of the victim. It did, however, further the slow progress of this nation toward the ideal of equality under the law. That was why I wanted the record. Not that I was part of the process, but that the process had resulted in a fair and reasoned verdict. I could have offered it to my students as an example, not shining and perfect, but an example, all the same, of rural American justice in operation.

But I can't do that. I can't recall all the testimony from a court case that was pled half a century ago. If it were not for some old news clippings, I wouldn't have even the witnesses' names. I confess to a certain relief at the oblivion of that ungainly defense summation. Except as an example of how to numb a jury, it would serve no purpose in my classroom.

As for the future, I cannot predict even when we shall climb out of the terrible, wasting idleness that has seized the civilized world in the four years since the stock market toppled and so many banks and businesses failed that able-bodied workmen, veterans of the war that was to save the planet, now stand idle in the streets without the means to feed their families. In the midst of such a crisis, I cannot summon the zeal to uncover or redress this old injustice, or misuse of judicial privilege, if that's what it was. I am not even certain whose advantage was served by burying People versus Jackson, or by abandoning the search for Gertrude Hover's killer. There must be other examples of such racially motivated practices of expungement. But I am old (or lazy) and too preoccupied to undertake the project of baring them. I do not have the energy for a crusade. I just want to ease my conscience and placate the benign spirits that still urge me to take one step forward, when for the most part I am content to slip two steps back.

For all the achievements of my nation in its short history, there still remains a great weight of failed promises, a burden that is borne unequally on the shoulders of those least able to endure it. The current catchphrase for America is the melting pot, as if, like Black Sambo we might stir the ethnic strains of our society fast enough to dissolve their differences. However, as I was fond of pointing out to Elena, seethed hot enough and long enough, the pot itself will melt. Wade in that water, chilleren. God'sa gonna trouble those waters. The offspring of immigrants and slaves may turn on the children of selfish privilege before that happens. They might cast off the burden, disown the promises of freedom. No wonder the fear of Communist Russia dominates our foreign policy, even in this time of economic crisis.

I don't believe we should be 'melted' or homogenized. I think a finer solution would be for us to be individualized, regarded one by one for our amazing gifts, our mysterious uncommonness. I prefer to encounter people singly and begin to know each one while I can. I look ahead and see one more river. Whatever lies beyond it exceeds my hope or comprehension. The next adventure is all any of us can see in this brief and narrow existence. Most of what we know is our past. In my mind I yet can hear, faint and far in memory and softened by time, a cloud of voices, a swell of music that slowed the seething panic of a captive crowd in that old gaslit courthouse. I was there. It happened. All of it happened. I have written here what I recall of it in the hope that this record will honor those dear to me, who thought me kinder, wiser, better than I am.

Now, here are some namess we all should honor. First, Gertrude Margaret Hover, who chose to live among the colored folk of her village. She was unappreciated, her stern ethics and unbending social principles at odds with her time and place. She was for all her faults, a good woman, a good citizen. Second, Jacob Jackson, a defendant of singular courage and composure, who emerged with dignity from an ordeal no one can contemplate with equanimity. Third, John V. Whitbeck, who defended Jacob Jackson with thoroughness and passion and won his acquittal.

Then there are the twelve jurymen, whose sharp perception and thoughtful choice should have been an example for American justice in the generations since. Their fairness, their wisdom, goes unmarked in our legal history. It is wrong that their contribution to the cause of equal justice has been buried and forgotten. As a small redress, I set down their names here.

Samuel M. Bush, a farmer of Taghkanic
Lott Cook, a hotel keeper of Copake
Samuel Coon, a farmer of Livingston
Derrick Hallenbeck, a farmer of Greenport
Newton J. Miller, a clerk, the last juror chosen
Webster Miller, a farmer of Livingston
Samuel Myers, Jr., a farmer of Taghkanic
Thomas Peer, a butcher of Taghkanic
Peter R. Rockefeller, a farmer of Germantown
Benjamin Sheldon, a farmer of Taghkanic
Herman Stickles, a farmer of Livingston
Martin Wagoner, a farmer of Taghkanic

I regret that there has never been a resolution in the matter of Gertrude Hover's murder. I regret that the effect of this accusation and trial on the lives of Jacob and Cynthia Jackson is not known to me. I am keenly sorry that the matter of a lost trial record has come to my notice only after so many years. When I cross that one more river beyond which no path lies, I hope this small effort of restoration can serve as my entry fee.

Royce Tilden
at Loudonville, New York, November 1, 1933.

Sources

Bennett, Lerone, Jr., *Wade in the Water*, Great Moments in Black History, Chicago, Johnson Publishing, 1979

Bial, Raymond, *The Underground Railroad*, Boston, Houghton Mifflin, 1995

Collier, Edward A., *A History of Old Kinderhook*, New York, G.P. Putnam's Sons, 1914, (reprinted by Higginson Book Company, Salem, Massachusetts)

Ellis, Franklin, *A History of Columbia County*, New York, Philadelphia, 1878

Farley, Ena L., *The Underside of Reconstruction New York*, New York, Garland Publishing, 1993

Finkelman, Paul, ed. *Race, Law, and American History, 1700-1990*, Volumes 1-11 (volumes 3, 4, 8 referenced: Voluma 3, *Emancipation and Reconstruction*; Voluma 4, *The Age of Jim Crow*; Volume 8, *Race and Criminal Justice*) New York, Garland Publishing, 1992

Franklin, John Hope, An *Illustrated History of Black Americans*, New York, Time Life, undated

Higginbotham, A. Leon, Jr., *In the Matter of Color, Race and the American Legal Process*, New York, Oxford University Press, 1978

Hine, Darlene, Wilma King, Linda Reed, eds., *We Specialize in the Wholly Impossible*, Brooklyn, NY, Carlson Publishing, 1995

Hughes, Langston, *The Dream Keeper and other Poems*, New York, Alfred A. Knopf, 1994

Hughes, Langston, *Selected Poems of Langston Hughes*, New York, Alfred A. Knopf, 1987

Katz, William Loran, *Black Legacy, a History of New York's African Americans*, New York, Atheneum Books, 1997

McManus, Edward J., *A History of Negro Slavery in New York*, Syracuse, Syracuse University Press, 1966

New York Public Library Schomburg Center for Research in Black Culture, *African American Desk Reference*, New York, Stonesong Press, 1999

Sernett, Milton C, *Abolition's Axe*, Beriah Green, Oneida Institute and the Black Freedom Struggle, Syracuse, Syracuse University Press, 1986

Sherman, John R. Ed. *African American Poetry, an Anthology*, New York, Dover 1997

Shetterly, Robert, *Americans Who Tell the Truth*, New York, Dutton, 2005

Siebert, Wilbur H., *The Underground Railroad from Slavery to Freedom*, New York, Macmillan Company, 1898

Washington, Jack, *The Long Journey Home*, a History of the Black Community of Princeton, New Jersey, Africa World Press, Trenton, NJ, 2005

Wideman, John Edward, *My Soul Has Grown Deep*, Classics of Early African American Literature, Philadelphia, Running Press, 2001

Wright, Giles R. and Edward Lama Wonkeryor, *Steal Away*, A Guide to the Underground Railroad in New Jersey, Trenton, New Jersey Historical Commission, undated